ACLLAHUASI

UNTOLD FOLKLORE OF A RAVAGED INKAN CIVILIZATION

J.D. Lanctôt

ACLLAHUASI

This book is a novel based on research performed by the author concerning the Inka (Inca) Empire. The author takes no responsibility if historical, or geographical facts are inaccurately portrayed. Should factual errors exist, please contact the author.

All information, techniques, ideas and concepts contained within this publication are of the nature of general comment only and are not in any way recommended as individual advice. The intent is to offer a variety of information to provide a wider range of choices now and in the future, recognizing that we all have widely diverse circumstances and viewpoints. Should any reader choose to make use of the information contained herein, this is their decision, and the contributors (and their companies), authors and publishers do not assume any responsibilities whatsoever under any condition or circumstances. It is recommended that the reader obtain their own independent advice.

You can contact the author at publishing@pachacutipublishing.com

Paperback ISBN: 978-1-7367223-2-9
Ebook ISBN: 978-1-7367223-1-2

Printed in the USA
First paperback edition February 2021.

Pachacuti Publishing
4133 Kansas Street
San Diego, CA 92104
United States of America
www.PachacutiPublishing.com

Published by Happy Self Publishing
www.happyselfpublishing.com

HAPPY
SELF PUBLISHING

To Joy.
She helped me find the hidden author within me.

Contents

Preface

It has taken several years of research to write this book. I believe it to be the most historically accurate novel of Inkan life that has been written. This is the end product of years of research, writing, and travels to South America. The biggest lesson learned from my research is that we will never exactly know what it was like to be an Inkan, too much has been lost to history. We will never know the details of rituals or ceremonies, or what the meaning was behind significant structures. Still, we know a lot and I portray as much as possible into this novel. I can confidently say that the reader will be closer to understanding what it was like to be an Inkan by reading this book than they would by reading what is available elsewhere. Having said that, this book isn't perfect. I ask the reader if factual errors are discovered, please reach out to me so I can correct them.

The objectives of this book are 1) To give back to a culture its dignity that those from my continent of ancestral heritage unjustly took from them, 2) To increase awareness among the millions of tourists of the vast stories and sacredness of the places and objects that they visit, 3) To insult enough people by my ignorance to motivate them to better protect their own culture, 4) To provide the means for them to do so by donating half of the proceeds from this book to them.

This book contains over one hundred terms that may be unknown to the English reader. There is a glossary of terms and a character glossary in the back of the book. I try to define unknown words in the text without sacrificing the flow of the story, but sometimes it wasn't possible. This glossary will add further depth and teaching to the story. For example, there were many institutions in the Inkan Empire that were unknown to Europeans. One of these is the 'tampu' which was essentially a state run inn every few kilometers along the major roads for traveling armies and rulers.

I feel a level of unworthiness in writing this book. I believe it is the descendents of those of whom I write that should write it. I cannot say that they have not tried, they have obstacles that prevent them from taking on such an undertaking. I am privileged to have the ability to spend thousands of hours performing research and writing a history that is not mine.

I went into this project with an open mind and an attempt to understand a culture and people that I cannot comprehend. Still, I have read textbooks' worth of research and have visited the sites of which I write. I have interacted with the descendents of the characters in my books to the best of my ability while living thousands of miles away. Despite my due diligence, I cannot accurately depict many areas of Andean life such as

1. Vocabulary. I have removed all mention of colors because there is ample proof that those are an invention of modern language. Other problems exist, such as shapes, modern descriptions, and concepts that I either did not identify or could not substitute.
2. The layout of the Acllahuasi is unknown. We know some features of it, but no schematic exists. I recreated the Acllahuasi according to narratives that are available and based on the remnants of the walls that are still erect. These walls have been turned into a shopping mall in Cusco and serves as an example of the traditions of the Inkas being trampled upon by people that are unaware of the history. The Acllahuasi as described in the book is based on educated guesses of what it was like after reviewing the research available.
3. Sexuality. The art that survives from the Andean cultures and Inkas suggests that these people were a hyper-sexual culture compared to the modern-western world. There are depictions of widespread public sexual acts, homosexuality, insest, polygamy, what would now be considered pedophilia, and a mix of all the

above. I omitted nearly all sexuality, choosing to pursue it in a forthcoming book.

4. Ambition. Should the chroniclers be believed, the population of the Andes lived a content life void of ambition of personal gain, it was likely the closest thing to Marxism as has ever existed. By the nature of a story, a hero must have a quest and as you will read, Tara is bold and pulls of feats that there is no proof of having occurred. An overly ambitious character such as Tara would be rare in the Inkan Empire.

5. Festivals. The Inkas had a lot of festivals, all of which were celebrated differently. Unfortunately, few records were kept that do more than mention them, and thus, the details of how they were celebrated are lost. I have taken bits and pieces from different events mentioned by the chroniclers and created concoctions that are more or less accurate.

6. Spelling. Quechua is not a written language in the modern sense. They used the Quipu to record information and stories, but with only a few exceptions, they cannot be translated. Quechua has also transformed over the centuries and is now written with the Spanish alphabet. This resulted in a variety of spellings of even common words such as Inca versus Inka, Cusco versus Cuzco. I have stayed true to the most politically correct spellings such as 'Inka' instead of 'Inca'. I used 'huaca,' instead of 'waca,' and 'Acllahuasi' instead of 'acllyahuasi'.

7. Legends. I have included a few legends in the text, but I have paraphrased them. I sought legends that seem to have little Spanish or Christianity influence if any-many legends were changed to comply with the church's teachings. I encourage the reader who is interested in the legends of the Andes to look further into the subject. There is much fascinating work published on the topic.

8. Titles. I simplified titles as much as I was able to while remaining true to the heritage. The Inkas did not have titles as we understand them. Each place and person was believed to have

their own life energy that provided its individual characteristics. Instead of titles of position such as Bishop, President, or the such, the Inkas had a title for each distinct person and for each specific task they did.

9. Healing rituals. I have had continued difficulty finding information about healing rituals, so I have left them vague and they may be inaccurate. I based them off of what the archeological evidence suggests and what is still practiced in the areas of South America where shamanic practices remain prevalent.

If you would like more information about this fascinating culture, visit www.acllahuasinovel.com

If You are Planning a Trip to Ecuador or Peru

If you are reading this while preparing for a trip to South America, you can see ruins of several sites mentioned in this text. Aside from the fictional location of Milagro, which is based on a modern city, the locations mentioned exist and are in ruinous state. The first chapter of the book is 'Guapondelig" which is now called Cuenca and during the Inkan rule was called Tumipampa. There are several ruins in Cuenca, the most popular are Pumapungo and down the street Todos Santos. A few hours from Cuenca is the site referred in the book as "Hatun Cañari" which is now called Ingapirca. This was likely a shared estate built by Sapa Inka Tupac and his wife, the Colla of Cañari. You can find more info about many of the locations mentioned in the glossary.

Pronunciation

In reading this introduction you have already noticed that I spell the common word of Inca with a 'k.' I do that because that's the proper spelling, just as Cusco is the proper spelling instead of Cuzco.

I use Spanish pronunciation throughout the book. Please familiarize yourself with pronunciation.

Ñ/ñ is pronounced as 'nee' so Cañari is pronounced as Canee-ari.

'Ll/ll' is pronounced as an English 'Y' so Colla would be pronounced as "Coya."

'Que' is pronounced as the letter 'K'

'Qui' is pronounced as "Key"

Introduction

The Inka Empire is likely the greatest forgotten empire that has ever existed. Spanning from the 13th century AD until 1572 AD, when their last stronghold was destroyed by the Conquistadors, it is amazing what they accomplished. In the time span of hardly 200 years, the Inkas expanded from a small migratory group, to the rulers of an empire bigger than the country of Iran. People may know the name, Machu Picchu, Cusco, or the Inka Trail, but the significance of these institutions to the millions of inhabitants of the Inka Empire is not conveyed. This book will give the reader a small understanding of the everyday pressures and concerns faced by those that were being conquered by the Inkas.

The Inka Empire was composed of many cultures, tribes, and lesser empires that the Inkas conquered by war or diplomacy. Here, you take a journey to see the past. The book begins in what is now called southern Ecuador, where the Cañari culture still thrives. The Cañari civilization was once the center of their own empire with dominion from the coast of the Pacific Ocean to the Amazon rainforest. They were mighty enough to resist three invasions from the much mightier Inka Empire; however, they were eventually diplomatically outmaneuvered. In fear of another invasion, the Colla, the Queen, married the ruler of the Sapa Inka, the Emperor, and thus gave rulership to him.

The Inkas were a conquering people, their culture revolved around expansion and exploitation. They were the most ruthless military machine in the Andes. Once their eyes were set upon you, it was essentially over. This is one reason Atahualpa (not a character in this book), allowed the Conquistadors access into the Inka Empire. He thought that the 160 strange men were no match for his military of tens of thousands of men that did not know defeat.

The anti-hero in this book, Sapa Inka Tupac Yupanqui, was a highly successful military leader and visionary. His father, Pachacuti Inka Yupanqui, is credited with creating the Inka Empire into what it is known as today instead of a strong chiefdom, as it was before his reign. Sapa Inka Tupac Yupanqui continued the legacy as is shown in this book. The infrastructure of the Empire at the time of Tupac Yupanqui was robust, complete with the most ambitious road network in the world called the Qhapaq Ñan, irrigation, a communication network comprising runners called chasqui (chasquicuna for plural), inns, storages of food and supplies to last years of famine, and several other marvels. The bureaucratic structure rivaled their European counterparts. All of this was completed without a written language, pack animals, or a functional currency.

Once the Inkas conquered a territory, they set their fangs into it and devoured it. The level of dominance and subjugation of a culture was typically in response to their resistance to the invasion. As mentioned in this book, the culture called the Chachapoyas culture was annihilated by the Inkas to the point of having their language changed, utterance of their self-determined name outlawed, and tens of thousand of Inkan loyalists instilled into their land. Other civilizations fared much better, some had their rulers installed as Inkan rulers.

This is a fictional story that would have taken place around 1470 AD. I incorporated as much historical fact as available, but it's important to remember how much we don't know. History of the Inka Empire is marred with contradiction, myths, and re-writes. For example, there is an argument that Cañari was conquered by Pachacuti Inka Yupanqui; however, it's also thought that it was conquered by his son, Tupac Yupanqui. Another contradiction is who the Colla, Queen, was of the Cañari Empire when the Inkas Invaded. Colla is the Quechua word for 'Queen' (I would have used the Cañari word, but the native language of Cañari is extinct), but no one knows what her name was. Some say it was Mama Ocllo Colla, I believe it was, but there are reliable sources that name Mama Ocllo Colla as the Sapa Inka's sister. For this reason, I have left her without a name other than Colla.

The overarching message of this book is the power of forgiveness, even when the most grievous injuries and injustices occur. Throughout time, forgiveness has been shown to be the harbinger of progress and improvement. This story goes beyond forgiveness in how one can hold animosity toward one for a travesty but wish damnation upon another for something that was a misunderstanding. When one has forgiven and the energies of the universe are in understanding, the magic of truth, healing, and transformation occur.

Chapter One

Guapondelig

Tara felt the sticky monkey blood descend her robust back, down her short and skinny legs and into her sandals. She changed her stepping pattern from her natural soft steps to a stomp to prevent the dirt on the mountain path from mixing with the sticky blood in her sandals. It seemed to work, at least for now.

Tara was a slender girl of around the age when a girl realizes she's becoming a woman. Half of her face was dark like the depths of a cave. The other half of her face, split along the midline, was the color a light cloud, or as the tradesmen from afar would say, "The color of the foam of the ocean." She didn't know what that meant but thanked them in her soft-spoken and humble voice.

Her long dark hair, which flowed like the wind through a dense sun drown forest, was tied to her head to keep it from the bloody sack containing the dead monkeys meant for offerings. She walked with a forward gait and stood at the same height as her mother, Raura, who was beside her. Upon Raura's back was a large urn of chicha.

Tara was the favorite child of Raura, who was the leader of their region of Cañari, called Milagro. She allowed Tara to help rule, despite her young age because she had the wisdom and knowledge of a sage, and a love for Milagro that was unmatched. Tara said Milagro was the most beautiful, magical, and tranquil region in the Andes Mountains. She was right.

When Tara smiled a truly happy smile, which was often, the coy sprang from their burrows and scurried about. Her radiance was such that many men asked her mother for a promise to marry her when she reached of age. She replied with a request that they look at her again and when they did they saw Tara's divided face. They said they didn't notice it before and withdrew their request, not because she was ugly, but because they had never seen such a face and it scared them.

"Are you okay?" Asked Raura. She noticed Tara's uncomfortable march.

"Don't worry, I'm just a little tired is all," said Tara. "You always had to carry the monkeys before and I'm happy to help now that I'm old enough. Now you only have to carry the urn."

They were on a multi-day journey to Guapondelig for a festival and to meet the female ruler of Cañari named Colla.

"Your older brothers would be proud of the woman you're becoming. Colla will be proud of you too. Are you nervous about meeting her tomorrow?"

Raura didn't smile, she never did, not since her sons were killed and Guaman, Tara's father, became cursed. Since her voice lost its flavor and became taciturn, and she never smiled. To fill the void, she spoke with superiority, even to those that she loved or those that were above her.

Tara looked down, "I'm a little excited to meet Colla. She has done so much for us, and I won't have to carry the offerings any further."

"I know that's a fake smile, there are no coy running about."

"There are no coy because it's dark," said Tara.

Raura cleared her throat.

Tara moaned, "It's because you say I'm becoming a woman. You're a woman, mother, not I. I'm a child. I can't do what you do. I don't understand the gods and the living landscape as you do. You always make personal sacrifices for the greater good, but I'm selfish and always will be. You're so wise and you always recognize what to do. I'm just a young girl and when people tell me I'm growing into a woman, well, I'm worried that I'll disappoint them."

Raura moved closer to Tara, "I remember when I felt like that. One day it will all make sense to you and you'll discover in yourself what we all recognize." She stroked Tara's face.

Tara smiled and three coy ran from the brush beside the road and rubbed on Tara's foot and purred before running along to the other side.

"Now I believe you," said Raura.

They went further down the jungle path.

"Stop! There's a dead person over there!"

There was a bloodied corpse beside the road.

Tara dropped the sack of monkeys and ran to him. Raura waited behind.

Tara raised the man's head, "Mother, he's still alive."

Raura approached her, "Those are cuts. He was attacked."

"What do you think happened?" said Tara.

"Wait here, I am going to look around," said Raura.

The man moaned and opened his bruised eyes. Tara sat him up and he coughed up blood. He tried to speak, but Tara didn't understand him. He coughed up more blood and mucus and heaved the words, "The Inkas have taken control. Sapa Inka Tupac Yupanqui is here in Cañari. Don't go to the Capital. Run away!"

Tara jumped to her feet and dropped his head, unwittingly killing the stranger. She picked up a rock and scanned the dark line of the jungle. She threw the rock in the direction of the first sound she heard and picked up another rock.

"Tara. Tara, calm down," said Raura. She ran to her and held her arm and took the rock from her. "What happened that got you so worried?"

"He isn't dead!" She looked back at him and realized that he was dead, "Well, he wasn't dead. He said that the Inkas have taken control of Cañari and that Sapa Inka Tupac Yupanqui himself is here waiting for us in Guapondelig!" She bit her lip.

"Okay, calm down, and let's wait for your father and brother to catch up," said Raura.

"Calm down? Really! They murdered my brothers, your sons, and they placed the curse on father. Calm down?"

Tara's father, Guaman, had flashbacks of war and he suffered from violent mood swings. He sought help among the healers and huacas in the surrounding lands, but none fixed his mind. He had moments of his old self, but he was nothing like the caring and loving father he was before he went to war against the Inkas.

They knelt beside the dead man again. Tara closed his eyes and said a brief prayer and gave an offering of chicha from the urn that Raura carried upon her back.

Raura kissed Tara on the forehead.

Tara stood beside the bag of monkeys.

"The Inkas won't return ever again," said Raura. "Not after the offerings we gave Pachayachachic and Mamaquilla, they will protect us. We are safe. We will never have to fight the Inkas again."

Tara kicked the bag of monkeys. The arm of one of the five dead spider monkeys rolled out. She bent down to put it back in the sack her father created for this occasion.

"I will fight them. I want nothing more than to fight them and to kill Sapa Inka Tupac Yupanqui. I'm too young now, but I dream of it every night. I will do it even if I die trying. I have to go back to Milagro. I can't risk seeing him until I am ready to fight. I need to learn how to curse people. I need to learn how to use poison." She peered in the direction they came, "I have to go back."

Raura stood with her, "Tara, look at me. Look at me, Tara!"

Tara looked at her.

"You will be safe." said Raura. "There's nothing more that I want than for you to be safe, but remember, should you not go to meet Colla she will be offended and may resend the privileges she granted us. We don't know who that dead man is. He was probably robbed and was hallucinating; he could have been the thief for all we know. I promise you that if we are in danger, I'll be the first to teach you how to fight and I will get you to safety. How about we don't speak of those Inka monsters on such a beautiful night?"

Raura turned around and yelled, "Guaman and Achache, are you still back there?"

A faint yell penetrated the wall of darkness, "We'll catch up soon."

"Stay close," yelled Raura.

Tara still bit her lip, and she couldn't stop her fingers from fidgeting with each other.

"You're still pondering what he said, aren't you?" Said Raura.

"Yes, I asked the huaca of the giant spring what would happen to me and to us if the Inkas ever took our land."

Raura patted Tara on the back, "What did he say?"

Tara wasn't sure if she was being mocked or if she was sincere. "Tell me it isn't true, what he told me." She gathered some brush to cover the body, but really to disguise her fear. "He said that because of my beauty the Inkas would take me to a strange place called an acllahuasi and will use me for their pleasure—"

Raura huffed and opened her mouth to speak.

Tara ceased what she was doing and stepped in front of her mother. She made direct eye contact "—I'm serious, Mama. He's always right. They will take me to this place called the Acllahuasi and I will never be able to leave those barren walls. There, I will be used for the Sapa Inka's personal pleasure. When he is done with me he will give you to his-what do they call them, people in charge?-ah yes, curacas. He will give me to his curacas and apus. They will use me for their plaything for the rest of my life. When they aren't abusing me, they will force me to make textiles, clothes, chicha, and other manly work. These men will ravage my body and try to make it so I can't have children. If I conceive, they will starve me and beat me to make me lose the child. And should that not work and I deliver, they will treat the child poorly. They will allow me to raise it and love it but after it reaches a mature age, they will kill it in front of me, and mix its remains into my food. This is only the beginning of what they do. When I arrive they will—"

"—Okay Tara, that's enough," Interrupted Raura shaking her head. "The Inkas are not here. What you speak of is nonsense. They are not here, they cannot take you—"

Tara's twin, and only surviving brother, Achache ran up to them. "—eh, eh I, eh, I thon' like thi', can we go ba'—"

"—Shut up Achache! Can't you see we're talking? Why do you have to be so annoying?" Said Tara.

Achache pretended to throw something at her. "I thought you' wan' tho know wha' we thaw An Inka thcou' par'y, " said Achache, "Thad thold me tho wun ahead and thell you tha' they 'r' humming thowawd you. I'm thawed." He jetted past Tara to Raura and hugged her leg. Chicha splashed out of the large urn she carried on her back. Tara ran forward to support her from falling backward.

"Ha! Inkas here? Not possible, they are just another community that looks similar. It will look very suspicious if we hide from our Cañari brothers," said Raura.

"Thather thaid he knew they were Inka behauth they theak Quethua," said Achache. He spoke calmly and didn't share the fear of them that Tara did.

"Emmm, uhhh, whath ith tha'!" said Achache pointing at the half-covered corpse.

"It's a corpse, a dead person. You've seen one before. Stop being stupid," said Tara. She faced Raura. "We should hide!"

There was a long silence before Raura spoke, "I've seen no such thing, nor ever heard Quechua spoken since the last invasion."

Tara shuttered from fright. "I hear them."

Achache looked over his shoulder, "I thee them homming."

Tara's heart raced. Her knuckles were nearly as pale as her half-face. She constrained her legs from betraying her calm demeanor and taking her away in a frightened run. There were ten of them, and each of them wore the dark and light colored checkered tunic. They passed in a single file. Each of the scouts stared at the young Tara and continued without saying a word. Their shodden feet hit the ground in unison, offset by the sound of their spear's impact. On their belt, they carried a sling and several small rocks wrapped along the side of it. Two of them carried long wooden boards inlaid with sharp rocks along their spine, a signature of the Inkas.

"Hey you," said one soldier carrying the weird weapon. He spoke with a Quechuan accent.

"Are you speaking to me?" said Raura.

"Yes, you. What happened to this man?" he said.

"Nothing. We are plain people going to make offerings to Mamaquilla and came across him. He was already dead. We were covering it when we saw you," said Raura.

She showed no fear or curiosity about who they were.

"What's going on here?" Asked Guaman. He arrived behind the soldiers.

"Nothing Guaman, we are only explaining to these fine men that we found this body and had nothing to do with his death," said Raura.

The soldiers closed in on Raura and the leader peered directly into her eyes with a stare that made the night cooler, "Very well. All the best to you and your family, and especially to your beautiful daughter. I think we'll be seeing you again."

Tara wanted to hurt him, all of them. The rage inside of her exploded. She pictured when she would kill them, even Sapa Inka Tupac Yupanqui. She would do what her brothers died trying to do.

Guaman picked up two stones beside the road and lodged them in a pocket in his lush cloak.

The soldiers left. After they were out of hearing range Tara stepped in front of Raura.

"I don't want to go any further," said Tara. "I won't risk it."

Raura laughed, "Tara, oh Tara. If you do not go to Guapondelig, we will insult Colla. She gave us great honor and responsibility to rule over the neighboring settlements. What would she assume if my eldest daughter, the future ruler of Milagro, was vacant and didn't offer thanks? We are protected Tara, her favor with Mamaquilla has always protected us, and always will."

"You want the Inkas to take me and torture me for the rest of my life so you can hold on to your honor?" said Tara.

"Raurah," said Guaman. He put his hand on her shoulder. "My love, I think Tara may be right on this matter. We should allow her to return home. Those men weren't from here and their accent resembles those of some soldiers I fought during the last Inkan invasion. I can't bear to lose another child to the Inkas. At least our sons are at peace with the earth. Tara would be taken to their torture chambers."

Raura ignored her husband, her sarcasm turned firm and serious, "Tara. Your notions of what will happen are false. You are the most beautiful girl in Milagro but don't assume you are the most beautiful in all of Cañari or that you are beautiful enough to be taken to this so-called Acllahuasi. Because of the position that Colla gave us, Achache and Father will be saved from the front lines if war returns. Be a woman and think beyond yourself. Men that look like Inkan scouts will not take you away from us."

"I would rather put a knife into my gut than to be taken," said Tara. She lugged the sack over her shoulder and continued on the path. "And if you didn't notice, those Inkan scouts haven't left. They are atop the knoll watching us."

"I do not see anything," said Raura.

"Because your eyes aren't good. Their torches are plainly visible."

"They are still there," said Guaman. "Come, Tara, if there is any more reason to think the Inkas being here you can leave and return home. Right Raura?"

"Well, considering they are not here, I see little risk in your promise. I agree. Now, let us go."

Tara walked far ahead of the rest of the family, and no one pursued conversation until they reached the bottom of the mountain.

Fog filled the valley at the bottom and Tara saw only a few paces ahead, still, in the occasional breaks, she saw the torches of the stranger ahead. They never got closer, nor further.

"Tho you thin' they thee uth?" Said Achache.

"They absolutely can," said Guaman. "Anyone with trained eyes can see through this fog. It makes us appear as shadows against the moonlight. We used to track our enemies using similar methods."

"They can't see us," said Raura. "Why would they need to watch us?"

Tara bit her lip and glared at Raura from behind her.

The trail meandered along a stream that led into a field of flowers that resembled a sunset. The fog cleared, and the flowers were flowers so bright that they gave off the brilliance of daytime and the sweetest aroma filled the air. Tara was overwhelmed by a sense of peace. She ceased to worry about the strangers ahead, or of her argument with her family.

"Perhaps we could just stay here and hide from all bad things," said Tara. "A life among the flowers would be the most fantastic existence. Better than anything else. They will protect us," Tara said to no one in particular. She inhaled a long breath of the aroma scented air. An overarching sense of guilt overcame her.

She turned to Raura.

"I'm sorry I yelled at you. Forgive me. You know best and only want to keep me safe. I'm sorry I questioned you."

Raura didn't answer her but looked frustrated.

Tara removed the sack of monkeys from her back. She did not mind the gooey blood that pulled at her skin as she removed the sack. She ran into the field and danced.

Coy chirped from beneath the flowers where they played.

Achache ran after her to join the fun.

They ceased when they came upon the most beautiful of the flowers; a flower twice as tall and bright as the rest. It was multi-colored, like Tara's face. Half resembled the color of a deep cave and the other, like 'sea foam.'

Tara bent over, closed her eyes, and smelled it.

"I've never theen tha' hind of flowew befowe," said Achache.

"Neither have I. It's amazing! It must be a huaca, a portal into another world. Achache, give me something to offer to it," said Tara.

"I thon' have anything," he said.

Tara got on her knees and withdrew from her pocket a small wooden figurine of herself that her eldest brother gave to her the last time she saw him.

She buried the figurine beside the flower.

"Achache, the flower doesn't have any roots. It's floating upon the dirt."

"Ath i' fow thomething."

"Shut up Achache! I am asking!"

A thousand desires came to mind, and none of them stood out more than the rest. "Achache, do I want to be safe or do I want not to be here in Cañari. Do I want peace, or a war where we defeat the Inkas?What about—"

"—Tara! We need to keep going," yelled Raura.

Tara jumped.

"How abou' athk fow wha' ith bes' fow you?"

She peered at Achache for a moment and knelt again by the flower, "Please, dear huaca, give me the best life so I can live for my brothers that were robbed of theirs."

She ran back to her parents alongside Achache.

Raura put her hand over her heart, "You bring together each thing of a Cañari woman. You were angry with me, yet you forgave me. You were having a good time in this flower field, and still, you listened to me when I called for you. You are strong, yet sentimental. You carry a heavy load on your back, yet enjoy the scent of the flowers. You are wise but humble. I do not know how I was given such a daughter."

They spent the night in a nearby mud and straw hut. Instead of dreaming of the Acllahuasi and the strangers, she dreamt of the flower.

Chapter Two

Mamaquilla

The strangers were nowhere to be seen the next day, but Tara felt they were being watched, almost as if it were the insects and the animals of the jungle that were watching them. To her, it felt that instead of going to Guapondelig that they were approaching a storm, a torrential murderous storm. She didn't mention her worries to her family; she could only imagine her mother's response. She distracted herself by kicking a stone down the pathway. The silence lasted until they reached the clearing around Guapondelig. It was filled with the thousands of boisterous people who arrived for the festival, yet didn't fit within the confines of the city.

Achache ran ahead toward the city, "Yay! We'e finally hewe!" He tripped on a hidden mound of dirt.

Tara laughed.

Guaman ran to him and helped him up.

They made their way through the throngs of people to the city entrance.

"Mother," said Tara. She interrupted a conversation between her and an old friend they happened upon, "Look at the entrance, who are those people?"

Raura looked in the direction. "We will find out soon enough."

"They don't look like they belong here," said Guaman.

Tara and Guaman slowed their approach.

Tara referred to a select few people dressed in clothes and ceremonial decor that she hadn't seen before. They were dressed in animal costums with features both of humans and pumas; others dressed as serpent looking people. The man that caught Tara's attention most was a man wearing a large checkered cloak made of feathers and a chest plate of gold. He wore earplugs large enough for Tara to put her arm through. Beside these foreigners were idols of Inti, the Sun God of the Inkas.

Guaman stopped and grabbed Tara's arm. "I'm scared for you to go any further because if they are the Inkas, then, no. No, no, no. You will experience things far worse than me if they are the Inkas. Stay here until we figure out what's going on."

"Come on you two," said Raura, "this is nothing. They are merely trying something new."

"I don't know my wife, I think these are Inkas, straight from Cusco."

The strangers from the trail the previous night appeared behind them. They came toward Tara's family with a quick march.

"We would know if the Inkas was here because if they were, there would be war," said Raura. "I'm sure there's a reason why. Let's keep going, Colla will explain all. Remember, all it takes is a slight insult to Colla and she can strip us of all the privileges and honors she has given us. Do you wish to go back to the fields? Do you want to have to return the new clothes and only have the one pair allowed to normal people? Remember, they itch." She pointed toward the entrance to the city. "Come."

The man with the golden chest plate approached them.

"Mama!" said Tara in a trembling voice.

Guaman's breathing grew deep and he gripped his chest. He was slipping into a flashback.

"Tara, go. Go now," said Guaman. "They'll take you! Go back to Milagro. You'll be safe there."

"What are you talking about?" said Raura. "Do not insult the family and the llajta. Tara. I know you're scared, but there is little risk of that which you fear. They won't take you," said Raura.

"I think there is a huge risk," said Tara.

"Tara," said Guaman. He breathed heavily and lowered himself to the ground as he spoke. "If you want to avenge your brothers, go now. Go now!" He cowered his head into his arms.

The decadent curaca dressed as a jaguar was only a few paces away from them. The scouts were sprinting toward them.

"Guaman, what happened to your fearlessness, your courage? You're an embarrassment to me. To all of us," said Raura.

"Mother, the Inkas are what happened to him, and you'd let them ruin me as well if only to protect your honor. You promised you'd help me."

Guaman wheezed, "Run."

Tara dropped the monkeys by her mother's feet and cried, "Here are the offerings. If Colla doesn't understand, I hope Mamaquilla will."

She ran.

"Tara! If you don't come back, you will no longer be my daughter!" Yelled Raura.

"Run!" Yelled Guaman harder than Tara ever heard him yell.

Chapter Three

Waranga Hualpa

Tara focused on the tree line. The scouts chased her and they were only a few paces behind her.

Faster!

Faster!

"Little girl! Stop!" Yelled one of the scouts.

Each step she pushed further into the ground. She panted.

Almost there!

A low hanging twig cut her eye. She felt the blood run down her face like a tear. She collapsed into the towering jungle underbrush and crawled in it until she found a hidden log.

"Where did she go?" Asked a scout.

"I think she went this way. I'll go that way and you two search over here," said a scout with a deep voice.

Tara heard their footsteps come near her as they combed the thick brush.

She tried to hold her breath, but her heavy panting won. She hoped the sound of the birds and insects were loud enough to drown the sound.

She found a spot that burrowed into the earth. She lowered herself into it and something sharp cut deep into her leg. She was too scared to feel the pain.

A monkey screeched from afar and several birds took off in flight.

"You think she's over there?" said one of the men combing the area.

"Who knows, it might be her, or maybe it's a snake," said the other man. "Well, anything really. It's impossible to say."

They continued to search the area. The footsteps come near, other times they were distant. She felt powerless because her view of what was happening was blocked by the foliage above her.

"We will not find her, it's not like looking for someone in Cusco, this jungle is too thick. Let's go back," said a scout.

They searched for a short while longer and then their footsteps disappeared and their voices grew fainter until they were gone.

Tara's courage returned, and she pushed herself out from the hovel beneath the log. She poked her head up from the thick foliage. They were gone.

She limped down a game trail at a quick pace but didn't run. The pain of her leg worsened and the trail grew hazardess. The only way to continue was to walk on the smooth road.

The day grew hot, much hotter than it ever got in the mountains. Beads of sweat rolled into her cuts and stung them, others rolled down into her mouth. She spit out the sweaty saliva. There was the sound of the rushing cool river on the other side of a narrow stretch of thick trees. She found a path that led from the road to the river. The water felt refreshing and helped numb her throbbing leg.

She swooped her hand into the water and destroyed her beautiful reflection, "I wish I were ugly! I hate you! I hate being beautiful." She scooped up some mud from the beach with her fingers and spread it upon her face and hair until she felt it dripping off of her. She picked up a handful of gravel and threw a rock into the river, "I hate being beautiful!" She threw another and then another until she was throwing handfuls.

Rocks went everywhere into the water, and onto the opposing bank.

"That's for abandoning us, Pachayachachic, and allowing the Inkas into our lands!"

She threw another so hard it hit the other bank, "That's for abandoning me! And not allowing me to be ugly and safe!"

She kicked the water, "That's for...that's for...that's for protecting me and helping me escape. She lowered her head and sat down on the beach and allowed her feet to flow in the current. "Thank you, thank you."

She rested her head on her lap and raindrops landed on the back of her head. The gentle drops warded off the bugs and darkness chased away the daylight within a few moments.

A shout from the road on the other side of the trees woke her. The sun had yet to rise from behind the towering mountains on the horizon, not that she saw through the fog that blanketed the jungle.

The shout that woke her sounded like Quechua, the language of the Inkas. Hundreds of men yelled in response.

She tried to discern what was being said, but the sounds of the awakening jungle muffled the commands.

The sun rose and the fog lifted. The jungle heat arrived a moment behind the sun. She splashed her face to wash off the dirt from the night before.

Footsteps and voices approached. They came from the small trail that lead to the river. She cautiously looked over her shoulders at the path, but her vision was too blurry from the water to discern anything. The men's voices became clear as they approached. The voices spoke in Quechua.

She grabbed her sandals and darted into the jungle.

"Mother, Father! Why aren't you here? Dear Pachayachachic, help me. Oh my God, please. Anything, help me!" She said under her breath.

She hid in a plant that had leafs the size of her body. From her hiding place she saw the road and a regiment of soldiers and a group women upon it. A few men broke off from the regiment and approached the river followed by two women with empty urns.

Tara's heart pounded so hard that it shook the plant she hid in. She held in sobs that seemed on the verge of breaking through despite her resistance.

The soldiers splashed each other in the river and swam. One of the women filled her urn and she called out. "Men, look. There are footprints!"

The soldiers in the river swam to the beach.

FOOTPRINTS! Tara bit her lip so hard that she tasted blood. She cowered into the bush to conceal herself. She didn't want to breathe anymore. She looked around for a heavy branch or any weapon, should it come to that.

There was nothing.

The soldiers followed the footprints to the edge of the jungle. They grabbed their weapons and took a step into the thick vegetation.

"Topa and Manco, come here! Look at this," yelled the commander from the road.

The two soldiers gave up their inquisition and ran up the path to the regiment. The others with them followed.

Tara gradually stood up and moved to another bush where she could better plan an escape. There, she saw what had drawn the soldiers' attention: two speckled bear cubs playfully fought one another. They tumbled down and across branches high in the trees.

One bear tried to flee the other and jumped to the adjacent tree. Its pursuer tried the same maneuver. He missed and landed with a thud on the road just in front of the commander of the Inka troops. He took a step back. The soldiers laughed.

Tara examined her options to escape, but there weren't any, she knew the soldiers ran faster than she and there weren't any other trails. There was the river, but she didn't trust the current of an unknown river-she watched more than one friend disappear doing that.

Tara sank into the shrubbery where she watched the soldiers and the bears.

The bear that played in the trees ran down and mauled his friend across his head. The bear that fell did not move. The bear mauled his friend again. Still nothing. The bear lowered his head and smelled his fallen playmate. Failing to arouse it, the bear laid next to his playmate and cried. The soldiers awed. But then, the bear that appeared dead jumped up and landed upon his friend with such rapid movement that his friend did not have time to react.

The soldiers yelled and spooked the bears. They vanished into the jungle. Two soldiers ran after them and after a moment returned with several scrapes across their faces and their tunics torn. Their comrades laughed at them, as did Tara from behind her hiding place.

The soldiers nearest her, those that were at the beach, looked at her.

She covered her mouth. She laughed louder than she realized.

They approached the edge of the road and the wall of the jungle. The tallest soldier stepped forward, "I would bet you half of my field of potatoes that there's someone there watching us."

"What are you two looking at over there?" yelled the commander.

"There were footsteps going into this area from the beach, and I just heard someone laugh."

"I saw the footprints as well," said a women. "They were recent. I think we're being watched."

The women ventured to them.

"A week's worth of coca leaves for whoever finds the spy!" said the commander.

The soldiers ran into the jungle.

She stood up and stepped backward. The pain from her injured legs returned. After a couple of backward steps, she turned intending to run to the river. She no longer feared the current. But she was trapped, there were soldiers in front of her between her and the river. The pain was too great. She tripped on a raised patch of soil and fell backward into a thorny bush. Before she wiggled herself free, the soldiers picked her up and pinned her against a tree. Her breath ceased, and she felt her pants become wet.

The commander emerged from between the ensuing crowd. Two guards held her, both holding one of her arms and brought her to him.

A man with a heavy accent introduced the commander, "This is Waranga Hualpa Inka of Hanan Cusco. That means he is the commander of many men, and he belongs to the Inka family, the most powerful family in the world. Whatever he tells you is the law, and whatever he says is the truth."

The hareld withdrew a towel from his bag and wiped the mud off of her face and hair.

"Oh my god! Would you look at this girl!" said Waranga Hualpa. He spoke loud and seemed drunk. "You are beautiful. You could be an aclla."

He appeared exactly what Tara imagined an Inkan Waranga to be, a normal man with an overconfident affect. He wore the same tunic and cloak that his men wore, which were the checkered tunic and dusty cloak, but unlike his men, his apparel was exquisitely clean. The plugs in his ears were the size of his eyes, which were as dark as any other eyes she'd seen.

Tara struggled, but the soldiers held her tight.

"Relax, that was a compliment. Many girls wish they were as beautiful as you," said Waranga Hualpa. He caressed her cheeks and then moved his rough hands to her shoulders and arms. "You Cañari women are so beautiful. It's a shame we didn't conquer you earlier, and it's a bigger shame your men make you do all the work. If the women in Cusco were nearly as beautiful, we should never run out of children to offer to the sun. We shall fix that though, now that we have control of Cañari. Isn't that right men! WE HAVE CONTROL OF CAÑARI!" said Waranga Hualpa.

The soldiers yelled.

Waranga Hualpa's caresses continued. He pushed on her chest, "No breasts yet. How old are you?" He asked.

Tara kicked him in his shin. He raised his hand to slap her, but stopped before her cheek.

Tara did not flinch. "I won't be an aclla!" She said.

She tried to kick him again.

"This little girl is braver than most of you," said Waranga Hualpa to his men.

They laughed.

"If you don't want to be an aclla, we can make you ineligible to be one. You see, the Acllahuasi only accepts virgins. If you're not a virgin, you can't become one. There are one hundred and ninety-nine men here, well, two hundred if you count me. One of us, despite your youth, would be so inclined."

Tara slammed the back of her head into the stubby nose of one of the guards holding her arm. He grasped his face and freed her arm. She gouged the eyes of the other soldier. He let go.

Tara, now free of their grasp, looked around. They surrounded her, there was no escape.

Everyone laughed.

Five more soldiers grabbed her.

"Don't hurt her men, don't hurt her," said Waranga Hualpa. He turned to Tara. She dripped with sweat. "We are here to help you, but a little laugh doesn't hurt now and then. Tell me, what is your name, and what happened to your leg?"

Tara ignored him.

Waranga Hualpa yelled something in a language Tara didn't understand. Another man dressed differently than all the others emerged from the thick of them and lowered himself to look at her leg. He said something Tara did not understand to Waranga Hualpa.

"Beautiful girl," said Waranga Hualpa. "This is the man that can heal your leg. Whatever you did, you hurt it extremely bad."

The man examined her leg and withdrew some ointment from a bag he carried. Tara moved her leg away from him. He looked up, "Please—" with such a strong accent Tara didn't understand his Quechua.

Tara succumbed to the stranger and he gently applied ointment to her leg.

Waranga Hualpa caressed her snow cheek.

Tara screamed.

"Woooo, calm down. Just answer my questions and I'll be able to help you. What are you doing out here, do you need food or shelter?" asked Waranga Hualpa.

"Waranga Hualpa, don't take me to the Acllahuasi, please! Don't take me there. Let me go!" said Tara.

"First, don't call me Waranga Hualpa. To such a beautiful girl as you, it is Hualpa. Next, it is not our duty to take you to the Acllahuasi. I was joking with you, do you remember that laughing thing I said? You should try it. There are special men who come and find girls to be acllas and we are not them. We are just soldiers. Besides, it's ordered that there be no acllas gathered from Cañari without Colla's permission. I only meant to compliment your beauty. Our orders are to only find those in need along the road and see that they are provided for and safe. That is why we are here, now, I ask again, are you hungry, and do you have a place to stay?" Asked Hualpa.

Another man approached Hualpa and gave him a sort of maize bread that Tara had not seen before. It had a paste spread on it.

"Eat this." Said Hualpa. "It's ají, it's a pepper that adds good flavor to the bland bread. Try it!"

"I don't trust you. You are evil, you wish to ruin everything we have here. You killed my brothers, *purun rur'a*!" said Tara.

Hualpa pushed the bread closer to Tara, "I'm not purun rur'a but even with your insult, I'm sorry for the loss of your brothers. This is the first time I am in Cañari so it couldn't have been I that killed them. I'm here to care for you, look at your leg, it feels better, doesn't it? Eat this and let us know you are okay and we will be on our way."

Tara looked at her leg. The man wrapped it with a soft cloth and it didn't hurt anymore. She looked around at the soldiers.

"What choice do I have?" said Tara.

"You don't actually have a choice," said Hualpa. He smiled.

She pulled her right arm free from the soldier holding it and took the bread. First, a small bite to see their reaction. There was none. The maize bread and the ají were delicious. As per custom, she returned the bread to Hualpa, and he took a bite before returning it to her.

"The rest is for you," said Hualpa.

She devoured it.

Another soldier came and gave Hualpa a ceramic cup with two nozzles protruding from the top.

"It's morada," said Hualpa.

Tara looked at him questionably,

"Maize juice," said Hualpa. He pushed it closer to her. He nodded at the soldier that still held Tara's arm, and the soldier let go.

Tara's leg no longer hurt, and each part of her wanted to run, but if he wanted to take her, the deed would already be done. She put one nozzle to her lips and took a sip. The morada was sweet and pacified the spice of the ají in such a way that it left a sweet, desirable taste.

She gave the urn back to Hualpa who drank from the other nozzle.

"Why are you here?" said Tara. "We won the last war, and you were not supposed to return," She looked Hualpa in the eye when she asked.

"It's called diplomacy. Sapa Inka Tupac Yupanqui married Colla and gave her his word that he would protect the Cañari's as if they were his own children. We are fulfilling his orders to do such. You didn't hear that we are friends? No wonder you were so afraid, you thought we were enemies," said Hualpa. He put his arm on her shoulder. He became very serious. "We are no longer enemies, but friends. I'm sorry you did not know that. Here, take this as a token of my remorse. It's called a chuspa. It's a small bag that you wear around your elbow, it's a convenient way to carry things."

The small chuspa was full of food.

Tara raised her head and gave a small smile to Hualpa, "Thank you for your kindness to me. My name is Tara. I am from Milagro and my parents are expecting me in Guapondelig. Now please allow me to go. You have fed me and healed me and I have a place to stay and I will be safe. But I must go now if I am to make it before night," said Tara.

"You're from Milagro, did you say? That is where we are going. I'll look forward to your return there," said Hualpa.

Tara squinted at him. She hoped he was joking.

Chapter Four

Mullu

The soldiers departed toward Milagro and left Tara standing on the side of the road. It was quiet and the humid air felt empty. There were no sounds from the thousands of insects or birds. No branches brushed against each other in the wind. Even the sound of the river seemed quieter than before. She took several steps toward Milagro. The squish of her sandals against the mud path disrupted the serenity.

"No. NO!" She yelled in the direction where the soldiers disappeared. "You don't know Milagro exists. That's my place, that's my home!" She paused and looked down, "No. Please, no."

Next to the road was a tall hill that offered a vantage point of the surrounding areas. She climbed that hill to one of the many clearings on the top to see if Waranga Hualpa and his soldiers were in sight.

She saw in the lowlands below, toward the enormous field of flowers, Waranga Hualpa and his 199 soldiers on the road that led to nowhere but Milagro. He didn't lie to her.

Her breathing deepened as her desperation grew. She picked up a rock and threw it toward Waranga Hualpa as hard as her small body was able. She saw another small Inkan band near the base of the hill she stood upon; they marched in a different direction. Where ever she looked, she saw more Inkan soldiers as if they were ants devouring a fresh morsel of food. She heard faint war horns and disciplined shouts of men carried in the wind of the looming storm. No matter how faint or loud the sounds were each pierced her ears as if saying "Cañari is gone. It is gone."

She crouched on the ground and hugged her knees. She wished to cling to her mother, she would know what to do. But for the first time in her life, she was beyond reach.

She laid down and stared at the sad and heavy sky. A raindrop hit her cheek, and soon another followed. Thunder shook the ground.

The clouds grew thick until it was dark as night. She imaged the cloud was a warm embrace to help her feel safe. The rolling thunder drowned the sirens and sounds of the armies.

She lied on her belly with her cheek on the dirt and mumbled to herself. "What have I done? What have I done by abandoning you mother? I ruined our favor with Colla, I ruined everything. Now here I am on top of a mountain, cold, wet, and crying to myself. I'm so sorry. I'm such a horrible person."

She lost sense of time and wished that one of the multiple lightning strikes would hit her and take the shame away.

The thunder ceased for a moment as the hideous screeches of a condor filled the void.

"Leave me at peace, condor. I want to be alone."

The condor hissed again.

"Leave me!"

Tara heard a thump as something hit the ground. The condor screeched again.

Tara rolled over to see what hit the ground. The unknown object illuminated the dreary meadow overtaken by the drab clouds.

Lightning struck next to it.

Tara wiped her eyes and crawled through the wet grass to it. The light emanated from the same flower that she encountered on her way to Guapondelig, the one she buried the figurine beneath. There the flower stood, just like before. It was dry despite the rain. It stood without a leaf or any sign of a root.

She sat and stared at it for several moments.

"But how?" She said. "You can't be the same flower, or can you be?"

She dug a hole in the mud beneath the flower with a pseudo-curiosity if the wooden figurine her brother made for her was there. To her surprise, she felt it and withdrew it from the mud. The object she bore was not the figurine but a mullu shell, the most prized item in the world.

The clam-shaped shell was smaller than her palm and long blood-colored spines protruded through the layer of mud that encapsulated it. She held it in the pouring rain; the mud dripped off and the bloody brilliance was as great as the glowing flower.

Mullu shells, Tara was told, were only found in distant water lands called oceans. She was told that the lands turned to water and there, different Gods and monsters ruled. Men, chosen by these strange gods, devoted their life to discovering where mullu shells hid far beneath the sea foam—sea foam like the color of half her face. She didn't believe in such tales, but it was the only explanation as to where the shells came from.

"Thank you, Pachayachachic. With this, I will find forgiveness with mother and she will regain the favor that she lost due to my selfishness. It will also protect me from the Inkas, if they try to take me away I can give this to them instead."

The sun rose shortly after and Tara returned to Guapondelig with the shell hidden in her clothes.

Chapter Five

Window

One of the first festivals that Tara remembered attending as a child, she and her toddler friends spent the time running around the fields outside of Guapondelig. They chased each other and played different games as their parents performed ceremonies and visited each other. While playing, she noticed a large stone tower built into the wall of the city that had a window on the outside, a feature that was very rare among Cañari buildings. The window looked large enough for her to squeeze through, and she wanted to hide from her friends. After failing to reach it after a few jumps, her friends found her and she forgot about it until now.

She woke from her reverie when she came across an Inkan patrol. Each muscle in her body tensed and she shook, but the memory of her mother's confidence calmed her. She allowed them to pass as she walked along the other side of the road, just as her mother did. The patrol didn't stop her, but many of the men admired her beauty as they passed. They muttered such phrases as, "Boys, an aclla walks among us.". Or, "It's Mamaquilla's child." She returned their praises or insults-she was unsure what they were-with a small smile.

She emerged in the crowded clearing between the jungle and Guapondelig where she used to play as a child. She casually moved through the thousands of people that surrounded the city. It resonated with lively music as each group celebrated with their own songs. The air was perfumed with the aroma of foods as diverse as the music: roasted corn and aji, llama meat, monkey meat, coy meat, potatoes with salt, fish, maize bread, and the sweet aroma of chicha. But no men were present. No men at all.

She found the window without delay and stared up at it. It seemed too narrow to fit through and too high for her to reach.

It will be risky but Mama needs me. The family needs me.

The window was in sight of hundreds of people. She considered waiting until nightfall but decided to try once and if she failed, she would return later. She ran to the window and lept as if she were leaping across a great chasm. Her fingers gripped the ledge of the window as if it were a branch on a tree so high that letting go would mean death. Her feet planted on a ledge, and with a small squirm, she pulled herself through with enough force that she tumbled down the other side. She landed on a wooden box.

The room was an empty storage room with a foul smell and filled with several ceramic vessels. A commotion filled the room as if the main gathering were on the other side of the wall. She tiptoed through the room and spotted the door drawn by the daylight spilling through the sides. The wooden door opened with a creak and she peered through to a small, empty, and walled courtyard consisting of entrances to several stone houses. There, on the far side, a gap between two of the houses appeared to lead somewhere. She sprinted through the courtyard to the opening and went down a passage between tall brick buildings, one painted as blood and the other of glacial ice. The noise of the songs and horns echoed between the buildings as she cautiously made her way to the end of the passage where there was another wooden door, albeit larger than the first. She slipped through it and emerged at the front of the festival. Thousands of people stood before her.

"Hey, what were you doing in there?" shouted one of the two guards that watched the door.

Tara looked at them, smiled, and then disappeared into the throng of women. She dashed through the masses and forced her way between the strangers to the densest part of the boisterous crowd. She found herself in a small gap between the bodies. The dense crowd blocked the way forward, and the looming Mamaquilla Huasi, plated in silver, rose in magnificent reverence beyond them. It was built atop the gentle incline and created a beautiful scene that touched the innermost parts of her heart. Tara paused for a moment of awe.

Colla approached the edge of the platform.

The crowd hushed.

Colla spoke, "My people, Mamaquilla gave us an abundant year as never before, but it was marred by war and fear. Now, after the offerings we gave Mamaquilla, she provided a way for us to live in peace. Never again shall we starve. Never again shall we have to fight the people of the Sun. Always we shall be able to worship Mamaquilla. This security is given to us because of him," Colla pointed to the Inka tyrant that stood next to her. "I would like to present to you my new husband Sapa Inka Tupac Yupanqui."

The crowd gasped and several people, including Tara, yelled.

Colla, dressed in a silver-colored tunic and a burning headband stood tall and proud beside her new husband who looked down upon her. He wore a blood-colored fringe wrapped around his head with three feathers ascending from it. His ear lobes bore plugs the size of a grown man's wrist and he wore a wide golden collar. His sky-colored tunic was checkered with gold. A cloak that resembled urine covered his back and his long obsidian hair flowed down it.

Colla continued, "You know him as an enemy, but now he is the greatest friend and ally we have. He will assist in the ruling of Cañari and ensure that we always have plenty. He promised me—"

The more Colla spoke, the further forward the audience moved. They thrust themselves toward the platform with such zeal that Tara was unable to maneuver between them. She shifted and shoved to no avail. She squirmed when the swelling women pushed against her. The force and pressure of the crowd lifted her off of the ground. She floated among the crowd as a branch in a river caught in the current, toward the platform.

She panicked and kicked those around her until it exhausted her. She thrust her elbow into the person next to her whose walking stick was pressing into her armpit.

She pushed herself to the ground and crawled between the legs of the spectators. Colla finished speaking, the crowd loosened, and before long she continued on her way to her family.

"Tara, is that you?" said one of Raura's best friends named, Latacina. She pushed the onlookers aside and ran to Tara.

Latacina was skinny and tall, and worked harder than any other woman in Milagro. She laughed at everything and played jokes on everyone, always at the worst of times. She was the complete opposite of Raura, and that's why Tara thought they were so close.

"We've been worried about you. Your poor mother, she looks like she's aged 10 years in the last couple of days. Dear child! Doing things like that to your poor mother will come back and hurt you. Oh you child, oh you bad child. Come with me, you will go to your mother and apologize for the rest of your life."

She grabbed Tara's upper arm and pulled her with such force that Tara almost lost balance.

Chapter Six

Cañari Women

Achache threw his food, ran to Tara, and hugged her legs, "thither, you'e back'!"

"Achache, come back here. Don't make her trip," said Raura.

Tara kicked him off of her legs and scowled at him. His shoulders slumped over, and he returned to his meal.

Tara reached into her bag and withdrew the shell.

"So you came back, huh?" said Raura. She was a few paces away and was yet to see the mullu shell.

Tara's kin that were present at the gathering assembled around them.

"Mother, I'm sorry. I was selfish and did not consider how my actions would affect us. I brought you something so you can regain the favor with Colla," said Tara.

Raura noticed the mullu and almost jumped for it. She refocused on her daughter, "Did you learn anything from your venture?" asked Raura.

"I did. After I left—"

Raura pushed Tara's hand to the side and hugged her. "I did not realize how afraid you were at being taken as an aclla." Raura held her for such a long time that Tara wondered if she'd ever release her.

The other gathered women urged Raura to let go. She released her and held onto Tara's cheeks.

"You were right. The Inkas are here. I spoke with Colla and she said not to fear. She made special arrangements with Sapa Inka Tupac Yupanqui and they won't allow any Cañari girl to be taken away."

Tara jumped and hugged her mother again.

"Thank you!" She released her and looked around. "Where's father and the rest of the men?" Asked Tara.

Raura didn't answer, but took the mullu shell from Tara and examined it. After studying the shell she answered Tara in a flat voice, "The Inkas ordered that our men be instructed on how to be men of Inti. He says men should do more work and not only be warriors as they are now. They are away learning how to farm as they do in Cusco and how to perform other tasks. They will teach us women how to sew and make textiles the Inkan way; it's all so weird. The men should be back soon."

She admired the mullu shell again and glanced back and forth from it and Tara.

"Now, tell me, where did you get the mullu shell? Never before, I mean, it is magnificent, but," she paused. "We're in the mountains, and it comes from the ocean. Did you go to the ocean? And how did you get to Manta and—" Tara put her hand over her mother's mouth.

"I'll tell you mother, I'll tell you everything, but first, I promised Pachayachachic I would give it to you. I want you to regain the favor you lost because of my disobedience and to seek your forgiveness. Really, Mama, I'm so sorry. I learned soon after I left how much I need you."

"I need not regain my favor with Colla because your absence did not cause her to be angry. She inquired of you, and I explained that you ran away because of your love for our gods and that the idols of Inti scared you. She laughed, and we spoke of other things. We shall offer the mullu shell to the gods as a thanksgiving at the Mamaquilla Huasi to thank her for your safety," said Raura.

"Mother, let's just stay here, far away from the Mamaquilla Huasi. I think it's better this way. We can give it as an offering in Milagro when we return home," said Tara.

"You are growing paranoid again, Tara," said Raura. She turned toward Achache. "Come Achache, we are going to the Mamaquilla Huasi again to the place of offerings. We will eat when we return."

Tara hesitated but followed her mother's direction and followed her to the Mamaquilla Huasi where the offerings were made.

"She's right. I'm paranoid is all," she whispered to herself.

Tara allowed the thought to escape her mind and told her mother of her adventure. Before she finished, they neared the Mamaquilla Huasi amongst the thick crowd of thousands of people.

"Hurry up, Achache!" Said Tara. She looked behind her at Achache. He stared at the platform atop of the Mamaquilla Huasi.

"Achache, you're not supposed to stare at the platform, didn't you hear—"

"—Thara, tha' man in the weiwd 'clotheth' ith looking a' you."

"What?" She followed to where he pointed, her eyes locked with Sapa Inka Tupac Yupanqui's who was looking directly at her from atop the platform. She jerked her head away and shook.

"Tara and Achache, hurry," shouted Raura from a few paces ahead.

Tara ran ahead to her mother. She wanted to tell her, but no, she didn't believe that out of the thousands of people in the courtyard that the Inka Tyrant, the most powerful man in the world, the Son of the Sun, commander of 100,000 soldiers, noticed her. No, it was just a coincidence.

They got to the long line of people waiting to give their offerings. At the end of the line was a large stone altar with fire upon it as tall as Tara. Above the flame was a golden idol of Inti and a silver idol of Mamaquilla. On each side of the altar was a person, one Tara recognized as a priestess from Cañari, a woman and dressed in traditional Cañari. She wore leafs in her short hair, and a golden nose ring that hung over her mouth. A silver necklace made of several small plates hung between her bare breasts. She wore a vibrant colored feathered skirt that ended above her knees.

"Who is the man standing on the other side of the altar than the Priestess?" Said Tara.

"He is what the Inkas call a Nina Kamayaq. He serves the same purpose as the priestess but for their God, Inti. His name is Amaru Tupa Inka; he's Sapa Inka Tupac Yupanqui's brother."

Amaru Tupa Inka's ears were gauged, as Tara knew was Inkan tradition. The gauges were large enough for her to put four fingers through them. His llautu was inlaid with several feathers, the color of the sky on a clear day. He wore a traditional Inkan checkered tunic, and over the front of it hung a large golden chest plate. His snow colored hair was braided and descended his back and was lost in a fur cloak, the same color as his hair. The cloak fell to his knees. His lower legs were naked.

Seeing him made Tara want to run, but her mother had been right so far, she trusted her.

Tara felt a heavy gaze upon her from above as they waited in line. She shook her head and picked up her story where she left off. She was at the part of the story where she found the mullu buried beneath the flower. She stumbled on the details and interrupted the narrative with long pauses as she considered what would happen if the Inka Tyrant was, in fact, looking at her.

They drew nearer to the looming Mamaquilla Huasi; its shadow fell upon her. Tara gave into her yearnings. She looked, just for an instant. Colla was so close that she saw all the imperfections on her face, the texture of her hair and the knots of her clothes.

Sapa Inka Tupac Yupanqui's gaze met hers again. He stared at her with such an intensity that Tara didn't turn away. Their eyes locked and he examined her, all of her. Inside and out, her shame, her thoughts, the small hairs upon her legs. She felt violated. The world faded from her mind. The surrounding sounds echoed within her head. An invisible person punched her in the chest. Waranga Hualpa's words bounced back and forth in her head. "We were told that there would be no acllas gathered from Cañari without Colla's permission. You're safe."

There was a nudge on her shoulders, "Are you okay, Tara?" Asked her Raura.

"Huh?" Tara mustered the strength to break the stare.

"What is wrong, Tara? You don't look well."

"He saw me. He stared at me. He knows exactly who I am," said Tara in wisps.

"Who?"

"The Inka Tyrant," said Tara.

Raura rolled her eyes and laughed. "There are thousands of people here, why do you think he saw you?"

"No! Don't look," said Tara. "He has powers, and you can't look away."

Raura looked up to the platform where Sapa Inka Tupac Yupanqui sat and turned back to Tara. "He is standing upon the edge of the platform looking directly at you. Quick, say your prayer and leave."

"I told you not to look!" said Tara.

"I know, but you also told me I would not be able to look away. I am not worried, but go! Present your offerings so we can leave. I do not like the way he looks at you."

"What does that mean? You said that Colla made a deal with him so he wouldn't take me, right?" said Tara.

"Yes, yes, I did. Now go say your prayers and leave," said Raura.

She glanced back up at the platform and then pushed Tara forward.

Tara's confidence dissipated and the pain in her leg returned as they approached the priestess and the man called Amaru Tupa Inka. They accepted the offerings for the silver idol of Mamaquilla and golden idol of Inti mounted to the side of the Mamaquilla Huasi. She sensed that every move she made, small or large, was being watched and admired from atop the platform.

I'm just paranoid, I'm just paranoid, I'm just paranoid

"Your offering, please," said Amaru Tupa Inka.

Tara jumped from fright.

She stared at the furs he wore.

"You like this fur?" He asked with a deep voice. "It's an albino jaguar. It's the same color as half of your face. I've never seen a face like that before."

Tara resisted and bit her lip.

"Such an animal as an albino jaguar would be revered as a huaca here in Cañari and no one would kill it," said Tara.

"You won't believe me," he said, "but Inti gave me the power to kill it with words alone. I spoke such cunning words to it and gave it such sweet gifts that one day it followed my commands. I led it away from the safety of its home and into a trap I made. I threw a rope around its neck and strangled it. Now, I wear the coat."

"Perhaps you should offer it to your God," said Tara.

"Speaking like that is a sure way to get yourself punished. Maybe someone will wear your beautiful skin someday." He laughed at his joke.

"The offering?" Asked the Cañari priestess.

Tara reached into the hiding place in her clothes and withdrew the mullu shell. "I present this offering to Mamaquilla for thanksgiving."

Amaru Tupa Inka admired the mullu shell. He tilted his head and looked questionably at Tara. He held it up so Colla and the Inka Tyrant on the platform above them would see it.

"For what are you so grateful to give such an offering, an item that is so precious they bury it with the noblest of people?" said Amaru Tupa Inka. "From which grave did you steal it?"

He lowered the shell but held onto it; he didn't put it into the flame along with the other offerings.

The priestess said, "Tara of Milagro, for your offering what message do you want to be conveyed to Mamaquilla—"

"—and Inti—" Interrupted Amaru Tupa Inka.

"—what are you grateful for, what favor do you wish to be bestowed upon you?"

Tara hesitated for a moment and then blurted out, "I'M GRATEFUL FOR EVERYTHING!" She covered her mouth, surprised by the volume of her words.

"Everything? Be more specific than that," said Amaru Tupa Inka.

"I'm thankful for my family, my life! My fields, my home, my llajta. And that Colla is not mad at Mother for my dishonorable and cowardly acts. I'm thankful that Hualpa let me go—" Tara continued listing more things, even down to the quality of the maize they grew.

Raura tapped her shoulder.

"—that's about it," said Tara with an exhale.

"I see now why you have such an offering," Amaru Tupa Inka smiled. "Now, Mamaquilla and Inti may return a favor upon you. If they were to do so, what is it that you desire?" He leaned against the wall, expecting her list to take a while.

"I don't think there is anything to gain from it besides forgiveness from my mother for my disobedience. But should Mamaquilla, in all of her wisdom, desire to reciprocate by giving something to me, I would ask her to keep me safe from being taken by the Inka Ty—" Tara paused before she finished the word tyrant. She tried to remember the proper name of the ruler, "I mean Sapa Inka Tupac Yupanqui and forced to become an—"

"—Raura and Tara of Milagro?" A voice interrupted her. The voice sounded smooth, like a clear night with a full moon reflecting with the stars off of a still lake.

Tara didn't finish her sentence and looked up. There stood the sister of Colla standing before them on the polished stairs that led to the platform.

Tara froze.

Raura pushed Tara down onto her knees, and they both kneeled before her. "Cora, what have we done to earn the presence of someone so great?" said Raura.

"Rise, I do not come down to you to be bowed to, but on account of your beautiful daughter. I ask that you would allow her to come to the top of the platform and present her offering to us instead of Amaru Tupa Inka," said Cora.

Achache ran off.

"I am Amaru Tupa Inka," he whispered in Tara's ear.

She jumped.

Raura stepped between Tara and Cora. "Allow me to bring the mullu shell to them. I know the rituals better than she and I would be better suited to present such a valuable object."

Cora smiled, "Colla appreciates your offer, but Sapa Inka Tupac Yupanqui wishes that your daughter go and present it to him and that you accompany her. Besides myself and Colla, she is the most beautiful girl among us. And Sapa Inka Tupac Yupanqui wants to see your face. He says he's never seen such a face before, the contrast is what he calls, perfect *yanantin*. He insists that he see it up close."

Tara bit straight through her lip. Blood flowed into her mouth. She gripped her mother's hand.

Amaru Tupa Inka put the mullu shell back into Tara's limp hand and held it there until Tara clenched it.

Cora extended her hand to Tara to escort her to the platform.

The color fled from Tara's sight, everything blurred, and she became lightheaded like her head would fly away, but it was heavy, so heavy she couldn't support it. Her vision darkened until it was a small funnel of light. She reached for the wall of the Mamaquilla Huasi to catch herself. She fell against it and felt herself slide down the brick wall. A crowd encircled her. She felt a burning sensation in her legs. Hands grabbed her and lifted her up.

She tried to stand, but the world faded again. She fell. Raura caught her and held her tight against her breasts.

"Help me, Mother," she wheezed.

"Oh, Tara, I should have listened to you, my baby. I promise he will not take you away from me," whispered Raura back to her.

Tara bit her lip.

"Now gather your strength and do what they command you with such confidence. You are a Cañari woman, show them what that means," said Raura in a louder voice.

Chapter Seven

Huasi

Tara grasped her chest, her heart beat so hard she heard it. She concentrated on lifting her legs, one after another, up the steep and narrow stone stairs with silver-plated walls on both sides. The light from above shined and reflected off of the silver-plated walls. She squeezed her eyes closed because of the blinding brilliance. Up she went, feeling the way up the stairs with her feet.

Amaru Tupa Inka followed behind her, and her mother in front. When the stairs ran out, she opened her eyes and locked them with the Inka tyrant.

"Do not look him in the eyes, he shall blind you," said Amaru Tupa Inka.

"Then blind me," said Tara.

The guard that stood beside the Inka tyrant stepped forward, "This is Sapa Inka Tupac Yupanqui, Ruler of Tahuantinsuyu, Son of the Sun—"

"—He's the man that's here to destroy Cañari," said Tara.

The guards jumped forward to tackle Tara, but the Sapa Inka raised his hand and the guards ceased.

"I'll have you thrown off of the platform for saying that," said Amaru Tupa Inka. The sun reflected off of his chest plate and stuck Tara in her eyes.

"You will throw me off the platform? Well here, I'll do it for you," said Tara. She dashed to the edge of the platform. It was higher than she expected and she saw Achache below her look up at her. She hesitated for an instant. Several hands grabbed her from behind and pulled her from the edge.

"I said I could have you thrown off, not that we would," said Amaru Tupa Inka. "Here, give me the offering and I shall present it to Sapa Inka Tupac Yupanqui."

"No, I shall take it directly from her," said Sapa Inka Tupac Yupanqui in a slow and deep voice.

"Aclla Tara Inka of Yanantin, you have a mullu shell that is as spectacular as you are, or do you not?"

He approached her. She did not break eye contact with him.

"My name is Tara Milagro of Cañari."

He caressed her face, first the dark side and then the light side, "No, of Yanantin."

She clenched her jaw and used all her strength to maintain her composure during this violation of her dignity. He moved his hand to behind her ear and removed an object. In Sapa Inka Tupac Yupanqui's hand was the same flower that gave her the mullu shell, the one that bore no roots or leaves.

Tara grabbed her ear, shocked that it was there. She never put it there, nor did she feel it.

The Sapa Inka put it to his nose and inhaled, "Never have I smelled such an aroma. Where did you get this?"

Tara did not answer him.

He walked back to Colla and gave it to her.

"You are a daughter of Mamaquilla and Inti. Only a daughter of gods can wear such a flower, and as a daughter of the gods you will no longer be considered of Cañari dissent but of Inka dissent. You will be an Inka by privilege. You shall be taken from this land of which you do not belong and go to Cusco. You shall reside only in the holiest Acllahuasi," said Sapa Inka Tupac Yupanqui.

Tara closed her eyes and cried.

"My dear brother," said Amaru Tupa Inka. He stepped between Tara and the Sapa Inka. "Such an honor cannot be bestowed on such a barbarian as a girl from Cañari. Such a privilege are only for those in the Cusco Valley!"

A guard hit Amaru Tupa Inka in the chest with a club. He attempted to block it and the club hit his hand but failed and it dented his chest plate. He showed no pain.

The Sapa Inka put his hands on Tara's shoulders. "You cry because of honor? That is an appropriate response."

"These aren't tears of joy. I would rather die than go there," said Tara. She lunged toward the nearest guard and gripped his sheathed knife. The guard grabbed her hands to keep her from taking it. She pried her legs against his legs to leverage it free, but she was not strong enough. Several men pulled at her shoulders and sides to get her off of their comrade, but she wouldn't let go. She twisted his hands so the knife pointed directly at her belly. She wiggled free and sent herself toward the sharp blade point with strength enough to impale herself. The guard with whom she wrestled collapsed causing Tara to miss the blade by a finger's width.

During this brief scuffle, Raura yelled and cried, but no one heard it. She ran to Tara and held her close. She turned to Sapa Inka Tupac Yupanqui, "Such a calling—"

"—No one shall not speak to Sapa Inka Tupac Yupanqui directly," interrupted Amaru Tupa Inka. He still held his bloody hand in his tunic. "unless you wish to be beat as well. What is it that you wish to tell him and I shall relay it for you?"

Several guards pinned Tara to the ground. Raura looked from the Sapa Inka to Tara and back to the Sapa Inka. She addressed Amaru Tupa Inka. "Such a calling for one's daughter is all a mother desires. Please forgive her and the family. It's an honor for her to go to the Acllahausi. She is afraid is all. Please remember, oh dear Sapa Inka

Tupac Yupanqui, she is young and unfamiliar with the customs of such a great one as yourself."

"I hate you," said Tara. The guard's weight on her jaw muffled her voice.

Amaru Tupa Inka relayed the message.

Sapa Inka Tupac Yupanqui stood up and approached Tara. He lowered himself next to her, "Colla told me that the women of Cañari are very strong. I believed her, but until now I did not see what she meant. Aclla Tara Inka of Yanantin," he said. He held her hand and lifted her off of the ground. "The women of the Acllahuasi are strong too, and they are what makes us Inkas so great. All girls want to go to Cusco, all girls want to go to the Acllahuasi."

"I'll never go," said Tara.

"Knowing my daughter," said Raura to Amaru Tupa Inka. "She would that you respect the tradition of Ayni that the Inka's practice. Offer her gifts or a feast and she shall then go to you without resistance."

"There is no other way. Ayni shall always be honored," said the Sapa Inka.

"Amaru Tupa Inka, see that Tara and her family are brought back to Milagro safely. See that she understands the privilege that has been bestowed upon her."

He dismissed them with a wave of the hand.

"Oh, and have Tara carried upon a litter," he added as they descended the stairs.

Chapter Eight

Ayni

Tara and Raura set on their way to Milagro as ordered. A guard of twelve surrounded her wooden litter, which was carried by 8 men and slightly larger than she. In front of her was Amaru Tupa Inka, draped in his albino cloak. Behind her were Raura and the other women from Milagro and her kin that were with them at Guapondelig.

Tara didn't speak for the rest of the day, nor the following day, or the next. Her desires and opinions were naught and so she had no reason to grace them with her voice, or with her breath that she wished would stop. Any desire for life was gone.

Waranga Hualpa stood in front of his regiment of one hundred and ninety-nine soldiers to welcome the residents to Milagro. He appeared more Inkan than he did previously to Tara. His average height, a head taller than she, his smooth dark face, his perfectly braided hair and his gauged ear lobes made Tara hate him.

"My men aren't here to cause harm. They are here to assist in building a brighter future for you." He proclaimed and then turned to Tara. "I didn't know if I should believe you when you told me you were from Milagro. Welcome home."

Tara jumped from her litter and passed him without a glance. She went to her family's small straw hut nestled on a nearby knoll. It stood in the midst of forested hills that smelled of guavas and the delicate flowers. The twelve assigned guards tagged along behind her, the litter behind them, and Raura behind it.

Raura convinced the guards to remain outside while she went inside the one-room stone house. Tara was in the darkest corner, laying down on the dirt.

"Tara," she said as she put Tara's head on her lap. "There was no way to refuse the Sapa Inka's request. Running or killing one's self is not honorable. Do not be mad. Our honor is higher than any other llajta because of you. The benefits given to our llajta have already started arriving because of your reputation. Did you see the sacks of coca leaves that Waranga Hualpa and his soldiers have for us? You being an aclla is an honor. Why are you not happy about all this?"

Tara only stared at her. Raura sighed as she realized that she wouldn't receive an answer.

"I have reason to believe that the guards do not know about Achache," said Raura. "I do not know where he is, but maybe that is best. I need at least one child left. Do not mention his name or refer to him."

Raura removed Tara's head from her lap and made her way to the door.

"After whom would you prefer that I name my children after?" Said Tara. "I mean, those children that will result from me being a sex servant? How about I name them Raura? It will be the name of the woman that's responsible for their existence and their ultimate miserable death," said Tara.

"I hope, I hope..." said Raura. She tore the worn cloth door from the fastener. She picked it up and threw it and left.

Tara didn't leave the hut for days. She refused all visitors and soon no one wanted to visit her.

Raura found another place to sleep.

The guards stood outside and occasionally peeked in for the first few days. After seeing her in the same place and position upon each inspection, they ceased checking. As she listened to their conversations over the days, she learned that only two of them remained. The others departed to join Hualpa's regiment readying the community for the Sapa Inka.

She awoke one evening by a man singing a reflective tune in the tone of one that didn't realize their song was being listened to. It reminded Tara of her eldest brother, who used to do the same. After several verses of the song Tara noticed a spark of energy within her, it was enough for her to emerge from the dark hut and discover the singer.

The two guards that remained to watch her sat against the wall of the hut, drunk and asleep. Their bronze and stone weapons stood beside them.

She imagined using the weapons to kill them and escaping into the dark jungle of the savages of the lowlands. The guards carried a small stone knife on their side. It was the same kind that she tried to stab herself with on the platform at the Mamaquilla Huasi in Guapondelig. Her mind ventured back to killing herself. Images of the warm blood flowing down her neck as life left her made life not seem so bad. How good the cut would be. She smiled for the first time.

Tara took large steps toward the guards, she was mindful to be quiet; she watched for branches, rocks, anything that made noise and could wake the guards. The closer she got to them, the more excited she grew. She would put the knife into her abdomen, one thrust and slice until she lost all strength, no, she would slit her throat. There is nothing to be done to save a life after the throat is slit. Or, she thought as she searched for her heartbeat.

A knife to the heart, like how my brothers died. The heroic way to die.

She bent over and put her finger along the knife blade and it bore blood. She laughed as she watched it come out of her.

"More! I want more blood!"

Her sadness and emptiness flowed from her with the blood. She sliced her palm and laughed louder as the blood flowed down her arm, but she got distracted from her moon-lit reflection in the polished bronze of a battle-ax.

What is so pretty about this face that even the Sapa Inka takes notice of it?

She hesitated, unable to decide whether to make the cut of death with the battle-ax that bore her reflection or the small knife.

The soft singing started again.

She picked up the knife and put it against her throat. As she pressed, she felt more alive than she remembered at any point in her life.

Just cut!

The song filled the air. It sounded like her brother's voice.

Brother, I'm coming to you!

She slid the dagger across her neck, but with little force. It produced a small bead of blood. She examined the blade and was shamed by the pitiful small streak. She put the dagger on her neck again, but a vivid image of her dead brother singing by the river flashed in her mind. It convinced her that it was him. The sweet idea of being free of the world didn't seem as fulfilling anymore, not until the singer was discovered.

With her bloodied hand, she held the slit on her throat to stop the bleeding of both. She placed the dagger by the guard's side and tiptoed to a nearby vantage point.

She poked her head around the corner of the hut next to hers. There was the river and a man next to it. The light of a million stars lit him up, and it was Hualpa sitting alone, making a pair of sandals and singing to himself. He looked up and smiled at her.

He looked spectacular for an instant. His shiny hair, eyes, and lips gleamed off of the stars and blended with the water.

"Tara! Where have you been? I've been wanting to say hello. Come, come sit with me."

The moment of infatuation disappeared, and she ducked back behind the corner.

"Oh, come on. Really, Tara? Come back here," said Hualpa.

She dashed back to her hut, where the guards were sleeping, but now they and were in a frenzy looking for her. She hid behind a tall tree for a moment while she looked for the knife. It was gone, along with the battle-ax. The guards moved closer to her hiding spot.

"—When we find her, let's make her hurt so bad she'll never be brave enough to venture away from mom again." Said one of the guards.

"If we harm her and Amaru Tupa Inka finds out, we'll be tortured to death." Said the other guard.

The guards were halfway to her.

"Oh, like he actually cares. Have some fun! I've done it several times, it's very simple to hurt someone so bad that they never speak of it. Especially little girls."

Tara crawled away from them and went back to the river and sat beside Hualpa hugging her legs. She said nothing.

"So now you come over here and act like we're best of friends, do you now? What do you want from me? Friendship?"

Tara didn't respond but wiped the blood from her neck.

"And what happened to you there? Every time we're together, there's something wrong with you," he said. He wiped her neck with a small towel he pulled out of his chuspa. "It's not that bad, it'll heal up within in a couple days."

Tara expressed no gratitude.

"You caught the attention of the Sapa Inka and he was so taken by you he gave you access to the Acllahuasi in Cusco. I don't recall any time other time that a non-Inkan girl was allowed there. I guess that's congratulations!" said Hualpa.

There was a tear in Tara's eye. He wiped it.

Tara pulled her face back.

"I remember you saying you are afraid of being an aclla, but really though, it's a wonderful life, or so I hear. I actually can't go inside of an acllahuasi but everything will be provided for you. You will participate in the holiest rituals in all of Tahuantinsuyu. You will be held in higher esteem than I am, a man that has sacrificed everything to fight for the Sapa Inka's glory. You! This little girl sitting in front of me will be a child of the—"

She stood up while he spoke and put her face right up against Hualpa's,

"—I don't want to be an aclla, I don't want to be raped or have my children killed in whatever ritual you think your god commands. I will find a way to rally men to fight you or I will kill myself. I hate you SO much," said Tara.

Hualpa scoffed. He moved backward and put distance between them.

"But really though, you need to calm down. You won't be raped, you have to be a virgin to be an aclla. Who told you that anyway?"

"How do you know? You just said that you don't know what goes on in the Acllahuasi. You have no idea. You don't even know what the guards will do to me when I go back to my hut."

Hualpa stared at her and then chuckled.

"After a long day, I finally relax and now you come to ruin it. Understand this, you may get your battle, but if you do get it, the Sapa Inka will order that your entire village be destroyed, everyone killed, farms burned and the fields salted—"

"—There is no salt here—" interrupted Tara.

"—Stop. Interrupting. me."

Hualpa pressed his hands together and made a fist. He didn't blink as he stared down at Tara.

Tara thought he might hit her.

He calmed down and then continued.

"The Sapa Inka will have salt brought here and it will render your land useless. But it will also be forbidden for anyone to inhabit this land again, forever. They will degrade your holy places, we shall erase your histories, your honor, and any prestige will be gone. In short, Milagro will have never existed."

Tara opened her mouth to interrupt again, but Hualpa's eyes become fire. Instead, she bit her lip.

"But really, you confuse me little girl. The Sapa Inka has given you the greatest honor a girl can ever hope to receive. He did more than that when he allowed you to live after insulting him. He then honored you higher than any other girl. You say thank you by threatening war? Look Tara, I have seen women less beautiful than you beg for mercy for their people in front of twenty-thousand Inkan soldiers prepared to wage an endless and brutal war. The women's wishes were granted. You, alone, are more powerful than any recruits you can muster and you've decide to waste such power." He picked up his drum and turned away.

Tara gaped as she watched him leave, "LIES! YOU ARE A LIAR!"

He turned, "But really, better a liar than a fool."

Tara was angry. Anger unto hatred. She ran past the guards and back to her hut. She collapsed on the straw covered floor. Exhaustion didn't come, nor did the sleep she sought. Instead, the depression lifted.

The two guards came into her hut.

"I WILL KILL YOU." She yelled and pointed at one of them. "I WILL BEAT YOU TO DEATH AND USE HIS SKIN TO STRANGE YOU. I WILL BURN THIS HUT DOWN AND HOLD YOU GUYS TO THE FLAMES AS WE ALL BURN TO DEATH. I WILL DROWN YOU IN EACH OTHER BLOOD."

The guards walked backward and left.

She paced back and forth for what seemed to her like a short while but was the entire night and the next day. She laid down again to sleep; it fled. Instead, she went to the cloth door and poked her head out. The world was moist and still, all was quiet other than the insects whose noises overtook any sign of human life. It was as if she was alone in the world.

The aura of a burning torch in the distance shown through the fog. Her guards were slumped over a log. Their heads were in a puddle of blood. She stepped over one of their arms and plodded to the plaza. She heard a muffled yell through the fog. And another yell from the other direction.

She jumped behind a bush and waited a moment. Both screams were silenced and followed by the same insect noises filled darkness.

Is everyone dead? There was a battle!

The more she thought about it, the more she realized it's what happened.

They are all dead. And now I am truly alone.

She continued on the path until she reached the torch. It stood alone and she saw no sign of why it was there or who put it there. She walked past it until she was almost to the place where she saw the plaza.

There was another scream in the distance. She was a few paces past the torch and the fog was lifting. She held her breath as she assessed what happened, or was happening. A hand covered her mouth and another grabbed her waist.

"Shhhh," said her captors.

They gagged her and threw her over their shoulders.

Chapter Nine

Milagro

Tara kicked and punched her captor as they carried her deep into the jungle.

Is this Hualpa? Who is the other person?

The darkness concealed the color of their cloaks and the style of their hair. She fought harder as her enemy carried her further into the jungle. The accomplice bound Tara's legs and arms to prevent her from kicking and punching.

When Tara gave up her fight and complied, her captor set her down with care not to hurt her.

"Tara, be silent! I'm going to remove the gag," said a woman.

Tara recognized the voice. She tried to punch her with her bound hands, but the woman caught her fist and laughed.

"You recognize my voice, don't you?"

"I'm going to let go of your mouth. Do you promise not to scream? I am a friend."

Tara shook her head in the affirmative.

The women struggled in the darkness to untie the knots. Eventually, one of of the women produced a knife and she cut Tara's bindings.

"Latacina?" Said Tara.

"Yes, Tanto and I are here to rescue you. You remember Tanto from the festival, don't you? She's your mother's friend from the Quillojos Llajta."

Latacina whistled identical to a bird call.

"That's the signal that I found you," said Latacina.

Tara was relieved but her gratitude promptly turned to scorn.

"Why didn't you just tell me and I would have come willingly? I thought you were the Inkas," said Tara. She spoke in a harsh whisper.

Latacina and Tanto laughed, "Where's the fun in that, my dear?" said Tanto.

Tara bit her lip and glared at Tanto.

"We were going to your hut to rescue you, but there you were in front of us," said Latacina. "Lucky we found you there or else I don't know what we would have done."

"Well, thank you both for rescuing me even though I don't appreciate how you did it."

"Some day, you'll laugh about it," said Tanto.

Tara ignored her, "Where is everyone? Where are we going?"

"Everyone is safe," said Tanto. She and Lacatina. "We'll fill you in as we walk. We must remain very quiet and can't use a torch in case there are Inkan Warriors hidden in here."

Tanto led them down a small path that Tara never knew existed.

"How can you navigate this path, it's completely dark," whispered Tara.

"Mamaquilla has given me exceptional eyes," said Tanto.

"I'm glad that you're talking again." said Latacina. "We were all worried about you. Now, for what's going on. Your brother Achache found your father and he raised a band of men to cover our escape from Milagro. After learning about your fate, all the women are afraid for their own daughters and demanded that we escape. When we learned of Achache's actions, we poisoned the chicha of many of the men, but the main force is still asleep. It's only a matter of time until they awake and see what happened. When that happens," she paused for a moment. "At least we'll have each other. That's the most important thing."

They entered into a star lit meadow with a turbulent stream of clear water cutting through the middle of it. Hundreds of women and girls huddling together, many of whom Tara didn't know. Everyone whispered and insects filled the air.

Raura ran to Tara and embraced her. Tara pushed her away and she fell backward.

"Don't touch me!" Yelled Tara.

"Shhhh!" Said Tanto.

Tara resumed in a whisper. "My life is ruined BECAUSE OF YOU! I hate you, I hate everything thing you've done for me. You're the worst person in the world, even the Sapa Inka is better than you! I hope whatever he gave you in exchange for me causes you to suffer as much as I will."

Raura got back up and hugged her again, this time harder to keep Tara from pushing her away. "I am sorry I did not listen to you, I am so sorry it took me this long to realize that you were right. You will not go with the Inkas, we are running. I love you Tara, please forgive me."

"You told me that honorable people don't run."

"Fuck honor! I want my daughter," said Raura.

Tara ceased resisting her mother's embrace. As angry as she was and as much as she despised her, there wasn't anything she wanted more at that moment than her mother's love.

The sound of a Cañari battle horn jetted over the jungle.

The women gasped and then it was silent.

A foreign horn, one much stronger and louder, answered.

A steady rumbling of drum beats overtook the sound of the awakening birds and wheeling insects.

"We should have already started our journey into the Forest of the Flatlands," said Raura.

She climbed a lone boulder that was in the middle of the stream that flowed through the meadow.

"Ladies of Mamaquilla," she spoke in a soft tone but louder than a whisper. No one but the women standing nearest heard her. "The Inkas have shown us that they do not care for our daughters, our customs, or the promises they made to Colla. They are forcing us to flee our homes and place the hope of our survival in our former enemies in the Forest of the Flatlands that reside on the other side of the river. Our fathers, husbands, brothers, and sons are fighting a much stronger foe so we can escape. Their victory is impossible but they fight so we can escape. If we do not run fast enough, the Inkas will destroy all of us, take our daughters to the Acllahausi, and will make it that we are forgotten forever. We will only be able to outrun them with the help of Mamaquilla. At this time, give your offerings to the Earth and beg her that she will help us."

Raura jumped from the boulder to the grass. She removed a blanket from her bag, it was the blanket that she swaddled her eldest son in when he was a babe. She wiped her tears with it, got onto her knees, cut a corner off of it and released it into the rushing stream.

The other women, mothers, and daughters did the same, some offered hair, others chicha, and others textiles.

A loud horn blared in repeated intervals. It was the Cañari command to arms.

"Let's go!" Yelled Raura.

She picked up her bag and ran along a game trail. Tara followed her and the dozens of women and girls behind her.

Tara sprinted to catch Raura and when she caught up she asked, "When will Achache and father be back with us?" asked Tara as she ran alongside her mother.

"They may not be back with us. They aren't fighting to win, they are fighting to provide us an escape," said Raura.

"Then who will honor them, Mama? When Papa and Achache die, who will tell their stories? And if running doesn't save us, who will remember our stories? And our gods? And...and...everything?" said Tara.

An Inkan battle horn blared from the direction they ran. Several birds took off in flight.

Raura stopped running,

"They've surrounded us," said Tanto.

"This way, down the cliff," said Raura. "Mamaquilla will help us."

They ran down a narrow trail that was cut through vegetation so thick that it cut out all light from the rising sun. The trail was steep; it, it cut back and forth and the switch backs seemed to never end. At the base of the towering walls was the river that led to the Forest of the Flatland.

The hundreds of women followed down the trail and formed a long slow moving line. Raura insisted that Tara remain with her in the lead.

The trail came and went, and much of the time they created a new trail through the dense bushes and shrubbery full of insects, spiders, and snakes. As they worked through cutting through one particularly thick switchback a vile smell protruded and made those in the lead vomit.

Tara and Raura hurled off the side of the cliff. A message was passed to them from the women in the rear that while running, a young girl tripped on a protruding root and split her head open. Tara listened while she leaned against the cliff side. It felt moist. Tara examined her hand. It was bloody.

"I think this is her blood," said Tara.

"Impossible," said Raura.

"Not if she's above us," said Tara. "I'm going back to help her."

"We must keep going!" Said Raura.

"The trail is cut and the sun is getting high. I can see better now. It will be quick to go back and help. A moment is all it will take."

Tara ran back, Raura followed her. The little girl was surrounded by her mother and her other relatives, all who carried supplies and babies on their backs.

Drum beats filled the air from above.

"Help us Mamaquilla, help us please!" said Raura. She looked down at the child lying in blood.

Raura lifted the child's arm and it was limp.

"She is dead, we can hardly outrun the Inkas carrying what little we have. We will have to leave her."

The mother of the girl who carried twins on her back yelled, and the other women gasped at the idea. Such an insult to leave a child's body on the trail wasn't even fit for the children of the enemy.

"No Mama, she's still alive!" said Tara. "Look, she's breathing, hardly, but more so than nothing."

"Tara, she is as limp as any other dead person, look at all that blood, there is no way she is alive," said Raura.

"Please Tara, carry her for me," said the mother. "I can't carry another child." She pointed to the two on her back.

"Nobody will be left here alive or dead for the sake of my life," said Tara. She picked up the child and put her body around her shoulders.

"I hope you will be able to keep up," said Raura. She ran back to the front of the line.

The blood from the child's wound trickled down Tara's front and down her legs until it wet her feet.

Once they reached the front of the line, their run was again reduced to a slow pace due to the difficulty of the trail. The cliff walls were no longer as steep and the morning sun continued to light up a navigable path.

Soon Tara's shoulders were numb from the weight of the small girl, but she didn't dare put her down or show any weakness.

She's still breathing, I know it!

"Tara," said the dead girl.

Tara jumped and almost threw the body.

"I'm died because of you. Should you have only done what you were supposed to do, I would have a long life ahead of me. How many more will die while you try to run from your fate? Do you really think you can outrun the most powerful man in the world, the Son of the sSn? Can't you see that Mamaquilla wants you to go with them?"

"It's too late!" Yelled Tara.

Raura, Tanto, and Latacina looked at her.

"Nothing, I'm just hearing—nevermind."

"We'll get to the river soon, don't worry," said Tanto.

"And then what?" said a woman that Tara didn't know. "We get to the river and what? We wait for the Inkas to kill us there?"

"No! We will follow the river to a place where we can cross it into the Forest of the Flatlands. To the land that is ruled by our new friends," said Raura.

"You mean, who we hope will be our new friends and not just more people that will kill us," said Tanto.

A series of horns sounded from above them. The women stopped and looked up. They only saw the canopy.

The dead girl spoke to Tara again, "Are all these women going to die just so you can live your life that you deem more important than theirs? You are, I know you are. You're just like your mother and only think of yourself and your honor."

"I won't ever be like her!" Yelled Tara.

"Tara, what's wrong?" said Tanto.

"The girl on my shoulders, she's talking to me."

Before Tanto replied Raura yelled. "It's the river! We're at the river, just a little further. I hear it!"

Tanto ran ahead along with the other women around them. Tara remained behind them. She was too weak to run.

"Everyone that tries to cross the river is going to die either by the current or by the savages on the other side," said the child on Tara's shoulders.

"Shut up!"

But the dead girl was right. The river was much larger than any river that Tara had seen. The women congregated on the banks and stared at it. It smelled of mud.

"There's no way we can cross this," said a woman.

No one replied.

"All the Inkas want is you," said the dead girl to Tara. "They are all trapped now, a death river in front of them and a cliff side behind them—"

Tara looked at the steep cliff that stood directly above them like a wall to the sky.

"—Once the Inkas get here, everyone will be slaughtered."

"Mamaquilla will guide us," said Raura moment later. "There has to be a way."

"No, Mamaquilla will not guide us!" said Tara.

Tara placed the child on a small patch of grass. Her little body sunk into the grass until her cold face was all that was visible.

"The only guidance Mamaquilla has given us has been given to me," said Tara. "Each time I try to run she guides me back to the Inkas, it's clear to me now. I must go and submit myself to them. It's the only way. I can plead for our lives and for them to forgive us. Hualpa told me that the Inka will always forgive. Because of me Milagro won't be erased from history. We will not be forgotten," said Tara.

Raura gave Tara a blank stare. "What are you talking about Tara? You have gone mad."

A barrage of rocks fell upon them. Tara looked up, the Inkas stood on a crag far above them and threw rocks.

One of the rocks hit Tacto on the head. She took a couple wandering steps and fell face first into the river. Raura and another tall unknown woman reached in to pull her out, but the current was too strong. Tanto's body floated away.

Another barrage of rocks were thrown. They hit four other women who fell over.

"Quick, get cover!" Yelled Raura.

They ran under overgrown vegetation at the base of the cliff. It protected them from the rainstorm of rocks.

Tara met Raura's glare.

"Mama, this is the day when I become a woman."

"I do not want to hear it daughter," said Raura.

"I was afraid for myself, but now I'm afraid for everyone else—"

—"No Tara!" Said Raura.

"The men are at war with weapons that are meant to fight, but my beauty is meant to win—"

"—we are running because of you, do not say you want to give up," Said Raura.

Tara looked at the dead child's face and then back at Raura. "I am willing to sacrifice myself to save the rest. We are all dead otherwise."

By this time, the other women that gathered beneath the vegetation voiced support for Tara to surrender herself. Three other women were stuck dead from the barrage of rocks. If all it took was for Tara to sacrifice herself to end the ambush, they argued the trade was well worth it. The women with daughters including Latacina didn't want to delay any longer.

The bodies of two Inka soldiers and one of the Cañari fighters fell onto the beach in front of them.

The women jumped from freight and huddled further into the thick vegetation.

"Absolutely not Tara," said Raura. "They will just kill you despite your beauty. Then, they will kill all of us unless if we get to the other side of the river. Think of all the men that have already died fighting for you." She pointed at the dead Cañari soldier on the river bank.

"Raura, listen to your daughter," said a tall woman. "Everyone will die! We can't cross the river! This is a hopeless flight and our men are fighting a hopeless battle."

"Mother, don't you realize, the flower that appeared behind my ear in Guapondelig was meant to win me favor with the Sapa Inka. The mullu shell I found was so he would see value in me. My face is meant to gain his attention, and my beauty is meant to win this war. Mother, I realize it now. My life is meant to be sacrificed. Let me go."

"By the end of the day," mumbled Latacina. "We'll all be floating down the river like Tanto. Tara is our only hope."

Muffled drum, yells of distant men, and an orchestra of bird songs filled the air as Tara and Raura stared at each other.

"If I don't go," whimpered Tara, "all those that fell will be forgotten. We'll all be forgotten. Even if you cross the river, the people of the Forest of the Flatlands will just kill you. I will go through torture for the rest of my life to give all of myself, so the rest of you can survive, so those that died will be remembered. Just, please, remember me."

Tara cried.

"I'm going to go with or without your blessing. Come, Mother, make me beautiful in all the colors and valuable textiles we have with us so that the men will be powerless in my presence."

She stroked her mother's cheek like how she always stroked hers when she was a little girl.

Raura opened her mouth to argue again but was drowned out by a chant of the women, "Let her go! Let her go!"

"Who has a basin? Fill it with water from the river and any soap that we have so we can wash Tara. Go and gather scented flowers so that we can make her smell good," shouted Raura to the women nearest her. "We must make her irresistible to the Inkan purun rur'a."

Raura placed Tara's hair in the basin of soap and water and washed the filth of the jungle out of it. She cried and stopped washing her hair. "I cannot do this Tara."

Tara grabbed Raura's wet hands, "Mama, I know you can. Listen to that loud screaming, the horns, and the drums. That's death coming for you that only I can stop. Please, mother, do this for everyone you love, for your home, for Milagro," said Tara.

Raura resumed.

Latacina put a towel into the water in the basin and wiped Tara's face, first the light side and then the dark side. "Come, we shall work on your face next. We will make your face look like a goddess painted on the finest ceramics from the land of Chimor. Inkan men like those women more than any other."

Another Cañari body fell from the cliff side onto the beach.

Chapter Ten

Beg

Tara went up the path and followed the screams and horns which filled the surrounding jungle. Near the spot where the young girl died, Tara stepped over the dead body of Latacina's eldest son. Beside him was an injured Inkan warrior who sat against a bush too injured to press on. From there, she saw the crag from where the Inkan soldiers threw rocks. Once atop the cliff side and back in the highlands, there was sporadic fighting, death and dying all around her. There were three men fighting a way off on the other side of a thicket. She continued on a different path but came across others fighting there too. When the soldiers noticed her, they ceased fighting, stowed their weapons, and followed her.

Her smooth hair was oiled and looked like obsidian flowing out of her beautiful head. It was coiled around her crown and held in place by a wooden ring. She put a feather behind one ear and carried a flower, the color of a vivid sunset.

She came upon four men engaged in a fight, two Inkan and two of her countrymen, their fight blocked her path through the dark jungle. Three bodies laid dead at their feet.

"Excuse me, may I pass? I'm seeking Sapa Inka Tupac Yupanqui," said Tara. All fight left them. They joined the three soldiers that traveled with her, some acted as a bodyguards, others cleared the path of the dead bodies.

Tara's dress was the color of the midday sky, inlaid with figurines of jaguars. She didn't give heed to the fighting. Each individual person that depended on her success busied her mind.

"Tara?" She heard a man yell. It was her father. He stood against a heavy tree. A thin trickle of blood dripped from his matted and soiled hair. It created a small puddle on the ground. Next to him laid four slain Inkan soldiers.

He extended his arms to her. She stood erect with no indication of going to him. A sensation of self-hate swept over her like a brisk breeze.

Guaman yelled, "What happened, why are you walking with them?" He pointed to the Inkan soldiers that escorted her. He pushed off the tree and limped to her. Tara commanded that her assumed guard lower their weapons and allow her father through. He looked confused.

"Papa, don't be mad at me. I am going to surrender myself. You protected me my entire life, and now it's time for me to save you," said Tara.

"I don't need you to save me. I was saved by your brothers and what have I got for it? They are dead and what remains of me is ruined and weak," said Guaman. "I won't let that happen again."

He raised his club to fight her escort.

"NO! NO FATHER!" Said Tara. She pulled down his arm and stood between the soldiers and him.

"Your sons saved you so you might walk with me at this moment, at this terrible moment. I go to surrender to save their memories, our gods, and our lives. If I don't do this, their memory will die with you, and I, and Mama, and Achache and everyone. The memories of all our heroes will be gone," said Tara. She whispered to him, "Walk with me. Don't let me do this alone. I'm so scared."

Guaman hugged her.

Tara put her chin on his shoulder. A way off behind Guaman was Achache. She gently released her father and ran to him and knelt next to him. He was still breathing.

"Achache, brother, don't die. I'm making things right, I'm going to fix this."

"I'm thowy. I thwied tho thave you but I'm no' throng enough. I will 'ome wethcue you fwom 'uthco. I pwomith! An' maybe you'll love me an' thweat me like I thee other girlth threat theiw bwotherth," said Achache.

Tara hugged his weak body.

"Don't come and save me, they'll kill you. Stay here and take care of Mama and Papa and live a good life. That is all I want. Live the life that I won't be able to!"

Tara held him.

"I must return now, the longer I delay, the more people die. Goodbye, brother!"

"Goodbye Thara," said Achache. He coughed.

Tara returned to her escort, who by that time had created a litter out of the available material and their clothes. They placed Guaman and readied him to be carried beside her. When Tara saw this, she kissed each man on the cheek who carried it.

Their wounds healed with the kiss.

Soon they arrived at the meadow where Tara and the other women gathered the previous night. The meadow was littered with bodies and the stream was colored with blood. Hualpa stood on the far side of it, engaged with a man that Tara didn't recognize. Tara's escort remained at the edge of the clearing.

"It's time," said Tara. She kissed goodbye to Guaman and instead of the kiss healing him, like it did the other men, his face softened and he smiled like a little boy. Then he died. She kissed him again and closed his eyes. She wanted to cry and hold on to him.

"Sleep well, Papa. You deserve a good rest."

She instructed the litter bearers to carry him to Milagro and that Hualpa would take her the rest of the way.

They obeyed her without question.

She turned to Hualpa, who sliced his opponent's abdomen open with his ax. The unknown man dropped his club and fell forward into the stream. Hualpa picked up his fallen opponent's club and gripped it with both hands. He raised it over his head and crushed his skull. The splash of water and blood flew far. Some landed on Tara's face.

Tara screamed and Hualpa looked up at her. He left the club where the man's head had been and raised his ax. He jumped over the stream in an intimidating leap and ran at her. Tara hardly recognized him. He wasn't the kind looking man she previously met, but savage and his face was covered with slime and human fluids.

Tara realized it was a horrible decision to surrender. She turned and ran. Tara knew it was her final sprint. These were her final moments. Hualpa yelled a yell that was just as savage as his appearance, and he lunged in front of her. Tara froze, and when she thought it was her end, Hualpa burst out laughing.

"Oh Tara, you should have seen your face. Oh my god, your face!" He laughed so hard and deep he couldn't stand up straight. Hualpa regained his composure. "Aclla Tara Inka of Yanantin, it seems like there are many men that want to die for you," he motioned around to the fallen. From where she stood, she saw 10 of her countrymen dead upon the ground and more moaning with their injuries. "I can't stop but wondering, does that increase your value to Sapa Inka Tupac Yupanqui or anger him? But I think that depends on why you come to me."

"Where is Sapa Inka Tupac Yupanqui? I want to surrender myself and beg for the life of my people and to give myself to him. He may use me for whatever purpose he desires so long as this battle ceases. You said you've seen a beautiful woman stop 20,000 soldiers. Do you think I can stop one made of only a few thousand men?"

Hualpa smiled his horrible smile. Blood dripped out of his mouth, "Whatever purpose he desires, you say?" He spit. "Didn't you tell me that he was going to impregnate you and then feed your child to you after you grew to love it, and you're telling me you're okay with that?" Hualpa spit more blood.

Tara bit her lips.

Hualpa put his bloody hand on her head. It was missing a finger. "I'll bring you to him. I don't know if you can stop us from destroying you guys, maybe. Maybe not. Or maybe he's going to tell me to kill you right then in front of him. Do you know what I'll do if he commands that?" He said.

"Kill me in front of him?" said Tara.

"You are correct, and without hesitation. You see this ax here? BOOM! It'll be in your beautiful face," said Hualpa. He swung it at her but stopped right before he hit her. He laughed again, "Oh your face. Your face! Be sure you don't let the Sapa Inka see how funny your faces are when you're scared, he might command me to kill you just to see it. Really though, I've never seen someone wince like that before. Like how your eyes go upward like you're already dead." He patted her on the back so hard she stepped forward to catch herself from falling.

"Enough of this Hualpa. Take me to him or I might go back" said Tara.

"No, no response to my insults? Nothing?" asked Hualpa. He laughed again. "Very well. He's back at Milagro waiting for you. He is very mad because of your betrayal, I've seen him massacre thousands of people for slights smaller than what you did."

He paused and gazed at her for a moment. "You are so beautiful. Here, let me wipe this off." He wiped the blood off of her face with a clean spot on his tunic and fixed her hair.

"Now, let's see how you beg. Follow me."

They found Sapa Inka Tupac Yupanqui in the plaza of Milagro. He sat upon his golden stool at the head of the feast that was supposed to be held between the leaders of the Inkas and of Milagro. The food was put out as if the feast was going to happen, although his guards were the only ones present besides himself. He motioned to Tara a place beside him on the ground where an Inka style plate was made.

"This is where you beg?" whispered Hualpa to her.

Tara lowered herself on her hands and knees and approached him. She forced herself to cry.

Once near to him, she lowered her face onto the ground. "Oh, dear Sapa Inka Tupac Yupanqui. You are the Son of the Sun and I always knew that you were, but I was afraid because of your glory. I beg you for forgiveness. You gave me an honor that is saved for only but the gods, and in my foolishness I was scared and I ran away. I did not run to insult you but I am afraid that I am too simple and that I am not who you think I am and that you will be disappointed in me."

While Tara spoke, Amaru Tupa Inka arrived and stood beside Sapa Inka Tupac Yupanqui. Tara didn't acknowledge him, but continued.

"I see the error of my thoughts and actions and I beg you, please dear Sapa Inka Tupac Yupanqui, forgive me and do not to punish my countrymen. They fight for me, they fight because of me, but I give myself to you to do what you may. Their reason to fight is lost, you have won. Please, I beg for mercy for them. If you take me and cease fighting they will stop, they know of your greatness and the miracles you perform and will become your most willing vessels. I personally am not worthy of mercy, if you are mad and seek vengeance, slay me and allow me alone to answer for my weakness and arrogance. I have heard that you are the protector of the poor, Most Powerful Man in the World. Please understand that they are the poor. They hope for your mercy, so much so that it was they that bade me to surrender. If you decide in your infinite wisdom to spare me, know that I will be your most loyal follower, the one that will preach your goodness and mercy to all people. I will go with you to Cusco and become an aclla that has learned the power and might of the Son of the Sun. An aclla that once feared your glory, to one that gives herself freely."

Sapa Inka Tupac Yupanqui turned to Amaru Tupa Inka and spoke to him, who in turn spoke to Tara.

"You may rise," said Amaru Tupa Inka.

Tara stood up but remained looking down.

"Your betrayal angers the Son of the Sun. What he would normally do, and what I told him that he should do is to kill you and continue the battle until everyone is dead. Then salt the earth to kill the land and the ancestral spirits that reside within it. But, the honor he gave you in making you an Inka by privilege is rare. He did so because *he* believes your mother is Mamaquilla and your father is Inti. He won't kill you now because he still believes it. He doesn't glory in killing people who don't deserve to die. You asked for forgiveness and he shall give it to you as long as you promise to never betray him again. He shall spare your people so long as they submit to him and allow the Inkas to control the land how as we see fit: they shall give the Inkas their most sacred idol to be stored in Cusco; they shall allow thousands of loyal Inkan families to settle here in Milagro to ensure loyalty and submission; they shall appoint one among them to report to the Apu of Tumipampa; they shall give the harvest of one third of their land to the Sapa Inka, and another third to the sun; they shall grow what the Inka commands that they grow; they shall provide men to fight when summoned, they shall—"

"—Stop. She understands," said the Sapa Inka.

"They will do whatever is necessary, just stop killing them!" Said Tara.

The Sapa Inka waved to Hualpa and he ordered that a litter be brought for Tara.

"We had this feast prepared," said Amaru Tupa Inka. "It was to pay offering to your people to provide Ayni in exchange for you. One party gives and the other reciprocates. Now, the gift from the Inkas to your people is that we shall not kill all of you. The food will go to the animals."

The litter arrived.

"Get on it, Aclla Tara Inka of Yanantin," said the Sapa Inka.

Tara did as she was ordered. She bit her lip to prevent herself from speaking or refuting her new name.

Sapa Inka Tupac Yupanqui closely watched Tara get into the litter. After she obeyed, he clasped his hands.

"Stop the slaughter," he said.

Hualpa raised his horn and played a staccato pattern. Scores of horns answered it and the Inkan warriors emerged from the thick forest carrying their wounded. The battle was over. Milagro and the surrounding llajtas were saved. She turned her head away so no one saw her weep the first tears of womanhood.

Chapter Eleven

The Drum

Tara covered her small ears. She didn't want to hear the beat of the drum.

"Don't do that, the Inkas will see and get mad," said one of the captive Cañari girls. She was tied to an imposing tree on the boundary of the Inkan military camp.

"I'd rather have them mad at me than listen to it. Do you know what that drum is made of?" Asked Tara.

The captive shrugged.

"It's made out of our friend Pirca. They commemorated their victory by making a drum out of her skin," said Tara.

What!" Said the girl. She had a disgusted face, the face one makes when tasting one's mouth after vomiting.

"Look at it, you can see her sad face sown to the side of it," said Tara. She covered her ears again.

The young captive girl covered her ears as well.

Tara knew she ought to return to the wooden platform that the Inkan soldiers built for her so she could watch the victory celebration. She looked back at it, it stood twice as tall as she. Atop the platform, she saw Amaru Tupa Inka, his chest was open and upon it rested a golden chest plate that reflected the fire's light. Aside him, were other Inkan nobles dressed in the traditional checkered garb.

When she left the platform, she told them she needed to relieve herself. She took the time to venture over to the edge of the camp to see the captives. She didn't have long before they would come looking for her.The celebration was taking place in a military camp that was built over the field of sunflowers that Tara loved. At least that's what Tara thought, but she wasn't sure because there weren't any flowers left. All that was left were the perfectly clean, triangle tents of the Inkan military and dirt paths that led to the gathering point in the middle of the camp where the celebration took place. There was a clay checkered urn of chicha at every path in the camp. The urns were as tall as children. The warriors' women stood beside them to fill their man's vessel when they ordered them to be filled. As the celebration, the women abandoned the vessels, removed their clothes, and joined the dances.

Sapa Inka Tupac Yupanqui and Waranga Hualpa Inka departed with their entourages earlier that day. They left to quell uprisings, similar to the one at Milagro: there were many llajtas that disagreed with Colla's decision of inviting the Inkas into Cañari. They fought to the last woman and child to keep their independence. Had the Sapa Inka remained, Tara figured these Inkan men and women under the command of Amaru Tupa Inka wouldn't have allowed themselves to descend into the disgusting state that they were in. Hualpa and Sapa Inka Tupac Yupanqui were to return after several days. Or many moons. Or seasons. It didn't matter. She would be long gone and in Cusco by then. For now, Tara was alone among hundreds of drunken soldiers that would want to kill her if they learned her true identity. Before Sapa Inka Tupac Yupanqui departed, he announced to the soldiers that she was an Inka, a daughter of Inti. A lie, but it protected her. No one dared question what he said except one man, Amaru Tupa Inka who was in charge now.

"You are so beautiful, Tara, in those jewels and the feathers inlaid in your robes and your oiled and braided dark hair," said the young captive girl.

Tara gripped the sky-colored gown she wore and resisted the urge to tear it.

"Tell me, who were you before you were a captive?" asked Tara. She addressed a captive on the tree next to the young girl. This captive was an older woman that Tara didn't recognize.

"My name is Sycri. I am the daughter of a tradesman from Amboto. He tasked me with finding a route to the rainforest to trade the sacred tea, ayahuasca, that allows for communication with Pachayachachic. He wants to bring it to Quito so that there would be peace." Sycri sniffled, "He told me not to go this way, but I told him it would be fine. Now look at me."

Tara wiped a tear from her cheek.

"My village of Milagro is near to the rainforest where they have ayahuasca. Should we have known each other in different circumstances, I would have helped you," said Tara. She stoked the thick ropes made of agave fibers that bound her to the tree while she spoke. "I've known many people that have partaken in the ayahuasca. When they wake from their conversation with Pachayachachic, they become wise and peaceful."

"You can still help me by cutting the ropes that bind me and setting me free," said Sycri. "The guards left us to go join the drinking. No one will see, they are all too drunk."

Tara studied the large knot on the back side of the old tree. "I can't cut them because I don't have a knife. I will find a way to untie them if you promise to go to Milagro and tell my family that I am well," said Tara.

"I promise I will," said Sycri.

The other prisoners who were tied to the trees beside Sycri echoed the same promise if she freed them as well.

Tara forgot about her troubles and began to untie them, "You must run fast. Go and live a good life, become who you are meant to be. All of you. And fight these Inkan invaders," said Tara.

"If you come with us, we'll be able to put up a better resistance," said Sycri.

Tara struggled with loosening the knot, but eventually figured it out and moved onto the next captives. Sycri ceased crying and helped her untie a boy slightly older than Tara who tried to appear brave, but his chin wouldn't stop shaking. Tara recognized him as a boy from a community on the other side of the large mountain.

He kissed her on the forehead and ran into the forest. Raura often talked about him as a future husband for Tara.

She pushed the thought out of her head and untied a young girl next to him, younger than her, that cried.

"Thank you beautiful Tara, thank you so much! The guards said they were going to sacrifice me by making me walk to the top of a mountain until I froze to death," said the girl.

"Don't call be beautiful," said Tara. She turned her attention from the bindings to the party.

"I think the guards are returning," said Tara.

Sycri shot a glance up at the party, "If they are, you have to come with us Tara. They will kill you for freeing us,"

"If I leave here, they will kill my family and everyone I've ever known. I have to stay and go to this dreadful place they call the Acllahuasi to protect them. You need to run Sycri. Once they discover you're gone they will come after you. Run!" said Tara.

She stopped talking when she felt tears coming like a volcano erupting. She swallowed hard, "Go! They are coming."

"You're going to the Acllahuasi?" Said Sycri, "I'm so sorry for you. We, in Quito, are taught to never allow our attackers to get the satisfaction of seeing us in pain."

"They won't ever stop," said Tara, "Nothing can stop them. It's my fault for being beautiful."

"I'm so sorry," said Sycri. She finished untying the boy who ran into the bushes without saying a word.

"GO! GO! GO!!" said Tara.

Sycri put her hand on Tara's shoulder that was covered with her robe made of the finest material, which was almost equal to the fabric which Sapa Inka Tupac Yupanqui wore. "I'm so sorry." She repeated.

"RUN!" Said Tara. She pushed Sycri's hand off of her. "Get out of here! I'll untie the rest."

She ran off.

Tara jumped to the next captive. He was naked and covered in filth. Tara used the base of her skirt to wipe his face. It was the husband of the former ruler of Milagro. She hugged him before sending him after the others.

The soldiers that Tara saw coming turned away from them and relieved themselves on a nearby tree. Afterwards, returned to the party with no regard to the prisoners.

Tara jumped from captive to captive, freeing them until all the captives were free.

The last captive that Tara freed, a young boy that once loved Tara, placed his hand on her shoulder. "Every day you are mistreated by the Inkan soldiers, remember that I will be in Milagro fighting any changes they try to make. I will make sure that you are remembered forever."

He kissed Tara on the lips and ran into the jungle. Tara looked back at the empty ropes limp at the base of the gigantic trees. It was as if the captives vanished. Tara was left alone, Tara Inka of Yanantin, Tara of Milagro, Tara of Cañari. Tara of whatever. It didn't matter, what does a name matter if there is no one to call it?

She returned to her post on the platform and sat down on the small stool reserved for the most important people in Tahuantinsuyu.

The large platform was empty, everyone had joined the party. She looked down upon them where the celebration had descended into chaos and an orgy. There were piles of chewed coca and the humid air smell of chicha. The monkeys descended from their sleeping places and joined the party and the drinking. They danced with their human companions.

At the beginning of the night, the songs were victory songs, but now they sang of the horrible things they did. Their dances changed from celebratory to reenacting events that never happened, dancing between human and monkey, monkey, and monkey, human and human, all to the beat of the drums, of one which was made from Pirca's skin. The men and women already too drunk to dance or have sex spread out on the ground slept.

Soon the songs and dances became about the invasion of Milagro. The dancer that portrayed her father was dressed as a lizard, her mother and herself as spiders, and Achache as a snake. The animals, taken as a whole, were believed to be the vilest creatures. They portrayed them as incestuous, lude, dishonest and dirty people who led their filthy followers to defy the glorious and wholesome Inkas.

Tara stood on the edge of the platform, "Stop! Stop! The Cañari's are kind people, smart and wholesome!" She didn't think anyone would hear her, but Amaru Tupa Inka dropped his vessel of chicha and pulled his penis out of a man's mouth. He glared at her.

He stepped toward her over his shattered vessel which cut his foot. He didn't seem to notice the thick trail of blood behind him emerging from the cut. Trying to climb the steps to the platform, his bloody foot caused him to slip. He hit his forehead on the edge of the platform but he continued his approach without indicating that he noticed it either. Tara step backward, away from Amaru Tupa Inka, until her heels hung off of the hard edge of the platform.

He regained his footing and went so close to Tara that when he spoke, the spit landed upon her face and she tasted sweet chicha on his breath. "What does the little spider say? You're the most disgusting thing I've seen. And you think you can be an Inka like me. We'll see about that. We'll see."

Tara pushed him away from her and regained her footing on the platform.

"Call me what you want," said Tara, "but you will portray the Cañari history and culture correctly. You will tell the stories of our gods and heroes accurately. You know it as well as I that our men defeated you Inkan trash twice and the only reason you won this time is because Colla decided to marry Sapa Inka Tupac Yupanqui. You would have never won otherwise."

Amaru Tupa Inka gripped her tunic between her breasts and held her over the edge of the platform. She resisted screaming and held on to his glacial colored cloak.

"We won without difficulty," he mumbled. "It was simple and it doesn't matter what you think because it's I that chooses how it's remembered. What I say is your history and culture now. Our heroes and gods are yours now."

"The prisoners are gone!" Yelled one guard. He ran from the area where the captives had been tied.

Tara smirked and her eyes met Amaru Tupa Inkas's. She didn't see the anger in his eyes like she expected, nor any sign of life. Behind the cavernous eyes was an abyss of humanity filled with stone, and hardened with hate and anger.

"How did they get loose, and where did they go?" Asked Amaru Tupa Inka.

"They turned into birds and flew away. Don't ask me where they flew away to, I've been here the whole night," said Tara.

"Tara," said Amaru Tupa Inka. He over pronounced each slurred word. "I once told you I would throw you off of a platform. I still intent to. Now, tell me the truth."

"That is the truth. If you believe all those lies, how about you just believe that they turned into birds and flew away? So sorry I can't help you," said Tara.

"Then you should turn into a bird and fly." He pushed her off of the platform. She fell onto her back onto the dirt below her.

"Bind the girl!" Yelled Amaru Tupa Inka, "She is an enemy! And chase down the captives."

The soldiers split into two groups. The smaller group grabbed Tara's hands and legs while other men and women disappeared into the jungle in search of the escapees. They were so drunk that several of them stumbled and fell onto the tent walls.

Amaru Tupa Inka descended the stairs. He slipped on the same step as before and slid down the remaining stairs. He threw a nearby figurine of Inti into the nearest tent and yelled.

The men that bound Tara brought her to Amaru Tupa Inka.

He wiped the blood off of his forehead and smeared it on her face.

"You will learn your place. You will! And you will learn that what you think doesn't actually matter."

"You can't treat me like this, you are under orders to protect me," said Tara. She spoke with the same spite that he addressed her.

Amaru Tupa Inka backed away and laughed, "I'm under orders to keep you alive and I'll be sure you don't die."

"Tie her up over there" he mumbled. One of the servant woman placed another vessel of chicha into his hands. He emptied it and the woman brought him another.

The soldiers dragged Tara by her feet. The dirt tore through her tunic and by the time they stopped her back was bare. They tied her to a pole near the fire in the middle of the celebration. They used larger ropes than had been used on the captives to tie her midriff to the pole. They tied her arms from her elbow to her wrists. The bindings were so tight she lost sensation in her fingers.

"Please, tie me up where the other prisoners were, not here. The fire is too hot, it'll burn me," cried Tara.

Amaru Tupa Inka picked up an armful of wood, "Sorry, I can't. Maybe your god Mamaquilla will save you from the fire."

He dropped the wood on the fire.

Tara scorned the bonfire.

Amaru Tupa Inka returned to the platform and ordered a new song and dance depicting what just happened. In the new dance, Tara turned into a snake and tried to kill several soldiers until the heroic Amaru Tupa Inka cast a spell on her that bound her.

The soldiers that pursued the escapees returned with some captives and brought them to the base of the platform. The dances ceased and the Inkas formed a circle around them.

"Kill them," sung Amaru Tupa Inka.

The soldiers laughed.

Amaru Tupa Inka spoke in a loud mumbled tone, "I am only under orders to make sure Tara doesn't die, not these creatures that tried to run. Stone each captive individually so the others can watch and then burn their body in the fire nearest to that traitor." He pointed to Tara. "While the body is burning, stone another captive, and then burn their body."

His orders were carried out and Tara and the other escapees were forced to watch as they burned the bodies until they were crisp charcoal.

Tara felt the skin on her face gradually wither. She smelled the scent of burning hair. Her hair. The fire increased in size to consume those she tried to save.

Chapter Twelve

Sycri

"Poor Tara looks cold," said Amaru Tupa Inka. "Make the fire bigger!"

The soldiers placed two more bodies on the fire and it ate them with a roar.

A soldier entered the circle with Sycri on his shoulder. As he passed Tara, Sycri said, "Tara, I'm sorry I failed you."

The soldier threw her down next to the other captives waiting to be stoned.

Tara yelled, but the gag muffled it. Tara tried to break free to speak, but the ropes were too tight. Her sleeve caught on fire and she put her face into the flames to burn the gag. After laughing, the soldiers dumped the latrine water on her to put it out. The putrid water felt like lightening bolts entering her raw skin and shooting down her legs. She knew she would be scared and ugly forever and the gag, although damaged, was still intact.

The soldiers threw another captive's stoned corpse into the fire while another picked Sycri up and dropped her in the middle of the circle. A stone flew from the crowd and hit her shoulder with a thud.

Another rock hit her abdomen.

She fell over.

Tara rubbed the burnt part of her gaga against the pole to which they bound her until it broke. "SYCRI, DON'T GIVE THEM THE SATISFACTION OF SHOWING PAIN SYCRI!" Yelled Tara.

There was no response.

The monkeys yelled and jumped from shoulder to shoulder of the murderers and threw stones themselves.

Tara struggled with the bindings of her arms and legs. "I'm going to tell Sapa Inka Tupac Yupanqui about my treatment! He ordered that you treat me well! And even I know Inkas treat prisoners better than this." She yelled in her coarse voice.

Mist made of human fluids sprayed into the air from the stones. It fell onto those present and painted their skin. Along with the droplets of fluids from Tara's friends, an ember from the fire landed on her leg. As it burned through the skin, she heard the sizzle.

If Sycri hasn't screamed, I won't!

Amaru Tupa Inka yelled and demanded silence.

"Men and women. If I remember, Tara is going to the Acllahuasi where only the most beautiful of women are allowed. Well, look at her. She's burned and ugly now. She no longer can be an aclla. After we are done burning the bodies, we will fuck her once for each captive that we didn't catch. After all, she need not be a virgin anymore."

Sycri ran from the circle where she was being stoned to Tara. The soldiers caught her before she reached Tara but she came close enough to be heard, "Tara, I will save you!"

Sycri picked up a rock that was thrown at her and hit a soldier across the head.

"No Inkan boy is strong enough to hurt me," said Sycri.

The Inkas clobbered her with sticks.

Sycri's screamed. The savages roared, they got what they wanted. Tara screamed, but a hand from behind her covered her mouth. She looked and there was no one.

"Let's all celebrate the dead girl's success in saving the traitor girl!" Yelled a soldier.

A pierce cracked the air and a roar of thunder so loud took the air out of Tara.

"The body!" said Amaru Tupa Inka. He ran to where Sycri's limp body laid, "Burn it! Burn it now!"

More thunder broke the sky, and torrents of rain descended on them. Such a downpour was unknown in Cañari.

Amaru Tupa Inka and three other soldiers brought Sycri's bloody and disfigured coarpse to the now dead fire. They tried to revive the fire, but the ash became a mud pit. One soldier fell into it and disappeared.

The other Inkan soldiers partied harder and louder than before, except now when they danced they sent mud stained with blood flying onto each other. It didn't take long before it covered Tara. The icy mud on Tara's parched skin hurt like she was burning all over.

They left Sycri's body on the ground to go get chicha that wasn't diluted by the rain and material to build a cover for the fire pit. They had to burn the body because a dead body was as bad as a live body if it remained intact.

Tara looked at the limp body and said, "You told the gods to save me. You sent the downpour, thank you."

The bloody lips of her Sycri moved and said to her: People believe they are incapable of committing such atrocities as this until they do so. Tara, it is up to you to spread the stories of what happened. Without you, our extermination and deaths will be forgotten and these crimes will continue to happen.

The soldiers dredged through mud up to their knees with the materials and two urns of chicha.   "Our camp is ruined," Yelled one of them as he dropped an urn of chicha.

"Don't be such a child," said another, "we're just getting —" he yelled as a wall of water washed through through the camp. The flood took with it all the tents and most of the soldiers and women. Tara, still bound to the pole, waded in the current. Sycri's body resisted the flood for some time, but eventually, she too washed away.

Tara later learned that her family discovered her body and buried it. Where they buried it became the choicest spot for ayahuasca ceremonies. It became a huaca, and people suffering from the worst problems came away from it with the greatest wisdom.

Only a few Inkan soldiers remained when the deluge ceased. They walked through the area that had been their camp and assessed the damage. The survivors organized search parties. None of them were successful, rather, they hid in the bushes and slept.

This was her time to escape.

They will blame my absence on the flood. I will be among those that were lost and they won't come for vengeance. Thank you Sycri.

Chapter Thirteen

The Burn

The embers from the fire damaged the ropes that bound her wrists. She reached for the rocks that made the fire ring. The only rocks she could reach were smooth like a baby's skin. She whimpered but rubbed the bindings against the rock that her freedom depended upon. She pressed on for the rest of the night. If the few Inkas that remained noticed, they didn't show interest.

Tara's bindings wore thin. Her arms cramped. She stretched and raised her head for the first time. The landscape had change. The clouds were gone and the sunflowers that the camp covered had grown back and retook their rightful place: they pulled the tents that remained from the deluge into the ground. The peaceful scent of the flowers replaced the sweet smell of chicha and burning bodies. The only proof of the previous night were the tent canopies lodged in the trees.

Tara smiled, the scab on her face cracked and she winced from the pain. She returned to escaping.

The sound of horns filled the air. They were the horns that accompanied the entourage of Sapa Inka Tupac Yupanqui and his soldiers in the uniformed checkered tunics.

She worked more furiously than before to cut her ropes, the final fibers were fraying against the smooth stone. Her arms cramped worse than before. She broke into a sweat. The horns and drums grew louder, and she heard the marching of the thousands of men and women.

She yelled when she realized she wouldn't be able to break free and hid her arms between her legs as the Sapa Inka and his golden entourage came into view.

Sapa Inka Tupac Yupanqui rode upon his golden litter covered with the most exquisite cloth and carried by 50 porters, just as he did when he departed days before. Beside him was another litter carrying Hualpa. His litter was made of wood with gold trimmings and a wooden seat built into it. He was covered by textiles that looked almost as fine as those that the Sapa Inka had. His litter had 12 porters. Behind them were thousands of soldiers, women, and administrators carrying quipus.

"I don't know where the flowers came from or where the camp went," said the soldier leading the entourage. He led a group of three other soldiers that walked beside Hualpa. Tara recognized them as the four Inkan soldiers that guarded her through the battle as she made her way to surrender.

"As I told you," said another one of the soldiers. "There were problems here from the moment you left. None of the orders given were followed. That's why we went and got you."

"Thank you for getting us," said Hualpa to the soldier. "As a reward, you can join the ranks of my men and replace those that I've lost in the battles."

They went and joined the ranks of Hualpa's regiment.

"Where is Amaru Tupa Inka?" Yelled the Sapa Inka to the remaining Inkas.

The horns awoke them and several fled. A few remained hidden in the tall flowers or in the trees with the monkeys.

Hualpa jumped from his litter and chased one of them down. Hualpa dragged him to the front of the Sapa Inka and threw him into the mud.

"Where is Amaru Tupa Inka?" Said Hualpa.

"He's pulling men and women out of the river," said the man as he trembled.

"What river? There isn't a river here," said Hualpa.

"There is now!" said the soldier. He hesitated, shaken by his decreased prospects of surviving the conversation.

"Don't harm him," called the Sapa Inka to Hualpa. "This was the work of gods, not a mere soldier." He spoke in a deep voice, almost as if the river itself had spoken.

Hualpa yanked the man up and pressed a small knife to his throat. "Should you have shown this much fear in any other circumstance?" Hualpa pulled the flat of the blade across his throat.

He put his knife away and said in a passive aggressive tone, "Run and get Amaru Tupa Inka."

The soldier ran off and Hualpa pulled a vine off a tent that was being pulled to the ground. When he pulled it off, two more vines sprouted and crept up the side of the cotton wall.

"I hate this place! Give me the order I will remove each one of these vines and flowers daily."

The Sapa Inka remained in his litter and his porters took him around. He didn't respond to Hualpa's comment.

Hualpa saw Tara slumped over and looking at the ground. Her arms were still hiding between her legs. "Sapa Inka Tupac Yupanqui, look who's still here!"

Hualpa went over and the Sapa Inka ordered that his litter be brought to her. Her hair was singed on half of her head and replaced with blisters. The blisters and bruises that covered the remainder of her body resembled all the colors of the jungle, and all the flowers and birds. Her festive outfit was in tatters and held over her shoulders by two strands.

The Sapa Inka got off of his golden litter, and both men stood in tandem and examined Tara in silence.

Amaru Tupa Inka arrived. His fur cloak was muddy and matted. The golden medallion around his chest had leafs and branches from the flood stuck in it.

Amaru Tupa Inka bowed and put his face on the ground before he spoke. "My dear brother, Sapa Inka Tupac Yupanqui, even though you were only gone a couple days I cannot express how happy I am to see you. Having you here gives me strength and wisdom."

The Sapa Inka told him to stand. He motioned with his hands to what had been the camp.

"I don't know what happened. There was lightening everywhere, and the rain was beyond anything I've seen." He walked to Tara and stroked her blistered face, "Ugh, she's become so ugly. I think we should kill her and return her to Milagro. She is not an aclla, never was, and now she can't fake it anymore."

"Yes, let me go back. I'm ugly now and of no service," said Tara.

The men ignored her whimper.

Sapa Inka Tupac Yupanqui stood motionless as he examined her for another moment.

"Why is she tied up and not on a litter?" said Sapa Inka Tupac Yupanqui. He slowly turned his head to Amaru Tupa Inka.

Amaru Tupa Inka fell into a slouch, "I saved her life. She revealed that she was born Cañari and the soldiers grew angry that she was an Inka by privilege and was to become an aclla. They didn't understand why their daughters, who are Inkan by birth, were not given the privilege. The women were jealous for the same reason. They wanted to kill her and they put her in the fire. I jumped in and pulled her out. This was the compromise that we should tie her up as a punishment."

"It's not true!" Yelled Tara.

"Quiet!" Said Hualpa.

Amaru Tupa Inka paused and seeing that neither Hualpa nor the Sapa Inka tried to stop him from speaking he continued.

"Now, her disrespect wasn't just revealing who she was after you tried to save her by changing her identity, but she freed all the prisoners we had taken. You see, dear brother, I did the best I could In fulfilling your orders. That is the reason she is tied up. I saved her life."

He appeared confident and showed no fear that his brother wouldn't believe him.

"And that is why you are my brother and my closest advisor," said the Sapa Inka. "You always find a way to fulfill all of my commands and you kept her alive."

"That's not what happened," said Tara. Her voice cracked.

"Tara, if you want to survive the day and have your stories heard, you will be quiet until told to speak," said Hualpa.

"I gave our soldiers and their women a celebration worth remembering, just as you commanded. We created dances and songs commemorating the events of the previous days. It was a great night until she sent the deluge," said Amaru Tupa Inka.

The Sapa Inka put his hand on his shoulder.

While the Sapa Inka spoke with the Amaru Tupa Inka, Hualpa approached Tara and examined her from top to bottom.

"It looks like you finally got your wish. You're ugly now, your face is ruined. It's covered in burns and you're covered in mud like the first time I saw you. Did you do this as revenge?" He pointed to the ruined camp, "Or as a thank you?"

"Amaru Tupa Inka is a liar. He tied me up moments after you departed, and he's the one that tried to burn me to death. Tell me, while he was assaulting me, how could I, this little girl who you pointed out doesn't even have breasts yet, have done this? Why do you even ask? You're ridiculous."

"You didn't answer my question, did you do this?"

"I was tied up so I couldn't have," said Tara.

The Sapa Inka joined Hualpa's and Tara's conversation.

"Of course she's the one who did it. Look at the flowers that have grown over my camp. You personally oversaw the removal of every flower from this area to be sure they were gone. But now that she's here, they came back." His voice was no longer as deep, but he spoke slowly and over enunciated each word.

Tara didn't lower her head or show any respect to him.

"That isn't what happened," she shook her head! "I was in a struggle for my life—"

"—How dare you contradict the Sapa Inka? What he says is what happened," said Amaru Tupa Inka. He noticed the sediment stuck in his medallion and was trying to clean it without taking it off.

Tara looked past him at the Sapa Inka "Look at me. Your evil brother tied me up next to the fire and it was burning me. My only focus was on saving myself from the flames."

"And so you sent a flood and killed his army?" said the Sapa Inka.

"Sapa Inka Tupac Yupanqui," cried Tara, "these are bad men and they are insulting my people. They stoned my friends to death and with their bodies fed the fire that burned me. If you insult my people, you are insulting Mamaquilla who would have sent the deluge, not me!" said Tara.

"Amaru Tupa Inka, what are the stories she speaks of?" Asked the Sapa Inka.

He looked up from his medallion. "I'm not sure. I mean, where's the proof? Everything washed away in the deluge she sent. She can say anything she wants at this point."

"Tara Inka," said the Sapa Inka. He lowered himself to her, "we are a civilized people. None of us would do these horrendous acts you speak of. Stoning children to death? Maybe that's something you did in Cañari, but I assure you it will not happen now that I am in control. We are more decent men than that."

He spoke kindly to Tara, and she saw from Hualpa's awestricken face that such kindness was not usual for the Son of the Sun.

"But he did!" Cried Tara. "Not only that he has everything wrong, he was calling my parents a spider and a snake in the stories."

"Tara, what you saw is not the history we record. I am the Sapa Inka and the history that we record is that which makes me look good." He looked to Amaru Tupa Inka to finish what he was saying.

"As I tried to tell you yesterday, dear Tara, changing the story is what gets you remembered how you want to be. The Sapa Inka is a God; what he says is the truth. He creates the world as he wants it. His father, the sun, gave him the power to change stories and pass them off as true for a reason. These soldiers around you didn't know that you weren't always an Inka, only I knew. By your insistence that the story we made up to protect you was revealed to be just a story, you revealed your heritage. That doesn't change the fact that you are an Inka. You are still an Inka because my brother, Sapa Inka Tupac Yupanqui, said so. Should you have gone with what he said, you would have been spared a horrible night."

"That is true," said the Sapa Inka. He turned to return to his litter.

"Someone loosen the poor girl's bindings."

Hualpa cut them and whispered to her, "Don't forget the promises you made The Sapa Inka. He only needs to say it and the massacre of your people will resume." He patted the top of her head and rejoined the other men.

"LISTEN TO ME!" She called after him, "You can't change what happened. No matter if you call me an Inka, I am Cañari. That cannot be changed no matter the lies you tell others."

The men paid her no heed. Tara stood up and continued.

"Should others treat me poorly for being a Cañari girl, fine, but it's better than being treated for something I am not. Those false praises hurt more than the true insults, it hurts more than being burned alive. I say this for Sycri. For Guaman. For Milagro!"

She felt smaller than a woodpecker trying to bore a hole through a monolithic tree, smaller than a drop of water in a cataract that would be lost in a grand river. She felt like a hair on an alpaca. She was a simple fiber meant to be shone, dyed, weaved, and formed into something that she wasn't.

The porters lifted Sapa Inka Tupac Yupanqui's litter. Several of the sunflowers were caught in it. The Sapa Inka covered his legs with several alpaca blankets, then picked one of the flowers from its stolen position and admired it.

"I make my own history." He crushed the flower. "That flower never existed." said the Sapa Inka.

"What flower are you referring to?" said Hualpa.

The three men looked at Tara. The last strand of her clothing broke and she stood naked.

"Amaru Tupa Inka," said the Sapa Inka. "I need you to search Tahuantinsuyu for the cure to Tara's new ugliness. I want her beauty restored. And Waranga Hualpa, you will accompany her to Cusco."

Chapter Fourteen

Oozing

Hualpa took command of the humble entourage that escorted Tara to Cusco. Sapa Inka Tupac Yupanqui remained in Cañari to quell the rebellions and to enjoy the company of his new wife.

Tara was told it would take two moons to get to Cusco along the Qhapaq Ñan. The hard wooden seat on the litter she was ordered to ride upon hurt her back. She became nauseous from the swaying of the litter as the bearers traversed the Qhapaq Ñan over the mountainous terrain. On the third day, she refused to ride in it, much to Hualpa's dismay.

Tara had a burned appearance. Half of her head was without hair, it was crusted, scared and oozing. They passed several huacas along the journey and Hualpa ordered that she give offerings to many of them so she would regain her beauty and learn to be grateful for her fortune of being an aclla. Her looks, along with her frequent visits to the huacas along the Qhapaq Ñan, raised suspicions among the soldiers. They believed she asked the gods to send another deluge, but what she really asked was that her people be saved from the Inkas and that a speedy death would come to her.

She felt like a little girl in an enormous world, in a world that used to be hers. In the rare moments that happiness graced her, usually because of an overpower view, or watching wildlife play, she didn't hear the coy chirp anymore. All the illusions went from her world and it was now a dreary place that seemed to be a cemetery of the fascination that used to exist in her life: the mountains that pierced the sky used to speak to her but now they were simply piles of rocks and dirt with ice on top; lakes of water that once quenched her thirst by a glance were now bodies of water-of urine; mystic plants that healed many afflictions were nothing more than what they seemed to the eye, a dying leaf.

As the moon changed and as Tara's dread of the Acllahuasi grew, she also saw a side of Hualpa that she didn't think was there before. Outside of war, he was a kind gentleman.

He went to great lengths to see that his men cared for her and no one touched her. He had one man punished for saying a mean thing about her, what he said Tara never was told. He gave her ointment that numbed the pain of the burns. He sat and listened to his men as if they were his brothers and even imparted supplies to those in ayllus they passed and were in need of aid. The man that invaded her homeland and killed with such indifference had feelings. He saw beyond himself, although it was rare that he did so. What amazed Tara the most was he appeared jealous of her giving other men any attention and ultimately made a rule that no man speak with her without his permission.

Nearly a full moon into the journey, they descended a stairway carved out the side of a steep mountain pass. The stones were slippery due to the persistent gentle rain that graced them for several days. More than once, someone yelled out in pain as their tired feet and legs gave out from beneath them and their feeble bodies hit the stone surface. They descended into a great plain where the city of Huaraz was located-a place with an acllahuasi, other than the one in Cusco.

Hualpa walked beside his litter that day. He always preferred to walk while it was raining.

"If I go to the Acllahuasi in Cusco, I know Amaru Tupa Inka will kill me," said Tara. "It will only be a matter of time. He's there waiting for me now. You heard Sapa Inka Tupac Yupanqui order him to be there, and to have medicines and omens ready to make me beautiful again. Which I don't want." She stomped.

He kept his eyes down. He pretended to focus on his footing while descending the slippery grade.

She jumped in front of him, and almost slipped. "LISTEN TO ME! He pushed her aside.

She pushed him over, "ANSWER ME, HUALPA!"

He hit the stairs but caught himself from falling down the steps. He looked up at her and laughed.

"You're so funny when you're mad." He stood up and poked her nose.

"What was it you were saying? I was busy thinking about how much you'll love Cusco."

"If. I. Go. To. The. Acllahuasi. In. Cusco—"

"—Men can't enter an acllahuasi," interrupted Hualpa. "As long as you stay in there, you will be fine. If you leave, I know Amaru Tupa Inka will kill you. He hates you, look at what he did to you."

"You mean you believe me?"

The soldier behind them interrupted the conversation, "Waranga Hualpa, must we remind you that we have to get down this mountain before sundown."

Hualpa tried to get Tara to continue to walk, but she refused.

"But really Tara, of course I believe you and always have—"

"—then why didn't you stand up for me?" Interrupted Tara.

"The Sapa Inka Tupac Yupanqui believed you too, but that doesn't mean that he *believes* you over his brother."

"Why do you think he believed me? He clearly sided with Amaru Tupa Inka," said Tara.

Hualpa glared at her for a moment.

"Sapa Inka Yupanqui ordered Amaru Tupa Inka to go to Cusco and prepare remedies for your burns. But did he order me to take you to him to receive the remedies? No. That's how I know he believed you. Why he didn't punish him, I don't know, but look how it turned out. I got to bring you to Cusco instead of him. It's us, and my soldiers and their women, all of whom I can trust not to hurt you. You're safer this way," said Hualpa. "He believed you."

He nudged her to get her to continue down the road.

She took a couple steps down and then stopped again.

The line of soldiers behind them moaned.

"You say that as if it was a good thing, it's not. He should be punished for what he did to me and I should be able to go back home," said Tara.

Hualpa closed his eyes and moaned. "Oh Tara, Tara, Tara. I've never seen Amaru Tupa Inka disobey the Sapa Inka before like he did the night. He often disobeys him, but not like that. He hates you, and he will do anything to kill or harm you. Part of me wants to say that you should be proud that it was on your account that he forsook his oaths. But really Tara, he's the brother of the most powerful man in the world. A punishment that equals what he did to you is death, and he may not want to kill him. I have my orders. Really, Tara, you'll be safer in the Acllahuasi than in Milagro. There, he'll just walk up to you and club you to death and receive no punishment."

"Don't say that Hualpa! Please take me to a different acllahuasi then, one away from Cusco. I heard from the soldiers that the one in Huaraz is good, and couldn't I just go to that one?"

"You'll be just as safe in any acllahuasi whether the one in Cusco, Huarez, Casamarca or any other one. If I disobeyed the Sapa Inka and brought you to another one, I wouldn't be as lucky as Amaru Tupa Inka to actually survive. He'd have me killed immediately. Do you want that?" said Hualpa. "Wait, don't answer that because I bet you do."

"No, I don't want you to be killed. You're my only friend now," said Tara. She spoke as softly as a butterfly.

He nudged her again to get her to continue down the road and she complied. Once they reached the plains of Huarez, the way to the tampu was blocked by a pack of thousands of llamas that came onto the Qhapaq Ñan. He left Tara's side to help the other men drive them off.

Chapter Fifteen

Proposal

The Qhapaq Ñan traversed the highest peaks and ridges of the Andes. They traveled far above magnificent views that she used to look up at, glaciers, mountain lakes the color of the sky, forests that spanned further than sight. The landscapes were only interrupted by other mountain peaks covered in puna and ice.

When the entourage was within days of Cusco, Tara sat and drank coca tea. It was the only remedy that calmed her headaches while in the highest of the mountains. Her sitting place was on a ledge beside the tampu where they stayed the night. She overlooked a glacier below her that melted into a clear river that fell into a cascade and lost itself in a dense forest far below.

Hualpa came and sat beside her. He didn't disturb her, she'd grown used to his oversized presence and occasionally felt lonely when he wasn't near. He put her arm around her. That disturbed her, but it made her feel a little safer as her fear of Cusco grew.

He looked down at the glacier. She knew he cared little for such views.

"What do you want, Hualpa?" she said.

"Well, since you insist, I'll tell you. I just received a chasqui from the Sapa Inka that asked me if I would accept you as a gift for marriage.

I was thinking about it, but looking at you now I might have to pass. Recover your beauty and I'll accept the offer," said Hualpa.

She removed his arm. "Is this how the most vile man I've ever met seeks my consent to marriage?" She paused. When she spoke the crusted skin cracked and she felt the ooze accumulate and a droplet ran down her cheek. She wiped the droplet and then continued. "And as you can't walk around with someone that is ugly as I, I can't be with a man that invaded my homeland."

Hualpa's mouth opened, Tara knew he didn't expect a refusal.

"Consent?" Said Hualpa. "This is how it works here? If the Sapa Inka says you are my wife, you shall be my wife. The only condition is that you become beautiful again."

"I just became very grateful for my ugliness. It's better to be scared and burned than have to be stuck with you for life," said Tara.

Hualpa laughed, "You're finally warming up to me. It's about time." Hualpa turned serious, "I know how much you fear going to the Acllahausi. You have night terrors about it in broad daylight, and no one can mention it around you without you wincing. If we marry, it will keep you from staying there very long. You'll come and stay with me in Cañari at an estate that Sapa Inka Tupac Yupanqui is building called Ingapirca. But really, I can't be walking around with someone that is scarred like you."

Tara wiped another droplet of ooze. She sat up straight and closer to Hualpa. She didn't understand why Hualpa cared so much about her beauty, she was a noble in Cañari. That was enough for any other man.

"You are not of age yet for marriage, you have at least another year to recover your beauty and to forgive me. Think about it, I will get you out of the most dreadful place and away from Amaru Tupa Inka," said Hualpa. "I will be your hero."

"Each time I try to forgive you for the horrid things you've done to my people, I find the pain and the hurt is deeper than I realized. I doubt I'll ever be able to forgive you, just like you may never see how I'm beautiful in other ways than my appearance."

She downed the tea, got up, and left. She hoped he wouldn't follow.

He didn't.

Inside, she was about to burst. Once out of sight she jumped with joy that she had a way out of the Acllahuasi.

The following days of the journey, Tara thought about this proposal.

Chapter Sixteen

The Qhapaq Ñan

T he entourage arrived in Cusco the morning of the second moon of traveling. The city of Cusco was in the middle of a large valley. Nestled among the forest, it gleamed in the first sunlight. The forests that surrounded it were colored as stagnant water in the jungle and ran into terraced hills, each terrace a different color than the next. They vanished into thick angry clouds. No matter the beauty, it fell upon Tara's empty heart and she felt no amazement by it. To her, it appeared as a colorful ant hole from which all the Inkas emerged and somewhere hidden within it, was Amaru Tupa Inka who stood in wait for her.

She shook.

Four roads exited the the city and went in opposite directions, one was the road that Tara was on. Hualpa explained to her that the four roads spanned Tahuantinsuyu and all came from one building in Cusco, the Coricancha the most sacred building in the world which stood near the Acllahuasi.

Tara had never seen a city that showed so much care in its construction as Cusco did. Everything was in perfect alignment, smooth, and polished. Hualpa told her that the shiny bricks that made the magnificent buildings were laid in a way to withstand Pachayachachic's tempers when she shook the ground. The roads were slanted for drainage for when the god's cried and sent floods. Each building, path, and structure was constructed for a specific reason.

They arrived the last day of Ayrihuay, the fourth moon of the year. It was a time of celebrations and festivals including Quicuchica, the celebration for girls that reached womanhood that year. Hualpa explained to Tara that although she reached womanhood that year, she could not go and she would never receive the anointing because she didn't know the rituals required to participate. She would be the only woman in the Acllahuasi who didn't have the ceremonial outfit, an ancalluasu and the accompanying shoes.

The festival of Capac-Cocha, also in Ayrihuay included the sacrifice of children. When she learned of this, she thought of the captives she freed. This festival was supposed to be their death, and because of her, eight of them were still alive and free, fighting the Inkas.

The escort left and only Hualpa remained beside her in his golden trimmed litter.

She saw Amaru Tupa Inka peering at her from a huasi within the confine called Pucamarca, a large, single level structure that opened to the road. When she looked back, it was empty. She quivered. She knew he watched her, he and his friends.

The streets were full of real Inkas, people who were born as Inkas, not fakes like her. They saw her for how she was dressed, as an Inkan woman of importance: she wore a jaguar mask that Hualpa gave her to cover her face and she sat upon a litter. She carried a bouquet and had her hair tied in llautu that matched the mess of colors of the bouquet. Her tunic was the shade of dark autumn leaves and the trimming a pattern between the shade of the morning sky and a thick forest. Her appearance worked. The Inkas looked at her with gleeful eyes and welcomed her. Hualpa smiled in delight of his masterful deception, but Tara knew it was all given to her based on something she was not, and detested the welcoming gestures and words.

"What do you think about your new home?" Asked Hualpa. He stood on his litter in front of her.

"It's dead and fake." said Tara. "It seems like a facade for the goodness and magic that used to reside here until you guys came and ruined it. You know, like it still exists in Cañari until you guys ruin it there too."

Hualpa laughed, "There won't be any fields of flowers springing up overnight and overtaking our tents, is what you mean?"

"No, what I mean is that you Inkas are only alive on the outside but your inside is already dead and decayed. You try to control everything, including that which awed you originally because it was uncontrolled. Apparently, you've succeeded in doing so to a point that there is no awe anymore."

Hualpa stared at her and raised his eye brows. He spoke slowly, even sarcastically, "I may have to rescind my marriage proposal. You make me feel stupid. How about you act you act your age."

"You speak of a marriage that I have not consented to," said Tara.

"You're still thinking that I need to wait for your approval, oh Tara," said Hualpa. "You want out of here, and I'm your way out."

Tara shrugged, "Marriage or not, I count on you to keep me safe." She paused for an instant and then said in a serious voice, "I saw Amaru Tupa Inka." She bit her lip.

Hualpa jumped from his litter with his spear in hand. His wooden sandals clapped on the stone road and echoed against the steep structures on both sides. He took a defensive pose, "I think we're trapped, Tara. It's all over for you—"

There was no one there.

Tara kicked him and tried to hold in her laugh.

Hualpa put the spear down, and grabbed her foot, "Stay within the Acllahuasi and you'll be safe," said Hualpa.

He let go of her foot and got back on his litter.

"You tell me to stay in the Acllahuasi so I will be safe, but they are going to torture and abuse me. I understand that men can't enter so I won't be raped, which is a relief. But the gods don't lie and they said that only pain awaits me within those walls. You say no, but what can you promise? Everything beyond those walls is a mystery to you. I think it might be better to be killed, at least then I won't be a prisoner."

Hualpa put his head in his hands, "Tara, you need to believe me and—"

"—But I don't."

"Then believe this," he reached over and grabbed her hands, "If you restore your beauty and become my wife, nobody will mess with my wife. Nobody!"

She took her hands away from him and put the ointment on her scared face, which hurt unusually bad. A large piece of skin flaked off.

The narrow stone road gave way to a crowded field in middle of the city called Huacaypata. It was the end of a multi-day party.

Tara moaned, "Don't you Inkas do anything other than party and drink?"

"Yup, we win wars and offer sacrifices to our gods so we can continue partying and drinking."

The Inkas who occupied Huacaypata dressed in lavish clothes resembling what which Amaru Tupa Inka dressed like: elaborate plumes of feathers attached to their long robes of complex patterns that meant nothing to Tara. The men wore golden breast plates, gold earplugs, and gold trimmings upon their heavy cumpi clothes. The women were adorned in jewelry. But no one had an albino jaguar cloak as Amaru Tupa Inka had.

Huacaypata was surrounded by compounds, the walls of which towered, as if the field were in the middle of a valley. The walls of one building were covered in gold, the others were either bare stone, silver or painted the color of blood.

Tara bit her lip.

On the far side of the plaza they came to the looming wall of the Acllahausi. It stood three times as tall as Tara. The front of the building which faced Huacaypata was narrow compared to the length of the building, which vanished down a narrow alley. The stones that made up the tall walls were raw and cold rock, and that so large that Tara felt a life energy emanating from them: they were nearly as tall and wide as

Tara was tall. A golden film laid between each stone and a golden and silver ribbon wrapped the circumference of the Acllahuasi.

Her muscles tensed and cramped. A putrid, neutral taste filled her mouth as her stomach folded in on itself.

A middle aged woman stood at the entrance, a trapezoid doorway. She stood taller than Tara and had shoulder length hair wrapped in a llautu that had two feathers inlaid into it, one the color of the water, and the other the pattern of a bee. She wore a cloak the color of dark rich quinoa and was made of perfectly weaved fabric. Her face was cold, but kind and it drew Tara inward like a chilly glacial stream on a hot humid day.

"That's Yachi. She's one of the servants of the Acllahuasi. Like I said, no man is allowed past the doors so she will bring you in. This is the end of our journey together," said Hualpa.

He got off his litter and he held out his hand to help Tara from hers.

Her stomach felt like one of the stones that made up the wall of the Acllahuasi.

She grabbed his hand and didn't let go.

"No, you can't leave me! You're the only person I know here. Please don't go," she cried and fell to her knees.

Hualpa removed her mask and stroked her cheek, "There are over a thousand girls in there. You'll make friends very soon." He put the mask on his litter. He laughed. "Actually, you probably won't."

"I forgive you for what you did to my people, you protected me all the way here, but I won't forgive you if you stop now. How do I know that Amaru Tupa Inka doesn't have people in there to kill me? I don't want to die! You need to be there to watch out for me," said Tara.

She held Hualpa's hand to her scarred face.

Hualpa placed his other hand on her other cheek and his forehead on hers and said softly, "Be weary of everyone and everything. That is what keeps me and my men safe from ambushes and it will keep you safe here. Restore your beauty and this won't be the last time we see each other," said Hualpa.

Tara cringed. Her breathing became shallow. "Come back for me. I will marry you, just come back," said Tara.

He let go of her, got back on his litter and left.

Chapter Seventeen

Yachi

Yachi grabbed Tara's hand with her short fingers and pulled her away from Hualpa. Her grip was awkward and cold, but her voice was sirene.

"I am happy you arrived, Aclla Tara Inka of Yanantin."

"That's not my name," said Tara.

"It's not?" Yachi paused as if she was going to say something but couldn't find the words, or had found them but didn't know if she should say them "Then what is?"

"It's," Tara looked down, "just Tara."

Yachi adjusted the cloth that covered her chest and pulled it down slightly.

"I'm Yachi. I'm a servant here. Um," she glanced at Hualpa. "I heard you were supposed to be here days ago and when you didn't show I feared something happened."

"You were counting?" Said Hualpa.

Yachi stared for a moment, grabbed Tara's nimble hand and smiled warmly. "Follow me." She spun around gracefully and entered the Acllahausi.

Tara froze. Her legs wouldn't walk.

"Come on," Yachi sang from inside the doorway.

"Trust no one and be weary of everyone," said Hualpa. She looked behind her and he was gone.

Yachi gave Tara a big smile. Her top lip exposed her big teeth.

"Are you coming with me? If so, hurry up. Come to your future."

Tara wanted to run. She pictured her father's last stand and her promise to him that she was going to go save Milagro.

She took a tiny step toward Yachi, then another and another until she was inside the horrid place.

Inside of the grand entrance of the abominable Acllahuasi was a ghostly bricked courtyard that was big enough to fit thousands of people but stood empty. The looming walls of the exterior of the Acllahuasi made up the equally impressive interior walls.

"This is where we have celebrations when the women of Cusco are allowed in," said Yachi. She entered the courtyard toward the back wall where there was another trapezoidal doorway.

As they went across the courtyard to the doorway, Tara noticed it was cold and stank of herbs. She went to cover her nose, but her mask prevented it. She scratched her shoulder instead.

The trapezoidal doorway opened into a tall and narrow corridor with only enough space for two people to walk shoulder to shoulder. Yachi led Tara. It was dreadfully long and scattered with dark wooden doors on both sides. Women dressed like Yachi stood by several of them."It's usually brighter than this," said Yachi. The corridor was dimly lit with sparse candles. "I'm not sure why it's dark."

"It's dark because I'm here," said Tara in an eerie voice. She didn't realize the words left her mouth.

Tara admired each of the servant girls as they passed them. She fell far behind Yachi, who stopped aways up the corridor. Tara ran up to her.

"These wooden doors, what happens behind them? These women waiting outside of the doors are waiting for their horrid fate, aren't they?" Said Tara. Her legs gave out and she fell on the ground at Yachi's feet. "I'm going to be one of them, won't I?"

Yachi laughed. She paused before she answered. "They are work stations. The women that stand outside the doorway are servants, like me. Since men can't enter we perform all the heavy lifting and physical labor that is considered undignified for acllas and mamacunas." said Yachi. "They wait outside the door for a task to be given to them."

Tara stood back up.

"What kind of work stations are they?" Said Tara. She focused on one of the doors, the darkest one.

"I'm not the one to ask I'm bringing you to someone that will answer all your questions."

Tara looked forward and didn't say another word.

There was a large trapezoidal doorway at the midpoint of the long corridor. It opened into another courtyard, which was much smaller than the previous. The courtyard was filled with beautiful and happy women and girls. The parameter of the courtyard was enclosed by rectangler stone houses with pitched roofs made of reeds. There were flower gardens and trees, and part of the courtyard was covered to protect the women from the common storms that accompanied the rainy season and the overpowering sun of the dry season. Several women scattered across the yard, all of whom Tara assumed were acllas and mamacunas. Many of them weaved while they walked. Some other women carried two large ceramic vessels in their hands while making chicha. They put some liquid into their mouth, swished it around, and spit it into the vessel in their other hand. Tara recognized the practice. It was the same in Milagro but it was usually the men who made it. Tara admired all the people and wondered which one, if any of them might have instructions to kill her. She shook when she realized all of them could bear such orders.

"I thought the women here were supposed to be indentured servants who were used and abused by the powerful men and women, not laughing, gossiping and dancing," said Tara.

"You thought wrong," said Yachi. "I am the indentured servant, and do I looked abused?"

Tara looked Yachi up and down and shrugged.

Yachi pointed at the opposite corner of the courtyard where four beautiful girls, the most beautiful girls that Tara had ever seen, were dancing. They had perfect skin, their hair was smooth and braided, their clothes were clean and fit their bodies, and their movements were smooth like trees swaying in the wind.

"Those are the acllas from further inside the compound. Sometimes, they come here to practice their dances."

"I can't be one of them. I think I'd be better as a servant like you," said Tara.

Yachi grimaced at Tara, "Yeah, you'd be better as a servant and I as an aclla, It's not up to us though."

She continued across the courtyard, but Tara stayed behind and watched the acllas dance. Yachi returned to where Tara stood.

"Ugh, come, I'll introduce you."

Tara wished that each step toward these beautiful women was one step backward so she wouldn't be noticed, but she was drawn to them.

The acllas ceased dancing and turned their attention to Tara. One by one, they introduced themselves. Tara didn't remember their names, except for one girl who was beautiful and bore a distinct Kasay than the others.

"Welcome Aclla Tara Inka of Yanantin. I'm Aclla Tata Inka of Moras," she said. She bowed her head slightly. "That's an amazing mask that you wear. It's a jaguar. It's not from Cusco, is it?"

"It's from—" started Tara.

"—it's from here, it was made just for her." Interrupted Yachi.

Tara felt ooze erupt from her blisters below her mask.

"I see," said Tata. "It doesn't matter. I like the colors, it's very unique. How is it that you're being admitted to the Acllahuasi after Quicuchica?" She spoke with a staccato and ended each sentence with a head slant and a smile.

Tara leaned over to Yachi and whispered, "What's Quicuchica again?"

"Ugh," said Yachi. She pushed Tara away from her. "Sapa Inka Tupac Yupanqui ordered that she come here now. He didn't say anything concerning Quicuchica," said Tara.

Tara felt the ooze run down her face. She pictured it dripping from her chin.

"Of course you're referring to his statue?" Said Tata. "Because I hear he's far away fighting."

"Clearly I am," said Yachi. Her face was blunt.

"I've just never heard of a girl being allowed in without first attending Quicuchia." Tata turned to Tara, "You must have made quite an impression on him. It was your mask, wasn't it?" She laughed. "We have to keep practicing though, it was nice meeting you Tara. We are performing at the celebration where they will anoint some elder women to the status of mamacuna."

Tara watched them perform their dance. She stroked her mask.

"Come on, Mamacuna Umita is waiting for you," said Yachi. She waved Tara on.

Tara ran to her, "Yachi, who is Tata, she seems special?"

Yachi didn't reply but led Tara back into the narrow corridor and they followed it past several more doors until they came to the end. There was another trapezoidal door. It opened into a small yard, too small to be considered a courtyard. The ground was covered with small stones and grass, and there was a fountain without water in the middle of it. The wide stone yard was surrounded by several rectangler enclosures which contained small stone huasis with pointed thatched roofs. The further from the entrance, the less space between the enclosures until the open space became a path that meandered through them.

Standing next to the dry fountain was an old woman who busied herself weaving what seemed to be a scarf. Her back was hunched and she leaned so far forward that Tara readied herself to lounge forward to catch her should she fall over. The ají colored scarf she weaved was draped over her shoulder so it didn't drag on the ground.

"That is Mamacuna Umita Inka of Inti." Yachi said. She paused and moaned. "She has been instructed to introduce you to life here."

Umita met them halfway between the fountain and the corridor. She smiled and embraced Tara. She smelled of the roasted maize.

"Welcome to the Acllahuasi in Cusco, the most sacred of all the Acllahuasis, Aclla Tara Inka of Yanantin daughter of Inti and Mamaquilla." She spoke in a sweet voice one expects from a matriarch who discovered a pure love of life.

"That's not my name," said Tara. She spoke with spite.

Umita lowered her arms and took a step backward. "You are likely tired from your long journey, I have something for you that will make you feel better."

"You can leave now, Yachi," said Umita without taking her eyes off of Tara. Her soft voice turned firm.

Yachi gave Tara a quick forced smile before turning away.

Umita went to the fountain without running water and waved Tara over.

Tara looked both ways and then went with her.

Umita dipped a small polished vessel into the dry pool of the fountain. She gave it to Tara. The vessel was shaped like a condor and with two nozzles that protruded from the wings.

"Here, drink some."

"Isn't the fountain empty," said Tara. She peered over the side and saw water in it. She gasped.

"Oh, did you now? Well, maybe it was empty. I forgot to look before I filled the vessel," said Umita.

Tara ignored the vessel. "Are those wooden doors in the corridor where I am going to be defiled?" She mustered as much strength as she could when she asked.

Umita lowered the water. "Oh my dear girl, that does not happen. No, not here. Inti watches over us and tasked his son Sapa Inka Tupac Yupanqui to keep us safe. It is in Milagro that you were at risk of such atrocities," said Umita.

"I am willing to take the atrocities like a grown woman. Please, don't lie to—" Tara stopped mid-sentence.

"You said Milagro? Why? How—"

"—That's right, I know your secret, and let me advise you that you be more mindful with your speech and what you say to the others so that it remains a secret. If the other acllas and mamacuna learn that you are Inka by privilege, they won't accept you. That means, for the rest of your life you will be rejected among those you are forced to work and live with," said Umita.

Tara's heart pounded and her breathing grew quick. She thought about all that she revealed to Yachi.

"But no one in Cusco is supposed to know, besides Amaru Tupa Inka. Did he tell you?" Asked Tara.

"It's okay Tara, it's okay," said Umita. "I trust Sapa Inka Tupac Yupanqui and if he ordered that you be here regardless of what I, or the others think, his order is all that I consider important. Obey our rules and no harm will come to you. No rape, no molestation, no pain. You will find companionship with the other women here, friends that will be come dearer to you than your mother, and a calling from Inti that resonates deep within you. Now," Umita raised the vessel of the condor back to Tara, "Drink my dear."

This time Tara took it and gently pressed it to her lips.

"Not so fast," said Umita. "First, pour some on the ground to thank Pachayachachic for such sacred water."

"You worship Pachayachachic?" said Tara.

"Yes, we worship all the same gods as you do Tara, Mamaquilla, Viracocha, Pachayachachic, but Inti is the sun and he gives us life so he is the most important to us."

The sides of Tara's lips raised in the smallest smile. She poured a little water on the ground, "Thank you Pachayachachic that even in this foreign land you provide water."

She pressed one of the nozzles to her lips and drank.

The sweet and cool water warmed her from the inside and awoke a dormant fire within her. She felt peace and safety. Her fears of the Acllahuasi disappeared.

Umita smiled, "It looks bad, but it's the best water in Cusco."

Tara gave the vessel to Umita and she drank out of the second nozzle.

While she drank, Tara admired her skin that appeared so thin and tender that Tara thought the mere brush of her clothes would tear it off.

"Take off your mask, sweet girl," said Umita.

"I was injured on the way here and the mask is covering my injured face," said Tara.

"No matter, take it off."

Tara removed it and dropped the mask to the ground. She quickly covered her face with her hands. On the palm of her hands, her skin felt like a cold fatty broth when the fat solidifies above the liquid beneath it.

"What happened to your face?" said Umita.

"It's nothing that a mask can't cover. When my hair grows back, I will cover it."

Tara peeked through her fingers at Umita.

"I asked what happened," said Umita.

"It will heal, but if it doesn't, does that mean I'm ugly and I'll have to leave?"

She lowered her hands a bit from her face and looked at Umita with wide eyes.

Umita moved Tara's hands from her face.

"Fine, you won't believe me. Amaru Tupa Inka tried to burn me to death on the way here."

Tara stared at her to see her response.

Someone yelled in the distance.

Tara jumped.

Umita put Tara's hands back over her face. "You are not to wear that mask again. This will be fixed but be ashamed of yourself if you only focus on your beauty and lose sight of why Inti wants you here."

"You don't care that Amaru Tupa Inka tried to burn me," Tara yelled. "You don't care about who I am or what I've done. You only care about why Inti wants me here. You people are barbarians!"

As she yelled at Umita, one of the few open spots of her wound opened and the puss dripped into her mouth. She spit it out and applied pressure with her finger.

Umita sat down and picked up her weaving tools and resumed working on the scarf. "We can fix your face and your beauty, but I'm afraid that we can't fix a disgusting person."

"I'm not a disgusting person. The Inkas are. They are the ones that took me away, the reason why all of this has happened."

"I thought we believed in the same gods, I was mistaken," said Umita.

"We do. Not Inti though," said Tara. The anger was out of her voice.

"I don't think we believe in any of the same gods. If we did, you would understand that it's not *us Inkas* nor just Inti that brought you here but all the gods including your principal god Mamaquilla." Umita glanced up at Tara.

Tara didn't know what to say. She stood frozen for a moment, then asked for water.

Umita nudged the vessel toward her with her elbow without ceasing to weave.

Tara picked it up and sipped a little while she watched Umita's fingers weave at a speed she didn't think the most skilled men in Cañari were capable of. Here, Umita, a woman whose skin was falling off of her hump backed body, was doing it without effort while maintaining a heated conversation.

Tara placed the vessel down and sat next to Umita on the wall of the fountain.

"Mamacuna Umita, acllas are supposed to be beautiful, right?"

"Yes, they are chosen for their beauty."

"I've seen older people that got bad burns when they were my age, or even when they were younger. The scars never leave. I will be ugly forever. Maybe it will get infected and become even worse. I've seen that happen too. Maybe it was a mistake to send me here. I will not be accepted by the others. I will always be an outcast."

"Remember, other people's fate is not your own fate. You are in a different place then they were and so different things will happen," said Umita.

Tara sat for a moment in silence.

"My dear girl," resumed Umita. "I already understand why the Sapa Inka sent you here. You see, Cusco used to be a place where nothing was as it seemed and everything was what it was not. The fountain flowered with clear and sweet water and given the right offering, any affliction was healed by its water. Back in those days, sipping the water as you did, would have fixed your face. Back in those days the landscape was alive just like us humans and we lived in a way where everything cared for us, and we cared for it. Now it's different. We create stories so it seems like it still is how it was in the old days. Now that the supernatural no longer happens, we made festivals and rituals to remember it by. With you, Tara, something is different. Tara. I know you felt it when you drank the water from the fountain."

Trust no one and be weary of everyone, echoed through Tara's head.

"Come, come, there is a lot to show you" said Umita. She nudged Tara on the back.

Umita, with her forward leaning gait, led Tara back into the corridor which was brighter than before. They entered the third wooden door. Tara acknowledged the servant girl that stood outside with a pitiful smile. The small room was well lit and rectangler. From each wall hung several looms. The floor was scattered with jars and urns of sewing material, threads, needles, broken needles, broken looms, looms that were carried upon one's back; partially completed tapestries, and a gold figure of Inti upon the wall.

"It's a mess," said Tara.

"Yes, yes it is," said Umita. She looked angry. "I will look into it after I'm finished with you." She smiled again and turned to Tara. "You shall have the honor of serving Inti as a weaver," said Umita.

Tara laughed, "That is funny, Umita, really funny. You can just point me in the direction of the fields and animals and I don't need to see anything else."

Umita covered her mouth, "No, none of that here. All food and animal products are provided from the outside. Here we only make textiles, chicha, and objects for offerings, and to be used by the Sapa Inka," said Umita.

She lowered her hand and gave Tara a spool and needle. It fit perfectly into her small hands, but Tara looked at it like a child looks at their parents when they realize how they were conceived.

"Let me see one of the sewing knots you know how to tie. Surely, you know some."

Tara tried to return the items to Umita with a pathetic smile, but Umita folded her arms.

Tara gripped the needle with a fist like she was holding a farm tool. She held the thread just as violently in the opposing hand. Umita remained crouched over with her arms folded until Tara tied a knot. It was rough and uneven

"No, no, no, not like that," said Umita. She coughed. "I've never seen someone do that before. Here," Umita took the needle and spindle back, "we will work on it tomorrow. You had a long journey and it is your first day here. Come with me and I will show you to your huasi."

She led Tara back to the yard with the fountain. They continued past the fountain, down the path that went between the walled enclosures of huasis. They entered the second enclosure.

"This is your huasi. It is where you shall rest and sleep," said Umita. She pointed at a small rectangle building with plain mossy stone walls and a steep thatched roof. It looked like each of the others beside it.

In the huasi, there was a single room. In it was a reed bed that sat upon the dirt floor. There was a raised part of the ground for a few items and a string across the room for her to hang her clothes.

"Sleep well," said Umita. "Your new clothes and all the processions you need will be provided to you in the morning."

She left.

Tara laid upon the bed.

"Please Hualpa, don't forget me."

Chapter Eighteen

Silo

Several moons passed and Tara grew more homesick each day. She developed the habit of wandering about the Acllahuasi after everyone went to bed. This night, she followed the wide path that meandered around the brick enclosures toward the back of the Acllahuasi. The path gave way to square block buildings, each built next to the other with small alleys between. What they were all for, and what purpose they served, she didn't know and didn't want to guess.

Against the walls and between the block buildings, were tall pottered urns that stood to her waist in height. The urns had the sweet smell of chicha and were painted with narrative stories. None made sense to Tara. Other urns had images of tasks that acllas did such as weaving, making chicha, and singing. She glanced at the narrative paintings that reflected against the torch's light. "I bet these stories are made up as well," she said to herself.

Several urns were stacked on top of each other, some stacks reached the top of the wall. She pushed the stacks around to create a staircase to the top. While she maneuvered them, one stack fell over. The top urn shattered on the ground and the noise echoed against the stone wall and buildings. It was so loud that she wondered if they heard it on the other side of Cusco.

She hid and waited for anyone to come, no one did. She resumed her work until there was an arrangement of urns that led her to the top of the wall. She gripped the rim of the first urn. It was sticky. She pulled herself up, and then up to the next one. When she reached the top, a cold gust of wind stripped any moisture from her face. She pulled her tattered cloak she found in her huasi snug around her body. The cloak stuck to her sticky fingers.

She crawled along the wall of the Acllahuasi and jumped to the thatched roof of one of the tallest building. She climbed to the top.

From there she saw the torches of Cusco and the surrounding frigid landscape scattered with shadows. There were scattered fires upon the hillsides that surrounded Cusco, and she saw lightening strike in the distant hills.

"What are you doing?" said a voice that sounded like it belonged to a child.

She caught herself from falling and looked down.

"I'm up here," said the soft voice.

There was a silhouette of a child that sat upon the wall of a compound outside the Acllahuasi and across the narrow road. The view was obstructed by the darkness, but she saw that it was a young boy.

She crawled to the edge of the roof and looked for the quickest way back into the Acllahuasi. There wasn't a way down without going back to the wall and thus showing her identity to the stranger.

"Don't leave, I'm just wondering what you are doing up there. I won't tell anyone, I promise. I've never seen someone up there before," he said.

She glanced toward him, "Who are you?"

"My name is Viracocha Inka of HananCusco. I live around here. I'm just lonely. What are you doing?"

The voice was soft and Tara didn't feel threatened by it. She ceased looking for a way down.

Tara told the boy she was longing for home and lied that she was from an Inkan settlement called Hatun Cañar.

"What is it like there? I've never left Cusco." Said Viracocha.

Tara described it to him and as she spoke of Cañari and Milagro she longed for it more.

He listened to her without interrupting, and it comforted her to speak.

"Come over here so we can see who we're talking to," said Viracocha.

"I can't leave the Acllahuasi," said Tara.

"Everyone else is in bed, I want someone to talk and play with. I can't sleep," he said.

Tara laughed to herself.

"Who are you really, young boy?"

"Tara, are you okay?" Yelled Yachi from below before Viracocha answered

Tara gasped, "Yes, yes I'm... I am just looking around. Cusco, it's so pretty."

"Come down here," said Yachi. "Acllas can't be seen and all of Cusco can see you up there."

"Meet me over there," said Tara. She pointed in the direction of the urns.

She motioned to Viracocha to run off.

He laid on his back and admired the distant lightening as if he never met Tara.

As she crawled along the roof back to the wall and climbed down the urns, she tried to get a better view of him, but his lying position kept him concealed. He never looked away from the distant lightening.

Yachi met Tara at the base of the urns.

"Oh my! What happened to your face?" Said Yachi.

Tara covered it, "Don't worry. Sorry. Umita doesn't want me to cover it with the mask anymore. She's been providing treatments, but they work slowly."

"She warned me, but it's worse than I expected," said Yachi. She looked away from Tara and raised her hand to block the view of it. "Acllas are supposed to be beautiful. You are very ugly!"

"I know," said Tara.

Yachi hesitated. "You were on the roof because you are longing for your home, weren't you?"

Tara wanted to scream YES and tell her that there was nothing more that she desired than to be out of that place.

"Listen to me," said Yachi. She grabbed Tara's hands but didn't look at her face. "You know I am your friend, right?"

"You're my only friend here," said Tara.

"If you ever want to escape, tell me. I will help you. Tara, you don't belong here. Obviously. You are from Milagro, you belong there. Leave the Acllahuasi, and I'm telling you that we will all help you leave," said Yachi.

"Who are we?" Asked Tara.

"I should also tell you that Amaru Tupa Inka is sorry for what he—"

"YOU'RE WITH HIM?" Tara pulled her hands away from Yachi's grasp.

"—He will help you return home. He's a man of honor, the Sapa Inka's brother, and he's ashamed of his actions. He still believes that it would be best for you and for the Inkas if you returned to Milagro," said Yachi.

"You're with him and I almost thought of you as a friend."

"Um, well, I'm not with him. Actually, he's with you. He wants to help you," said Yachi.

"HE HATES ME! HAVE YOU SEEN WHAT HE DID TO MY FACE," said Tara. She pointed at her scars. "Look at them!"

Yachi glanced at Tara's face. Yachi's face looked like that of someone who is watching a boulder tumble down a mountain and is headed for them. She turned around to avoid seeing it.

"Do you want to know what he did, this 'Man of Honor'? What his actions accomplished? Waranga Hualpa told me he would marry me if I was beautiful, and I would have been beautiful if it wasn't for what that bastard did to me! Do you hear me? He just ruined my hope of leaving here and his own chances of getting me out of Cusco. ISN'T THAT WHAT HE WANTED!"

"Um," is all Yachi said for a moment. "No, no he doesn't hate you Tara," She paused, and she kicked the dirt. "I, I, I know he'll help you become beautiful if that's what you want. A token, yes, I'll bring a token from him that shows his good will toward you. He apologizes about the night. He had too much chicha. He hopes you'll understand. It was the fever men receive after battle, and when mixed with chicha, it's all the worse. He owes you and he sees this as a way to repay you for his misguided actions."

Tara pushed one of the stacks of urns over and watched them shatter. Yachi jumped at the sound.

"If he wants to give me a token of his good faith, have him go into Huacaypata and tell the truth about the people of Cañari and Milagro. Have him tell the stories about our victories and how it was on our terms that we surrendered. Have him tell stories about our great men and women. There is no other token that I would recognize as meaningful. And have him restore my beauty so I can be with Hualpa."

Yachi grabbed Tara and prevented her from toppling another stack of the urns.

"Don't break those! They are precious and hold sacred stories," she said without looking at Tara.

Tara huffed.

Yachi turned around again. "I don't think that will happen, but I will ask him."

Yachi took a few steps away from Tara and turned back. She opened her mouth and hesitated like she usually did.

"And you want to marry Waranga Hualpa? Are you sure, he's um, he's not exactly what girls like."

"If it means getting me out of here, yes."

Chapter Nineteen

Weaver

"Wake up," said Yachi. "You should see the rain."

"Huh? What?" Said Tara. She opened her eyes. It took her a moment to remember where she was.

"Umita sent me to come get you. You were to begin work already. You're late. Hurry up!"

Tara jumped from her bed when she remembered the interaction the previous night. "GET AWAY FROM ME!"

"No," said Yachi. "I have a task to do and that is to bring you to your weaving lessons. Now come."

Tara dressed and refused to acknowledge Yachi's presence as she escorted her to one of the anonymous doorways in the dank corridor through the storm with raindrops the size of pebbles. Her anxiety was as disruptive as the thunder and lightening that shook the ground, the buildings, the people in the buildings - everything!

Umita stood in the corridor and tapped a wooden cane on the ground.

Tara smiled, she hadn't seen Umita since the first day she arrived.

Umita put her cane against the wall and wobbled to Tara.

Tara leaned forward and put her hands forward to catch her if she fell.

Umita slapped her hands away.

"*Little* girl," said Umita "I have received reports that you aren't devoting yourself to making textiles. It is the most important job in Tahuantinsuyu and you seem not to care about it. Well, now I am going to teach you. Today is the day that you are going to learn how to weave textiles of worth. Now, come inside."

Tara squirmed then followed her into the well lit room with looms in each corner and weaving tools scattered about.

"But weaving is men's work," said Tara. "I should be in the fields using my youthful fertility to grow the crops to provide nourishment as we provide it to babes and infants. Weaving provides warmth and protection, like what men provide to the family. You Inkas have it backwards!" said Tara.

"You mean, 'Us Inkas.' You are one of us," said Umita. The strength of her voice made Tara jump.

"The people in Cañari are the ones that have it wrong. Men are stronger so they should do the jobs that require the strength, like working the fields." said Umita.

"It's not a question of strength, there are plenty of men I am stronger than," said Tara. She raised her fist "Watch, bring me a man, even one twice my age, and I'll—" Tara interrupted herself, "NO! It's not a question of strength, it's a question of balance and using the gifts that the gods gave us," said Tara. She kicked the wooden stool next to the loom.

"You speak like a smart woman but you act as a child and your understanding is even less than that of a child. I won't provide the ointment and medicines to restore your face anymore. You aren't deserving of such a privilege. Perhaps we'll provide you as a sacrifice like other little acllas," said Umita. "The gods will know what to do with you." She pursed her lips, set down her items and went toward the door as quickly as her old body allowed her.

Thunder shook the ground, and Tara heard the rain start. She bent over and picked up the stool. She thought of Hualpa.

"I'm sorry. I'm sorry, Umita. I won't fight anymore. I want my face restored, it's the only hope I have," said Tara.

Umita snapped around, "Will you do everything I tell you to do without questioning?" said Umita.

Tara ran to Umita and clung to her sleeve, "I will. I'll be the best aclla that's ever been here."

"You will? Then tell me, who are you and what is your name, little girl?" Said Umita.

Tara let go of Umita's sleeve, looked down and mumbled, "I am Aclla Tara Inka of Yanantin, daughter of Inti and Mamaquilla."

A chasm opened within her.

"Say it like you believe it," said Umita. "Now, say it again."

Tara rubbed her face. It was smooth again, and there wasn't anymore oozing.

"Say it, Tara," said Umita.

Tara quivered and repeated it exactly how she knew Umita wanted to hear it. "I am Aclla Tara Inka of Yanantin, daughter of Inti and Mamaquilla."

She cramped up and wanted to vomit at the sound of the words coming out of her mouth. The chasm within her burned and smothered any glimmer of light and pride that remained.

"Very well, very well," said Umita. She supported Tara's arm and brought her to the loom. She extended the fabric hanging from it to Tara and instructed her on how to use it.

Tara did as she was told. As she worked at the loom, one by one the other acllas came into the room. Each of them stared at Tara's face as they walked past to their individual loom and said a brief prayer to an idol of Inti that stood in a nook on the wall. One girl was the seductive Tata. She didn't stare but walked past Tara and greeted her as if she was just another aclla.

"Let's see what you can make," said Umita. "Start with easy items, a towel, a sack, and a blanket."

She sat on the floor in silence as Tara struggled with the loom, needle, and thread.

Tara did as she was ordered and created a rustic sack, a coarse towel, and an itchy small blanket that looked similar to the towel. After she created the items, she threw the loom at the wall.

"There! I'm done."

"Those are items that a boy can create before he speaks" said Umita. She grabbed them and put them into a pile and lit them on fire.

Tata passed by Tara to open the door to let the smoke out. As she passed Tara, she said "You'll get it, Tara, don't worry."

The fire engulfed her work.

"We were all at your level at some point," said Tata as she returned to her loom. "Watch me. It's easiest that way."

Tara followed her to the other corner where she worked. She watched Tata's graceful yet firm hold on the needle as she worked the different colored threads in and out of the drawn strings. Tara returned to her loom and tried to replicate it. Her fingers wouldn't move in ways that seemed so easy to Tata.

"Keep trying," she said, and then ignored Tara for the rest of the day.

"Easy for you to say, but you were born an Inka," said Tara just softly enough so the other acllas didn't hear her. Umita hit her over the top of the head.

Tara bit her bottom lip.

"Little girl," said Umita loudly. She kicked the pile of ash at Tara. "You will be a weaver by the end of the rainy season. You will or I will drown you in the fountain."

"But—"

"—Again!" said Umita.

Through the rainy season, Tara continued to struggle. She lagged in each task set to her because instead of working she listened to the rain hit the thatched roof and thought of home and Hualpa. As the storms came and went, as the puddles filled and flooded sections of the Acllahuasi, and the fields around Cusco changed colors, Tara's ability only increased enough to keep the ointments coming.

By the end of each day, Tara doubted if she would ever weave. She stared at her hands and then at the looms, at the strings and at the amazing textiles that the other acllas created. She had betrayed herself, her identity, and her people to weave, and now she knew she would never be able to.

Her mind, always occupied by Hualpa, wondered what kind of life it would be with him, if there would be a life with him, if she didn't learn how to weave.

"Tara, what you need is concentration," said Umita.

"What?" Said Tara. She woke from her revere.

Umita glared at her, "Until you learn how to concentrate on what you are doing, you won't make the progress needed of you. It is nearly the end of the rainy season, and this is my last idea of what can help you. Wait here."

"I have nowhere to go," said Tara.

While she was waiting, Tara watched the other acllas weave. Tata stood at her loom and looked more confident weaving than before. Tara ventured over to her corner and asked what she was working on.

"I'm making a cloak to be a gift of Ayni to the Apu of Antisuyu. It's frigid there and he has given many of his men to help the Sapa Inka wage war," she said.

"You are so good at it," said Tara. "Do you mind if I stay and watch?"

"Watch Tata's methods as much as you can," said a different aclla in the opposite corner. "She's the best among us. She'll be made into a mamacuna soon or given to one of the most powerful men in the realm. We all know it."

Tata worked the quickly and with coordinated movements. Her beautiful fingers flowed like music.

Tata blushed, "Originally, I was supposed to be sacrificed, but when my work was shown to Sapa Inka Tupac Yupanqui, he was so impressed that he ordered another be sacrificed in my place. He said that my textiles were more valuable as offerings than I."

Something struck Tara with amazement. For an instant, she developed an appreciation of the worth of textiles and felt inspired to make them herself. The inspiration disappeared almost as if it never existed.

Umita returned with a blanket with an image sown onto it. She gave it to Tara to examine. It was of a landscape that was composed of cliffs covered in terraces, mountains that were shaped as a face, and surrounded by mountains. Upon one peak was a stone citadel that was so majestic, Tara thought the gods themselves built it.

"It's where I was born and raised. It's called Machu Picchu," said Umita.

Tara gazed at the wonderment. "Can you or Tata sew something like that of my birthplace Mila—I mean, Hatun Cañar, if I describe it to you?" Asked Tara.

Tata smiled, "Tara if you describe it to me I'll can weave anything."

Umita put her hand on Tara's back and looked at Tata, "Thank you, but you nor I can create it. Tara has to."

Tara glimpsed at the blanket of Machu Picchu. "What is this place you call Machu Picchu? it's spectacular." Her eyes stuck to the dynamic tapestry.

"Everyone who sees it asks me, so I rarely show it, and it hurts me to talk about it. For you, I'll make an exception," said Umita. She placed her hand on Tara's unburnt cheek and guided her gaze to meet her eyes instead of the blanket. "It is the personal estate of the father of Sapa Inka Tupac Yupanqui, his name was Pachacuti Inka Yupanqui. He was the greatest Inka to ever live. He is the one that conquered the Chimu and Casamarca. He brought the Chinchas to surrender, a feat the Huaca said was nigh impossible. He made Tahuantinsuyu the great place it is now. They taught me in Machu Picchu to be an aclla, but when Pachacuti Inka Yupanqui was about to die, he summoned me here. I was by his side as he died and I never returned. I miss it each day."

Tara closed her eyes to picture how she would create a portrait of Milagro, the grasslands bordered by vicious volcanos, the herds of vicuñas dotting the lush mountains, the forests that blended with the sky. The fields of flowers.

"Tara, dear Tara," said Umita in her frail voice. She put her hand on Tara's. "You're picturing it, aren't you? Show me what you see."

Tara's eyes got big as a sense of dread took over her. "You want to see it but you don't want to learn of our stories, histories, heroes, and gods?" said Tara.

Tata looked at Tara and squinted. She opened her mouth to ask a question, but Umita interrupted her. "Tata, the Inkan settlement of Hatun Cañar, where Tara is from, has a unique history and she wants to continue with the stories and myths she learned as a child instead of those we have here. That's what she means."

"Don't all Inkas have the same stories, though?" said Tata.

Umita picked up one of the tunics that was lying on a loom and focused her attention to it. "Goodbye, Tara. I think you're tired and need to retire for the day. Take the blanket of Machu Picchu with you. I hope you understand what it means to me. Treat it with care." Without moving, Umita continued, "Tata, please stay here with me. We need to talk."

Once outside of the corridor Tara looked at the blanket of Machu Picchu again. There were stains of tear drops and blood. Some of it was old blood and some of it was new.

Tara folded it carefully with her warn fingers and tried to keep more blood from staining it. She pressed it to her heart and left to her huasi. She looked forward to sneaking out after everyone was asleep to find Viracocha to tell him about Machu Picchu if he was on the roof again.

He usually was.

Chapter Twenty

Machu Picchu

"Hey Tara," said Yachi. She waited outside the enclosure that contained her huasi.

Tara turned away from her.

"Ugh," said Yachi. "We can get you out of Cusco, but you'll have to leave tomorrow morning before the sunrise."

Yachi stuttered before she spoke, almost as if she were ashamed or fearful of what she might say. "The only way you can make it back to Milagro is with his help. It's too far, you know that."

"I have a token for you from him."

Tara stopped.

Yachi caught up and withdrew a bag from her chuspa.

Out of the bag, she slowly withdrew a bi-colored flower. It looked exactly as it looked last time she saw it, when Sapa Inka Tupac Yupanqui pulled it out from behind her ear.

Tara lunged for it and took it out of Yachi's hands. In doing so, she dropped Umita's blanket.

Tara clenched it in her raw hand. The stem felt like wood but was as light as a feather. She raised her other hand and clenched it. She was going to rip it apart.

Yachi caught one of her arms and held it with both hands to prevent her from tearing it. Yachi looked terrified, "Tara," She begged.

After several moments of fighting to free her arm, Tara lowered the flower.

"I'm sorry. I'm so sorry! I'm sorry I scared you." She was going to cry, but there was still too much anger in her to allow any tears.

Yachi let go of her arm.

"This flower," yelled Tara. She took a deep breath and closed her eyes. She spoke in a calm but vengeful voice, "This flower is the reason I am here, the reason all of these bad things have happened to me. If it wasn't for this flower, I would still be in Milagro working on my farm with my family. NONE, NONE OF THIS WOULD HAVE HAPPENED!!! THIS FLOWER!"

Yachi peered back and forth, unsure of how to respond. She bent over and picked up the blanket that Tara dropped in when she lunged for the flower.

"Tara, is this Milagro?" said Yachi. She was taken by the beautiful image, "Is this where you are from? That's beautiful!" It was the first time that Yachi seemed sincere.

"It's called Machu Picchu, it's where Umita is from," said Tara.

"Wow, you should tell me more about that sometime. Is Milagro as pretty as this?" said Yachi.

"Give me that," said Tara.

She tucked the flowers into her tunic and snapped the blanket from Yachi. She hugged it close to her chest.

Yachi put her hand on Tara's back and tried to get her to move.

Tara didn't move.

"Go back to your huasi. Remember, tomorrow morning, meet me here and we'll get you out of this alien place and get you back to Milagro. It will be like that flower never came into your life."

"Stop," spat Tara. "Just stop."

She removed Yachi's hand from her back, lowered herself using the stone wall as a back support. She held her head like she had a severe headache. Something just didn't seem right, even with the flower as the promised token, the accursed flower.

She thought of the council Hualpa gave her to be weary of everyone.

"But what if they want to help me leave!" said Tara.

"What?" said Yachi.

Tara squinted at her.

Yachi slouched next to her and kissed her hands that covered her head, "We'll get you back to Milagro." She said, interrupting Tara's thoughts.

Tara lowered her hands.

"And the warriors that will be trailing me? What's Amaru Tupa Inka going to do about that?" said Tara. "You realize that it took me over a suyu to get here and I was being carried upon a litter. It will take me longer if I have to walk. Yachi, the warriors will catch us, and then kill us, and then go wipe out my family, my friends, my lands. They are the ones I am here protecting."

The tears came and she hugged Yachi and cried on her shoulder for a moment.

"I'm sure that Amaru Tupa Inka has a plan to protect everyone. He will give you a medallion that guarantees safe passage on the Qhapaq Ñan, and a small entourage that knows the way," said Yachi. She put her hand on the Tara's tunic, over the flower. "He is very sorry and wants to make it right. Come in the morning, talk to him and tell him your concerns. Let him tell you what his plan is. If you don't want to go, we can't force you to. We'll bring you right back here and no one will know you were gone.

Tara jumped up and went walked away from Yachi.

"WILL YOU BE THERE?"

Tara ceased walking, looked back at her, and then exchanged looks between the flower in one hand and the blanket of Machu Picchu in the other. "What do you think?" said Tara.

She got to her huasi and closed the door. She picked up the nearest vessel and threw it at the wall. It shattered.

"Why does it even matter what Hualpa thinks? It's my life, it's me that would be stuck here forever, it's I that am separated from everything I love."

Chapter Twenty-One

Nothing is Sacred

"You're not going to last very long here."

Tara jumped at the sound of Tata's smooth and seductive voice. She thought everyone was asleep and snuck to the wall to see Viracocha. Tata weaved as she walked. She weaved a similar scarf to that which Umita weaved the day she arrived. Her fingers moved so fast that the thread and needle were smoking. Tara looked closer at the cloth and embroidered into it was a repeated pattern of a mullu shell.

"What do you mean?" asked Tara. Her voice betrayed her fear that she'd been caught.

"You're up at night, sneaking around, you speak with a funny accent. You're obviously not from the upper classes of Inka nobility like we are," said Tata. Her voice no longer sounded seductive but repulsive, like a girl speaks to the boy that won't leave her alone in his pursuit of love.

"I'm from a mitmaq village in Hatun Cañar," said Tara. "You were told that when I arrived here. I am a full Inka, just didn't grow up here is all."

Tata didn't appear to be convinced, and so Tara continued.

"What you call weird is normal among my people. But I like you all so much that I've been trying to learn your customs. I guess I'm a slow learner."

Tara looked back at the sunset colored mullu shell Tata weaved. The smoke from her fast weaving increased.

"Well, you won't last much longer," said Tata. She came in very close to Tara. Her eyes burned as if they were on fire and her breath had the odor of burning peppers, chicha, and death.

"If I won't last long, then kill me," said Tara softly. "I've tried to kill myself several times to save everyone who hates me the hassle. I know as well as you that I don't belong here."

Tata laughed a laugh that sounded like a gale.

"You're so stupid you can't even kill yourself. That takes a special gift."

Tata circled Tara and examined her clothes and posture.

"A special gift like a mullu shell, wouldn't you say?" said Tata.

Tara didn't answer, but felt the burning heat of her gaze from behind her.

Tara shed a tear and closed her eyes. She pictured Raura and Achache.

Tomorrow, tomorrow, I go.

Tata reached around from behind Tara and suffocated her with the scarf she had been weaving.

"Don't worry that you can't kill yourself, I'll give you the death you wish for," said Tata.

Tara's throat closed and she coughed harder than she ever had.

She woke up from the dream. Her room was on fire and thick smoke obscured the view to the door. The thick straw ceiling came down around her. She heaved for air and coughed. She lowered herself to the ground and dodged the floating embers and falling flames as she crawled to the door hidden in the thick smoke.

She reached for the rope to open the latch door, but the rope was ash. There was no way to open it. Another part of the ceiling came down. Tara jumped out of the way. It blocked the door. The straw embers exploded when they hit the ground and some of them landed on her. She cried in pain. The tall flames blocked her exit.

She coughed harder and grabbed the alpaca blanket from her bed. She pressed it to her mouth and used it as a filter.

"Tara! Are you okay?" Yelled girls from outside.

"NO! I'm going to—"

She coughed. Her skin burned. It was exactly how she remembered it feeling from the night Amaru Tupa Inka burned her.

"Hurry! Hurry with the water!" Someone yelled.

She coughed harder. Her vision got blurry. She fell forward onto the ground and missed the burning wall by a fingers' width.

Her clothes caught on fire.

The shouts of the acllas, the whoosh of the fire, everything echoed in her head.

Tata was right. The end was near.

Cold water drenched her. She screamed. She never felt such pain, nor such cold. The acllas threw another bucket of water on her. One of them leapt into the fire. She put Tara's arm over her shoulder and pulled her out via the door they knocked down.

Tara kissed the cheek of the aclla, unsure who it was, and then succumbed to her exhaustion.

"You girls keep putting the fire out," said one of the girls. "I will go get Yachi and have her get some help from the servants and porters so they can bring her to a Hampi Kamayoc. They'll know how to heal her."

"No!" said Umita. She stood on the outside of the gathered acllas with a tray of urns, leaves and dried flowers. "Do not bring Yachi here, nor any of the porters. They aren't allowed to come to this part of the Acllahausi. There is no need for anyone but I."

The crowd of acllas parted and Umita passed between them.

"Oh my little darling, how many hardships do you have to survive?" said Umita.

She set the tray down on the ground beside her. She stroked Tara's face. "Oh, my poor child. Why do you have to suffer so much?"

After a moment, she stood up, "We will bathe her in the fountain in the courtyard. That will be enough."

A few of the acllas laughed.

"It hasn't healed anyone in a long, long time," said Tata.

Umita glared at her.

Tara said a small prayer to Pachayachachic and Mamaquilla that that the magic that followed her in Milagro would find her here.

Several acllas lifted her limp body and carried her to the corridor. The cold water felt like a million sharp icicles from the glaciers being inserted into her skin.

Tara screamed and then coughed so hard that she lost control of her body. She convulsed and the convulsions turned into vomiting.

The acllas sang a sad song.

"Aya oya uacaylli-aya oya puypulli-lluto..."

They pulled her out of the water.

"...puchac uamrayqui lluto puchac uacchayqui-uacalla Callamosumquim..."

She was on her hands and knees. She gasped for air, but each inhale was interrupted by vomit and coughing.

Four acllas supported her while Umita placed layers of ointment on her chest.

The retched smell of the ointments sickened Tara. Her stomach cramped, but she was empty and nothing more came out. She hurled.

At the conclusion of the song, Umita secured the leaves that compressed the ointment on Tara's burns. Six acllas lowered her into the fountain again and washed the tears and vomit off of her.

"I want all of you to stay with her tonight here. Make sure no one comes. This fire was not an accident," said Umita.

"You mean someone tried to kill her?" said Tata.

Tara shuttered from the sound of Tata's voice.

"I don't know, but we must always watch her from now on," said Umita.

"Why would someone try to do such a thing?" said one of the most beautiful acllas. Her words were interrupted by sobs. "Attempting to kill an aclla! Never before has anyone been killed in Cusco. Never! And in the Acllahuasi? Is there nothing sacred anymore!" She ran off.

"If you believe the oral histories, then no, no one has ever been killed in Cusco. If you believe the histories," said Umita. She put her hand on Tara's shoulder and spoke slowly. "Why would anyone try to harm a daughter of the moon?" She kissed Tara's forehead.

The pain disappeared, but Tara was exhausted, breathing required all of her energy. The acllas carried her into a building she didn't recognize. It hurt too much to open her eyes and she didn't try to. She drifted on and off to sleep.

Tara woke up unaware of how much time passed since she dosed, if felt like it had been days, but by looking around, only a few moments had passed. She didn't have the strength to move and listened passively to the conversation between the acllas.

"—I don't want to be a Mamacuna." Tata said. "I mean, I love Inti, and he always gives me life, but I want someone to hold onto, someone to make me laugh. I want to have children run around. I don't even care if I love him. It would be nice, I suppose, but I would have children that I would love."

"Speak for yourself, Tata," said another aclla who had a deep voice. "Here our days are simple, everything is provided to us. We don't have to worry about war, our husbands, or sons dying, famine or anything. This is the only place to be content."

Several of the acllas concurred.

"—Tata, I heard that Apu Atoc has just won a war," said an aclla named Ñuestra that Tara had once met. "He is handsome and brave. Imagine being with an Apu!"

The girl with a deep voice agreed, "Okay, if I was to be paired with an Apu I would leave the Acllahuasi, but only then."

"You know, that Waranga named Hualpa is a war hero now," said Ñuestra. "He will be made an Apu if tradition is followed. One of us will probably be awarded to him."

The mention of Hualpa made Tara wake up completely.

"Waranga Hualpa Inka who is he?" said Tata.

"He just beat those Cañari monkeys like he was chasing dogs," said Ñuestra.

Tara opened her eyes. Her sight was blurry and she was unable to make out who was who, but she glared in Ñuestra's direction.

"Everywhere Waranga Hualpa goes, he wins," continued Ñuestra. "That's why he travels with Sapa Inka Tupac Yupanqui now and why he'll be made into an Apu. Those two are unstoppable. Did you hear the story of how he is defeating the Chachapoyas?" Asked Ñuestra.

"The Chachapoyas?" said the girl with the deep voice. "They are done in Cañari? But I heard that the victory of the Cañari's wasn't as easy as you say it was. From what I heard, we invaded them three times before we won. And even at that, it was by marriage to their ruler that we the conquest was won."

"HA! No, not at all," said Ñuestra. "It was like fighting savage monkeys. They were barbarous, but since there were so many of them, they didn't know what to do. Waranga Hualpa came up with a great plan to burn the forest and force them—"

"—That's not true," scampered Tara softly. She rolled over on her side using all of her energy and coughed up a mouthful of sputum.

The acllas hushed when they heard her speak.

She sat up and she rubbed her eyes. Although her eyes were still blurry, she made out Ñuestra and Tata.

"We fought very hard to defend Cañari from the evil you guys brought—" Her voice was rough but flowed like a mountain spring.

"—I wish we fought harder. Two of my brothers died in the first wars, and my father and last brother were killed during the last one. We are not monkeys or barbarians. We're just like you!"

"I knew it!" said three acllas together.

"That's why there was a fire," said Ñuestra. She stood up and looked over at Tara. "You aren't allowed in here. Inti wants you out! Get out! GET OUT! You Cañari filth!" She pointed to the exit.

"No! Say it isn't true," said Tata. She covered her mouth. "You lied to us? You violated this sacred place. Truly, nothing is sacred anymore." Tata looked down at the ground.

"Make sure she doesn't go anywhere," said Ñuestra. "I'm going to get Umita. She needs to know."

Ñuestra ran off.

Chapter Twenty-Two

Conspiracy

"**D**o you think she'll come?" Asked Amaru Tupa Inka.

Yachi looked at him. He was dressed in his opulent clothes with the albino cloak. His flat toned face absorbed the starlight of the night, making the gold gauges his in ears appear brighter than usual.

"I'm sure she'll come. She hates it there enough to risk everything to leave." She spoke without the hesitation and the fear that Tara came to know her by.

She snuck out of the Acllahuasi through a secret passage she created. She wore a disguise of a wife of a ruler of a nearby allyu. Her cloak was humble but smooth, with imprints of llamas of different colors. Her hair was braided and her head was wrapped with a simple woven llautu the color of dirt. She wore tattered pants that went to her mid-shin.

Amaru Tupa Inka and Yachi spoke in a small ají colored room with patterned rugs with hanging from the walls. It was the huasi where Sapa Inka Tupac Yupanqui was born. Amaru Tupa Inka was one of the few men with access, and it served as a meeting point when secrecy was vital.

"I told my brother that she wouldn't like it at the Acllahuasi," said Amaru Tupa Inka. "He ruined her life, and the sanctity of the

Acllahuasi. I am only trying to fix things he broke. I'm always fixing things that he breaks, ever since we were little boys running around in Sacsayhuaman."

Yachi shrugged. "Does it matter who's fault it is. Let's just get rid of her. I have a feeling that Mamacuna Umita knows I'm up to something."

"So? Who is she and what does it matter?"

"Ugh, it does matter or else I wouldn't tell you. She's one of the Mamacuna that has been around longer than the world has existed. She's probably the Mother of Manco Inka. Nothing happens there without her knowing and approval."

"This Mamacuna Umita, can we kill her too?" said Amaru Tupa Inka. He smirked.

Yachi wasn't sure if he was serious or not, "If you want to kill her you're not the man I thought and I'd question your motives in wanting to kill Tara as well."

"My motive?" Said Amaru Tupa Inka. "I question your motives."

Darkness overtook Yachi. She felt it consume her from the outside and the inside. A pit of rage erupted. "Every time I see her, I feel inadequate. If any girl was made an Inka by Privilege, it should be me! I should be the aclla, not some stranger from a land of savages and beasts. I hate her!"

"I don't actually care about your motive," said Amaru Tupa Inka. "Just get Tara here in the morning and have her wear this." He gave Yachi a stack of robes. "History will give much glory to you and your family. The gods will forever provide you with your needs because you are sanctifying the Acllahuasi."

"Ugh, I don't care about glory, or sanctifying the Acllahuasi. You can keep your sooth-speaking and flattery for someone that wants it. Just get rid of her once I deliver her to you." said Yachi.

He escorted Yachi to the door.

Outside, smoke filled the air.

"It would appear there's a fire," said Amaru Tupa Inka.

"You think? You really think there's a fire. What else would cause this smoke and smell like this?" said Yachi.

"It was a joke, god, get a sense of humor."

"Ugh."

They went in together around the corner to see from where the smoke came.

"It's from the Acllahuasi!" said Yachi. She ran toward it a short way.

"Get back here and hide yourself!" said Amaru Tupa Inka. He pulled her back by the shroud of her tunic. "Get back in the building and I'll tell you what I see," said Amaru Tupa Inka. He climbed to the roof, using the notches in the wall that contained idols.

"It's a fire, and it's a big one coming from in the middle of the Acllahuasi," he said.

"What part is on fire?" yelled Yachi from within the building.

"The middle," said Amaru Tupa Inka.

"I mean what buildings, what structures?"

"Well, let me see. Oh yeah, I've never been in there so I don't know," said Amaru Tupa Inka.

A crowd gathered on the plaza in front of the building to watch the fire. He descended the wall.

"Let me get a look," said Yachi. She ascended half way but Amaru Tupa Inka pulled her back down.

"Oh yes, it will be much better for our plan if you get caught out here, won't it?"

Yachi sunk back into the building a little more and looked down. "Tara won't be able to come. Everyone in the Acllahuasi will be awake and on guard. I won't be able to sneak her out."

"What?"

"I'm telling you, whatever plans we had burned up with that fire," said Yachi. "She'll take this as an omen that she wasn't supposed to come. We'll have to find a new way to draw her out. We can always hope it gets Tara."

Amaru Tupa Inka laughed. "So, if the fire doesn't kill her, we'll try again tomorrow or the next day."

He leaned against the entrance wall in the building. "I knew this would happen. While performing chants and begging the gods for this chance to cleans Cusco, I had a vision that showed me a big fire on the moon. Now I understand what it meant. We'll find a new way to trick her into leaving. You continue what you are doing, keep befriending her until we have another chance. Make her trust you more."

"Ugh, I don't think I can keep doing this. Aren't you afraid that if your brother finds out that you are plotting against her, he'll kill you?"

"He disobeys tradition and I disobey him. We're the same. If Inti doesn't punish him, perhaps I'll escape punishment myself."

They stood in silence. Yachi broke it, "I have another idea that might get her to leave the city. So, she is promised to be gifted to Waranga Hualpa, well promised depending she restore her beauty."

"Tell me, please."

"Say, something finds its way into his food and he gets sick. He would return home, wouldn't he?" Asked Yachi.

"You really hate her, don't you? You are suggesting to harm one of our heroes and have him removed from a critical war just for a chance Tara might take him as bait," said Amaru Tupa Inka. He smiled. "I like the plan and I have just the method to get him sick. It will take some time."

"Must we bring her outside of Cusco, or would outside the Acllahuasi be fine to kill her?"

"It MUST be outside of Cusco. No one has ever been killed in Cusco. That is a tradition I intend to keep. I had a vision recently of another way to draw her outside of Cusco. In case if Waranga Hualpa doesn't come through, this will definitely work."

"What is it?"

"Oh, you'll see. You, though, must return to the Acllahuasi. They may need your help to put out that fire."

Yachi returned to the Acllahuasi via her secret passage, which no one knew about, not even Amaru Tupa Inka or her closest friends. She hid her disguise under a stone in a pile of rejected textiles outside her huasi and went in.

"Next time it may be your huasi that is on fire," said Umita. She stood at the entrance of Yachi's huasi. She didn't look up at Yachi as she weaved a tunic.

"What?" Yachi jumped.

"You are never to see Tara again," said Umita.

"You're not going to report me and have me killed?"

"No, I have a better use for you," said Umita. "And beginning tomorrow, you are to make five basins of chicha before Inti Raymi."

"That's impossible!" said Yachi. Her mouth dried up.

Chapter Twenty-Three

Blank Parchment

Tara pulled off some of the crusted bandages from her burns. The burns covered most of her body: her legs and arms, her lower abdomen, and the opposite side of her face that was previously burned. She lost feeling in her fingers and clasped her palms around the bandages to pull them. She yelled a little as the bloody cloth cleaved from her open skin.

Umita lowered the food she was trying to feed Tara.

"Oh Tara, stop pulling them or else I'll have to tie your arms down again and give you drink that will make you sleep again. Please stop pulling."

"I'm done here! I'm leaving Cusco! Help me get all of this stuff off of me."

She resumed pulling off her bandages.

Umita stood up and crossed the small wooden room that smelled of fermented leaves and roots. It had a large striped rug across the dirt floor the color of stone and dirt. She picked up a tray of ointments and bandages and returned to Tara.

"It will go the same way as it has the last several times you tried to pull the bandages off and leave. You don't have the strength and you'll just hurt yourself."

Umita cringed with each of Tara's moans as she continued to pull her bandages. I went to her. She placed her arm on her unaffected shoulder.

"Tara, my cute Tara, I can still restore your beauty, but you have to stop pulling at your bandages. You're looking so much better, just awhile longer, and you will be more beautiful than you have been since you arrived," said Umita.

Tara acted as if she didn't hear the soft voice.

She will say anything she had to in order to get her way. It's up to me to get out of Cusco now, Hualpa won't help me now.

She stood up. The dingy room moved back and forth and the floor came up. All of a sudden, she was in Umita's arms.

"GET AWAY FROM ME!" said Tara.

Umita lifted Tara with no difficulty, despite her frail frame and age, and put her back into her bed.

"There you go," she pushed her head back onto her pillow.

Tara looked up at Umita.

"It's been suyus since the fire. I'm ugly and can't walk or weave. Even I know I should be better by now! Look at my hands! I'm useless, let me go! Let me go back to Milagro! Send Yachi to me, I need to talk to her!"

Umita removed a stack of new cloth bandages and an urn of ointment from the tray. She dipped the cloth into the ointment and reapplied the bandages.

Tara didn't stop her, it felt good on her raw skin but the smell was bitter and she tried to cover her nose.

"Here, this will help with the smell and your anxiety." Umita gave her a thick drink. "It won't put you to sleep."

Tara grabbed it between her two bandaged hands. She drank some. It was sweet and the thick taste lingered in her mouth.

"Why is it only you that tends to my wounds? Do the others hate me so much now that they know I'm from Milagro that not one of them will help?" She paused and looked away from Umita, "Or because I'm so ugly? Yachi would help me. Please let her. Send her to me."

Umita ceased what she was doing and wiped her hands on a rag of the ointment. She put her hand on Tara's unburned cheek and pulled her face back toward her, "Oh dear Tara. When we nearly fixed half of your face, the other side had to get burned. You won't be ugly for long. You will be well by Quicuchica, so stop thinking you will be—"

"—What if I want to be ugly and don't want to attend Quicuchica? It used to be that I was singled out because of my face, now it's because I'm ugly. What's the difference? You know what! I think I'm happy ugly." She shoved the cup back into Umita's hands.

Umita put the cup on Tara's chest, "You will go to Quicuchica not because you are beautiful or because you are ugly. You will go because you are an Inkan girl in Cusco. Now, drink more."

Tara trank more.

"Will you at least send Yachi to me?"

"I will be the only one that tends to your wounds and your only company."

The drink took effect and even though Tara felt the anger going away. She laid back and relaxed.

Umita finished feeding Tara and tending to her wounds. She left the room with the dishes, ointments, and bandage and only left a basket of weaving materials on the ground next to Tara. Upon seeing it, which Tara did shortly after Umita left, she rolled on her side, grabbed it and threw it as hard as her strength allowed. It hit the wall on the opposite side of the small room. The small needles made of bones, and the spools made of wood hit a stone that protruded from the corner of the room. The echo of the simple sounds made the silence more ominous.

She shivered.

"You'll have to come back and put the basket back," yelled Tara.

The action spent the last of Tara's energy and she fell asleep.

Umita returned the next morning with Tara's meal and with a tray of ointments and bandages. She gently placed the food on the stone while she gracefully gathered the contents of the basket and restored it to its spot next to Tara. The only sound made was the sound of Umita's shuffle.

As Umita fed her a baked sweet potato and guavas, Tara looked from the basket, to her own hands, and to Umita. She tried to grab a guava out of the bowl, but it fell out of her numb hand and rolled onto the floor.

"It's okay, dear Tara, it's okay," said Umita. She picked it up, "The sensation in your fingers will be back in time. Just days ago you wouldn't have been able to get it out of the bowl."

Tara stared back at the basket of the tiny needles made of hallowed bone. She tried to imagine how she would pick up a small needle if she couldn't pick up the guava.

Umita gave her the last bite of food and fixed her bandages. She got up to leave.

"Don't leave," said Tara.

"I have to leave, there are acllas that are working on their weaving skills. I must assist them."

"Wait! I'm so lonely, I have to talk Yachi, can you send her to me to give me company, please!"

"Yachi is no longer allowed in the inner parts of the Acllahuasi."

"How come? I need to talk to her. I need company."

"I think you know why," said Umita.

"I don't know. Is she the one that started the fire, is that why?" said Tara.

"I don't know."

"Yes you do, and now I know it was she that started the fire. That's why I'm hidden away, everyone wants to kill me now. So let them kill me! It's better than being alone."

Umita went out the door and left Tara in the silence.

She threw the basket again.

The echo of the spools and needles hitting the stone echoed, and echoed and echoed. Each echo louder than the last. Tara covered her ears, but they got louder and louder until it sounded like a man shouting in a whisper.

"TARA!"

"TARA!"

"TARA! I KNOW YOU'RE NEARBY!"

Tara covered her ears, but the voice spoke to her from within.

"You can't run away, you will be here forever! You're ugly and not even the Inka trash want you anymore. Useless, Tara, you're useless. Tara of the Useless. Tara of the Useless TARA OF THE USELESS."

"I'M NOT USELESS," Tara yelled.

"You have no friends and family because you aren't worth it. Everyone hates you and everyone that doesn't hate you will die. You're ugly, Tara. Tara the Ugly. Tara the Ugly. Tara the Useless."

Umita opened the door, and the voices ceased. The light broke the putrid darkness and her foot steps sounded like a mother's voice to her lost infant. Her hunched back sent an ominous shadow across the room.

"I have dinner for you," she said.

She picked up the spindles and needles and put them back next to Tara. She fed Tara roasted dark quinoa and squash, then she changed some of her bandages, applied ointment, and left. She did all of this without saying another thing to Tara.

"Please, don't leave me," said Tara. She tried to sit up in her bed. "My mind is rotting with the silence and I know I will start seeing and conversing with the dead should my loneliness continue any longer."

"Very well, then converse with them. Maybe you will listen to them since you won't listen to the living."

Umita departed and closed the door behind her.

Tara reached over to throw the basket, but Umita came back in the room.

"Here," said Umita. "I brought you something to help with the voices." In her arms was a vessel, the blanket of Machu Picchu, and a blank cloth.

Tara put the basket down. Umita placed the embroidered blanket of Machu Picchu next to it, along with a blank cloth.

"It would be wise not to throw the basket again but to use the tools within to find your sanity in your loneliness." She placed a warm cup into Tara's hands.

Tara looked into it, it was tea and it smelled like dirt. Tara tried some. It tasted dull. Like dirt.

Umita kissed her forehead, lit a small fire and left.

"NO!" Yelled Tara. "Don't leave," she said in a whisper.

Tara sat up on her reed mattress and cried. She picked up the parchment of Machu Picchu. It was covered in more blood than when she received it. The fabric smelled of smoke and the once clean parchment was stained with burns. She compared it with the blank parchment, which was as if it were fresh snow. Tara picked it up.

"It feels like snow too," she said to herself.

She dropped the parchment.

"I CAN MY FINGERS AGAIN!"

She tried to stand, but her legs didn't listen to her.

She relaxed and returned her gaze to the parchment of Machu Picchu. The image became alive. Tara felt the energy: she walked along the narrow steep pathways lining the sheer cliffs towering over the thrashing rivers. She tasted the sweet air, humid with the moisture from the jungle.

Tara then looked at the blank parchment, but it wasn't empty anymore. It was Milagro and in the same detail as the parchment of Machu Picchu. She saw her father in it and in his hands. He held a cloth bag of his needles and thread that he used to make the clothes for the family.

He reached from the parchment and gave the bag to Tara, "Just as I clothed you to keep the family safe from the storms, you must protect Cañari from the storm of the Inkas."

"Look at my hands, father, look! I can't even feed myself. I can't hold the bag" She cried.

"You already have the bag." Guaman embraced her. She glanced away from the parchment to the basket Umita left behind.

"Your hands are injured, I understand, but I am dead and I still found a way to speak with you, am I not? Just try."

She reached for the needles but tipped the basket over. The contents fell into the dirt.

She looked back at the white parchment. Her father was still there. "What if I can't!" She raised her hands, one of the bandage and the other numb.

"The gods will restore them when they know you will use them and once you have done what you are supposed to, they will take them back again."

"So what if I can sew, and so what if I am good at it? I am ugly now. Hualpa won't marry me. He only cares about beauty. If I become good at weaving, then I will be stuck here in the Acllahausi forever."

"You must learn how to sew, my dear sweet daughter. Become the best weaver there is. That's how good things will happen to you. That's where all the good things for you begin. I promise. Weave well, get gifted to a ruler, then escape from him."

He left.

"Father! Father, please! Come back, I need you."

She felt an embrace again, as if a person was in the air around her.

Weave well, get gifted to a ruler, then escape from him.

Chapter Twenty-Four

Yanantin

"Umita!" said Tara next time she came in. "I can feel again! My fingers, I can feel them!"

"That is so good, my dear Aclla, and it's not only your fingers that have improvement. Feel the burned side of your body," said Umita.

Tara stroked her face, neck, and down to her legs. There weren't as many bandages as she remembered there being, and where the bandages had been was replaced with smooth skin.

A surge of warmth overcame her.

"I want to sew. Can you bring me ropes so I can practice? The string in the basket is too small and light for my fingers." She looked down at her hands.

Umita smiled. She put the tray down on the stone, went to Tara, and kissed her forehead.

"Oh you dear girl, of course I can. I will return shortly."

She returned within moments with a light rope made of llama fur. After feeding Tara and tending to her wounds, she gave the rope to her.

"Well, let's see what you can do," said Umita. She leaned so far forward that Tara thought she would fall over.

"You mean you're not just going to leave this time?"

"No, no, no, I must teach acllas to weave, and isn't that what I'm doing by staying with you?"

Tara picked up the rope and practiced the knots she remembered, which amounted to three.

"I thought I remembered more, all that time practicing, and I can only remember three knots, it's hopeless!" said Tara.

"No, no, no, don't even say that Tara. Remember, my dear girl, I am here to teach you," said Umita. She took the ropes and demonstrated. "You'll soon continue weaving and you'll be very good at it. I know you will be a good Aclla and Mamacuna."

"But if I'm a Mamacuna, I won't be able to be gifted to a war hero or ruler and will remain here forever," said Tara.

"Yes, yes, you will be here forever. I think that will be best for you and I will see that it happens," said Umita.

Tara lost all her strength and laid down. She looked at the blank parchment and for an instant of an instant she saw Milagro and her father in it. It filled her with energy.

"Mamacuna Umita, I want to be gifted to a deserving man, not to remain here."

Umita gave the small ropes back to Tara and she took them.

With little effort and practice, the knots that escaped Tara's memory returned to her and she learned more knots and sewing patterns in the next days, then in her time at the Acllahuasi.

That night, long after Umita left, Tara woke from her sleep. She felt uneasy, like the moments before she was burned.

"Tara!" Called the deep voice again that called her before. "Tara, where are you, Tara? Will I ever see you again?"

"TARA!"

The call ceased, and she didn't hear it again until several lonely nights later.

"Tara! Where are you?" said the deep voice, "I know you're still here. Why are you hiding Tara?"

Then nothing.

"It's just loneliness," she told herself.

Umita returned each day and put a unique and unfamiliar ointment on Tara's fingers and the areas that were still injured. Tara didn't mind because whatever she was doing worked and she felt happier and more energetic. What bothered Tara was that Umita took each item that she sewed, "to be offered to the gods as an offering of gratitude."

Tara followed Umita's commands and gave her the items she sewed, no matter how simple or how emotionally attached she was to them.

"Can't I keep just one of them?" Said Tara after Umita took her best work yet. It was a cloak with a spiral pattern weaved into it.

"The gods have been kind to you thus far," said Umita. "They gave you health and you gave nothing back to them. You must remember Ayni in all that you do. You must remember that whenever something is given to you, you must give something back and when you give something to another, expect something back from them. This is what keeps existence in balance. It keeps us alive and the world around us in order, it's why this ointment works."

By the next moon, Tara created a small image of Milagro on the side of a chuspa.

"What is it?" said Umita.

"It's Milagro from the vantage point of my home, I mean my old home, I mean Hatun Cañar, my old home. Ugh, whatever. Just, what do you think, Umita?"

Umita stroked Tara's short hair. The thick charcoal hair that was burned off was returning thicker and so dark it was as shiny as obsidian.

"Remember this image, so that when you are better at sewing, you see how far you've come," said Umita.

She took the needle and thread away from Tara.

"Practice more tomorrow, your fingers are still weak and I don't want you to injure them."

"A loom is easier on the fingers than the needle," said Tara. "Can you bring one tomorrow so I can practice on that?"

Umita opened her mouth, but no words came out.

"Or am I well enough that I can come out and practice?"

"I will bring one here," said Umita immediately.

Tara tried but failed to use the loom the next day because of the fine finger movements required and leaving forward hurt.

"Do you want me to get the sewing basket?" said Umita.

"No, please just teach me. Can you weave slowly so I can watch and learn?

Umita hung the loom in a way to give Tara a clear view. She placed the large wooden pluck in one hand and in the other she held and picked at the separate strings that formed a field of colors of threads on her lap. The other hand plucked and worked them with the needle.

Tara mimicked each movement to the best of her ability. All else in the world was forgotten besides her father in the back of her mind, encouraging her.

Days later when Tara felt well, she grabbed the loom and needles as she saw Umita grab them and not the way she remembered her father or brothers having done so. She did one pass with the wooden needle across the strings. She dropped the needle. She bent forward onto the loom and cried.

Umita put her hands on Tara's back, "Oh no, dear girl, what's wrong?"

"Mamacuna Umita, when I came here I was ready to be tortured and hated. That's why I never cried or complained about my pain, or my burns, or not having friends. What I never expected was to find someone like a parent. That's what you are to me, you are my mother as much as my actual mother in Milagro."

Tara dropped everything and lept onto Umita and hugged her. Umita's body felt cool and Tara's reach didn't go around Umita's humped back, but the hug was what Tara needed.

"Oh no, no, no. I am not so lucky to have you as a daughter. The only mother that can claim such perfection as you is Mamaquilla."

Her tears wet Umita's shoulder. "No more about Inti, Pachayachachic, Mamaquilla, or any other god. You were the one here for me, the one who fed me, the one who loved me through this time. You are my mother."

"I understand, but remember, you must not say such things. The gods are the ones that gave you your health, not I. It was they that assisted me in restoring balance to you and the earth and air around you to restore your health. It was not I."

"I was out of balance? I thought I was sick." said Tara. She pushed away from Umita.

"That is what any change, good or bad, is: a loss of *yanantin*. Or as you call it in Cañari, balance, a loss of balance. When you lose *yanantin* things fall out of balance and a change happens and we call this a *pachacuti*. See, a pachacuti must restore yanantin when it is disrupted in anything that possesses kawsay, an object, a body, a culture, an environment. Really, anything. When a young girl comes to the Acllahuasi and is full of malaise and anger, a pachacuti must happen that breaks her, and then she is a girl of yanantin. Your face, how it's evenly split between the light and the dark, represents this yanantin." said Umita.

Umita picked up her needle and the llautu she was working on.

"I was only mad because I didn't want to be here. Everyone hates me and I hate all of them too," said Tara. She spoke in a muffled tone.

Umita looked up from her weaving. "Tara look at me,"

Tara complied. She didn't want Umita to think she was mad, she wasn't, but this conversation was boring.

"Be thankful for this fire and who ever started it. You are here suffering, yes, but now you have *yanantin* again and your former family and people are safe in Milagro from your poor decisions. You will leave the safety of the healing chamber when the first rain arrives during the rain season. Take the pain of the pachacuti as a warning, don't try to leave again."

"What, what?—" Tara asked how she knew of her plans of leaving the Acllahuasi before the fire. Umita reached forward and covered her mouth.

"I know everything that goes on in these walls."

She pulled her mouth away from Tara's mouth.

"You know who started this fire, don't you?" Said Tara.

"It was Inti who started the fire."

"It might have been Inti that started it, but who spread it to my huasi that night?"

Umita set down her sewing, picked up the tray of food and ointments, and left.

Tara curled up in bed.

Be weary of everyone and everything.

"Oh please, Hualpa, come back and rescue me, get me out of this horrible place. Or anyone, anyone please ask for me as a gift and get me out of here."

She fell asleep and woke to the deep voice.

"Tara, oh Tara, did you actually leave without me knowing?"

Tara heard people running on the other side of the wall next to her pillow.

"He's over here!" said a woman. Tara didn't recognize the voice.

"Goodbye Tara," said the deep voice.

"I heard him again, this way!" said another woman.

"Are you sure," said the first woman.

"Yes, you stay here and I'll go this way."

Tara felt a hand within her own. She opened her eyes, but there was no one there. The voices disappeared.

Chapter Twenty-Five

Viracocha

Tara peered out the door each day, hoping for a rain cloud so she could leave, but the dry season seemed like it would never end. She spent the days weaving, during which time Umita sat with her. The rain arrived a suyu late and on the shortest day of the year. The thunder shook the ground and was so loud that Tara plugged her ears with small balls she created out of the string.

The rain turned into a sprinkle in the second half of the day. Umita came in and offered Tara a hand to the wooden doorway to leave.

Tara grabbed her soft and wet hand with her fully healed hand. Umita assisted her to the door and Tara peered into her surroundings for the first time.

Lightening stuck nearby and the thunder split the air.

She took a couple steps into the rain and smiled when the drops hit her face. She looked around and realized that she was inside the building that she crawled on top of when visiting Viracocha.

She laughed.

"Did you see that?" said Umita.

"What!" said Tara.

"A little coy just ran across the path. I haven't seen one in the Acllahuasi in a long time."

"Hmm, a coy?" said Tara. "I wonder why."

"It's because of the rain. Such things happen when Pachayachachic and Llapa come together," said Umita. "Have you ever considered the relationship Pachayachachic and Llapa?"

Tara realized it was the beginning of another speech about ayni and yanantin, and she took a couple steps away from Umita. Her attention turned to the rain. It was the most beautiful thing she had seen since her arrival at the Acllahuasi.

"You see, everything in existence is because of Yanantin and Ayni, even this beautiful rain which is a gift from Llapa."

Tara jumped into a small puddle.

Umita continued, "Llapa, the God of thunder, is releasing the daily thunderstorms and gifting Pachayachachic the moisture she needs to have things grow. As a thanks, she gives creates clouds and storms in the mountain peaks so Llapa grows more powerful. The exchange between Llapa and Pachayachachic gives us the needed moisture and vegetation, and the high places and low places, so that we can live. Because of that, we give thanks to them and provide offerings or else they may forget us and withhold their gifts from us. Do you see how it all works now?"

"I've understood since the first time you explained it," said Tara. She smiled at Umita. "I need to make the best textiles so that people realize what I'm worth."

"And?" said Umita.

"And so people have something worthy to sacrifice to the gods so that there is reciprocity for all they give us," said Tara.

"And what does that matter for you individually?"

"So that I can give offerings to thank them for a return of my beauty and ability to weave," said Tara. She jumped into another puddle, then ran to Umita and gave her a hug and kiss. The embrace left the front of Umita's tunic soaking.

"Now, now, where are you going to do, sweet woman?" Said Umita.

"Become the best weaver that the Acllahuasi has ever known, so I will be gifted to a good man."

Umita put her hand on her forehead, "Tara, you already found a good man and he is Inti."

"Of course," said Tara. She left and chuckled to herself on the way to her old loom, jumping into each of the puddles on the way.

She passed Ñuestra and Tata, they were in a nearby building making chicha. Neither of them acknowledged her until she passed.

"Bye, snake!" said Ñuestra.

Tara bit her lip and turned around.

"What?" Said Tara.

"Yeah, you know you're a snake." Said Ñuestra. "You are going to wish you were never born by the time we're done with you. Just wait, we'll make your life here so bad you'll wish the fire devoured you. You're a horrible person."

Weave well, get gifted to a ruler, escape from him.

"We'll see," said Tara, and she continued to her quarters dancing.

She spent the rest of the day weaving. After the sunlight vanished, she lit a lamp, but it went out before she wanted to finish so she weaved by feel until her fingers became raw. She departed the loom only after she dozed off and fell over.

Her clothes were still wet from the rain, and the cool air outside the small room gripped her like the water of a mountain lake. The chill woke her up. She glanced in the direction of her huasi and thought of the fire. She turned away from it and instead made her way to the back of the Acllahuasi where the chicha urns were stored. They remained in the same places as before the fire. She gently pushed two of them over to empty the water and then stacked them. She climbed to the top of the wall and followed it to the roof of what she learned earlier that day was the healing chamber. She peered through the cloudy darkness to see if Viracocha was there, but he wasn't. She fell asleep on her own lap.

She spent the next day at the loom and once again left after she fell over from exhaustion. She went to wait for Viracocha on the roof, but he didn't come. She waited for him each night through the rainy season and he never came, not when it was clear, nor when it was raining or hailing, not when the sky was full of meteors, or when lightening danced between Llapa and Pachayachachic.

The long hours at the loom made her into a better weaver than she thought she was capable of. She wanted to show someone her works but the other acllas and mamacunas shunned her. She hid them from Umita because she smiled and took them away to be made as offerings.

"Oh my dear Aclla, that tapestry is good, but it's not as good as you can do. Here, give it to be for an offering."

Other days Umita would tell her, "You need to get away from that loom, tomorrow I will show you how to make chicha." Tomorrow never came and Tara continued weaving. She placed her textiles that escaped Umita's watch into a large urn that she used to create the stairs to the top of the wall. She used several of the urns to store her personal items to avoid returning to her huasi, which she hadn't yet returned to. Each time she thought of returning, an unexplained anxiety overtook her and she found herself going in the opposite direction. It was like another person was in control of her body.

Each night, she took her most impressive work with her to the roof to show Viracocha. He would appreciate her new skills, she hoped. Without that hope, she would be completely alone in the Acllahuasi.

The lonely nights on the roof accumulated.

One unusually cool night, as cold as the loneliness that dwelt within her, she went to the wall. The urns had been moved to the opposite side of the small storage place between the wall of the Acllahuasi and the adjacent buildings.

She looked around. She felt someone was watching her.

"You think you can stop me from my only pleasure of this horrible place, ha!" said Tara in a muffled voice.

She pushed and pulled the urns across the bricks to the wall. She started with the heaviest of them, which formed the base of her pyramid to climb. After it was in position, she moved one of the lighter ones. It broke when she put it on its side to roll it. Scores of snakes slithered on the ground around her.

She shrieked and jumped on top of the larger urn.

Laughs echoed down the corridor, "You're done, Tara," said a voice Tara recognized to be Tata's.

The terrible yet beautiful snakes had large heads and were as long as Tara was tall. They were striped the dark color of leaves and the shiny luminosity of stagnant water. They slithered in each direction looking for shelter, but several of them surrounded the urn she stood upon and struck at her feet.

Tara jumped to avoid their bites, and the first two snakes missed her.

Vines of sunflowers emerged from between the bricks at the base of the urn and wrapped themselves around the snakes and pulled the snakes to the ground. They hissed and slithered, but were bound too tightly by the flower stems to escape.

The laughs ceased and Tara stared at the flowers. They were the same sunflowers as in Cañari that pulled down the tents of the Inkan military. She stared at the ground, not knowing what to think.

Tara bent over and touched one of the snakes when their struggle ceased. It was as cold as snow.

"Thank you, Pachayachachic! Thank you!"

She got off of the urn and looked into each of the urns before she moved them. The rest were empty except for those that had her textiles and clothes.

She looked around again before getting on the top of the wall.

"So tell on me," said Tara to the void.

She proceeded up the urns, across the wall and over the healing chambers wall to her usual spot. As she expected, Viracocha wasn't there and she quickly went to sleep.

"I wondered if you'd ever return," said a deep raspy voice. It sounded like a croak more than a voice.

Tara woke and gave a little jump.

"You were caught in that fire, weren't you?" he asked.

She focused where the voice came from, across the alley and on the roof where Viracocha typically was.

"Don't worry, it's me, Viracocha. Were you in that fire?" He said.

"Oh, Viracocha! I thought I'd never see you again." She was on the verge of yelling. "I'm so happy you're back. I've come here every night waiting for you. Can see my burns?"

"No. You got burned? That is unfortunate. I can't see them, I can only see your outline against the torches behind you and that your face that is split evenly between the light and the dark. I just figured you were in the fire because it's been awhile," said Viracocha.

Tara bit her lip. Viracocha was different, not just his voice. She sensed he was no longer the boy that wanted her to play.

"What do you mean it's been awhile? I've come up here every night during the wet and dry season, and you've never been there. It has been awhile for *you*. Where have you been?"

"I tried to say goodbye to you before I left. I thought you were one of the girls that came looking for me when I called for you."

She thought back to the night in the healing chambers when a man called her name.

"That was you that called for me? I thought it was the voices in my head."

"You heard me?" Said Viracocha.

Tara blushed. "I think. Maybe."

She squinted at Viracocha and examined the parts of him that the faint light provided by the stars and distant torches illuminated. He appeared short, but she figured he was sitting. His shoulders were massively wide. The light reflected off of his face, it seemed to have a hue like a sunset. She easily identified a large medallion worn upon his chest and even though the night was cold, he didn't wear any warm clothes.

"I left Cusco for Huarachicoy," said Viracocha.

"What's that?"

"It's the rite of passage for boys to become a man." There was sarcasm in his raspy voice. "Everyone knows that. Something amazing happened to me, though. I spoke with a condor and they revealed to me that which I must do with my life."

"Oh, that's good. I want to hear all about it another time," said Tara. She paused. "I can weave again! I've been doing a lot of weaving. Look at this tapestry I made." Tara put a little rock in it and threw it across to him.

"It's good, isn't it, just like the textiles that a nobleman would want his wife to make, right?"

He held it close to his face and looked at it for several moments. Longer than Tara thought he would, and it made her uneasy.

"It is beautiful. Tell me about it," he said. He spoke with caution in his raspy voice.

Tara smiled because of the compliment. The tapestry had the desired effect.

"It's an image of my homeland, Mila—of Hatun Cañar. It's an Inkan settlement in Cañari," Tara told him the story that influenced the image.

"I want you to tell that story to my friends," said Viracocha after Tara finished. "When I'm a Waranga and my friends are my soldiers, we will go there and make peace between everyone and bring civilization to the natives of that land. I mean, if Inti desires that, of course."

He placed the rock into the parchment and threw it back to Tara. She didn't try to catch it and watched it as it made a thud when it hit the thatched roof. It rolled off of the roof and onto the Acllahuasi floor below her.

"What if the native's of that area don't want your civilization?" said Tara.

"What? Everyone wants it. Everyone is better under the dominion of Inti and his son, the Sapa Inka," said Viracocha.

Tara stood up to leave but sat back down, "Let me tell you another story, this one about the natives who are called Cañaris," she said.

"Tell me tomorrow. I want some of my friends to meet you and learn these stories," said Viracocha.

Tara didn't answer.

"It will only be those that I trust. You'll be safe and your secrets will remain secrets," said Viracocha.

"Tell them to tell no one else."

"I promise," said Viracocha.

She returned the following night and Viracocha was there with several other young men. They all sat on various parts of the steep roof. They hid themselves in the low light, so Tara saw nothing but their outlines. She told them stories of Cañari and of what life was like in the Acllahuasi.

The young men promised they wouldn't speak of their midnight ventures, but more boys came each night. It worried Tara, but Viracocha assured her it was fine.

"Tara," Viracocha said in his raspy and hiss-like voice, "these men are here at greater risk to themselves than you are at risk of getting caught. They want to learn the stories of this magical place you talk about of Cañari, where the coy sing when you are happy, where huacas provide items immediately, and where kisses heal the injured."

Tara thought about what he said, "What would happen then," she asked herself. "At best they'd kick me out, at worst, they'd make me stay? Or try to kill me, again?"

Tara told them everything because she realized this was her chance and it was only a matter of time until her showtime was discovered.

Chapter Twenty-Six

Big Step

Q uicuchica Festival was drawing near, and an increasing number of acllas made chicha. As for past Quicuchica Festivals, each of the urns in the Acllahuasi were filled with chicha and covered. Tara prepared for when the urns she relied upon to climb the wall would be utilized for such purposes and no longer available to create a stairway by moving her items into sacks and hiding them around the Acllahuasi. She loosened the bricks at the base of the wall to use them for her makeshift stairs.

The night came when the urns were gone, and she stacked the loosened brings atop each other. Rain came down especially hard that night and the occasional hail pellet hit her. They left little dark marks on her skin.

"Tara," said a soft voice from behind her.

Tara looked, and Tata stood directly behind her.

"I have a message for you from Yachi," said Tata.

Tara stared at her and looked at her nearly completed staircase. She picked up a brick and held it ready to throw at Tata.

"You are a disgusting person--" thunder rolled through the air and muted Tara.

The hail grew larger and Tata ran to take cover. Tara clenched the brick harder and followed Tata, impervious to the hail that bounced off of her.

"—and now you have a disgusting message for me?" Tara yelled over the noise of the storm. "How do you expect me to trust you or any message you carry? I know you hate me. Now you act like it's all okay and come with a message."

"I never told you to believe me," yelled Tata. "Let's not forget who the liar and plotter is, Tara of MILAGRO. Filth who tricked her way into the Acllahuasi. Liar who made up a story about who you are. I'm passing a message on from Yachi and that's it. Do you want to hear it?" said Tata.

"I don't want a message from the person who tried to kill me with poisonous snakes."

There was more lightening and thunder. The two girls glared at each other through the hail. Tara still stood in the thick of it. The rolling thunder continued.

"You don't deny the naked?" said Tara.

"No, because that was me and if it wasn't for your sorcery with the flowers, they would have killed you. No one can survive a bite from that snake."

Tara smirked, "Yeah, that's right, you're not strong enough to kill me, no one is."

Tata yelled louder than was necessary to overcome the hail. "What matters is that Waranga Hualpa Inka is here in Cusco. He's dying and wants you. That's the message. Take it or leave it."

"Impossible."

"Goodbye. Oh, and about that trust thing, should I hate you as much as you think I do, I would report your nightly adventures to the top of the wall."

She left before Tara replied and her personage disappeared behind the hail.

The moment Tata was out of sight, Tara ran through the vacated pathways and courtyards to the corridor that connected the lower and upper courtyards. The pathways and corridor were empty this late at night and everyone hid in their huasis, away from the storm. Tara ran until she arrived at the lower courtyard. As she approached, a guard dressed in gold emerged from a corner.

The guard caught her mid stride. "Who are you?" said the guard. She grabbed Tara's shoulders and pushed her to stand squarely in front of her.

The guard was a fierce looking woman, the likes of which Tara had only seen in Cañari. Large in stature and dressed in a gold plated suit, she terrified Tara. Her hair was tied in braids with inlaid feathers the color of the noon sky.

"I am an aclla. Let me pass!" said Tara.

"Let me see your face, aclla," said the guard. She peered closely at it.

"What does my face have to do with anything?" Tara ducked away.

"Awe, you're the one. I received instructions not to let you pass."

"How dare you stand in my way? I am stronger than you and can force my way past you," said Tara.

"You are welcome to try, but it might hurt."

"I don't need to, I spoke with Mamacuna Umita earlier and she said it was okay that I pass," said Tara.

The guard laughed, "She would have told me, Aclla. Now, be gone." She flicked her hand like Tara was a fly.

"Fine, you can stop me from crossing here, but you can't stop me from going," said Tara.

She returned to the wall, but instead of crossing to the top of the healing chamber, she continued onward toward the lower courtyard. Viracocha and his friends on the roof waiting for her.

She went a way that hid her from their view.

The wall wrapped around and became the divider between the lower and upper sections of the Acllahuasi.

She used her arms to lower herself onto the wall that formed an enclosure of huts where the servant girls lived, and from there she climbed onto one of the huasi roofs. She slid down the pitched thatched roof and fell onto the ground. A bone crack. She moved each limb, one by one. There was no pain. She jumped up. Still no pain.

"Yachi!" She whispered loudly into a huasi.

No answer.

She tried the next one. "Yachi!"

A girl responded, "Shut up! She's one over."

Tara ran to the next huasi. Yachi sat in the middle of the yard in front of the huts as if she was expecting her.

Yachi said nothing, but raised her arms as to hug Tara. She moved in her usual stiff movements.

Tara glared at Yachi for a moment but gave into her yearning for an embrace. She leapt to her and hugged her.

"Oh Yachi, how much I've missed you. It's okay you're friends with Amaru Tupa Inka, just be my friend. I can't be lonely anymore! I was going to come that night but then there was a fire and now Umita said she won't allow us to visit each other anymore."

Without letting go of Yachi, she kissed Yachi on the forehead.

Yachi stood still. "Tara, it's Warana Hualpa Inka, he's not well," She paused.

Tara let go of her.

"He's here in Cusco and he's very sick."

Tara's face went cold.

"He can't talk and can hardly move. Something horrible happened to him in Chachapoyas, where he was leading his men in war. I'll lead the way if you want to go with him," said Yachi.

"I'm safe in here," said Tara. "I want to go to him, but he's the one that told me never to leave the Acllahuasi."

"There is no difference between leaving with me tonight and leaving with me when I was going to help you escape. It's the same. Come on, let's go."

"That was then, this is now. Prove that it's not some trap."

Yachi stood perfectly still but seemed to want to hurt Tara, "Before Hualpa lost his ability to speak, he asked for you. He said to tell you this: Your laugh, like the one he heard when he met you while watching the speckled bears, would help him recover." Yachi shrugged her shoulders. "He said it would mean something to you."

"Okay, I can go," Said Tara. She thought of the terrible day, the last day of her freedom.

Yachi gave no response. She went to the side of her huasi and dug through the pile of rejected textiles.

"Here, wear these," said Yachi. "This will make you match the women of Cusco, so if anyone sees us they won't suspect anything."

Tara took them from her and changed.

"And what about the gods, will these hide me from the gods?"

"If the gods didn't punish you for being in the most holy of places, the Acllahuasi, I don't think they'll punish you for leaving."

Yachi led the way to the exit of the Acllahuasi. The guards who watched the exit and entrance were absent.

Tara stopped. Something was wrong. She promised Hualpa she wouldn't leave.

Yachi grabbed her hand and nudged her forward like she was trying to open a door against the wind. Yachi's hand felt like bones and skin against Tara's chilly hand.

"There are a lot of people that will kill me outside of the Acllahuasi."

Yachi dropped Tara's hand. "The big and scary monsters you imagine won't have time to find you. Hualpa is basically across the street in the Sondorhuaci Tower, you can see it from the corner and it doesn't matter how far we have to go because we are in a disguise."

Tara felt an invisible hand on her shoulder that pulled her backward into the Acllahuasi.

Yachi bobbed her head side to side, "I mean, we don't have to go visit Waranga Hualpa Inka, I just thought you might want to. We can go back. It means nothing to me."

Tara tapped her foot and bit her lip, "Are you sure it's Hualpa?"

Yachi ceased moving her head and gave Tara an upward glance. She went back into the Acllahuasi, "Ugh, we won't go then. Let's get you back inside before anyone notices—"

"—No, I'll go," said Tara. She took an exaggerated step into the street. It was empty of the horrors she imagined. It was just like any other street in any other place.

Chapter Twenty-Seven

Sondorhuaci Tower

"Follow me!" Yachi ran past Tara to the corner beyond the Acllahuasi.

Yachi pointed to the tallest tower in Cusco when Tara caught up. Tara recognized it from the roof of the healing chambers.

"We're going there, it's called the Sondorhuaci Tower." said Yachi.

"That's really close, I thought it would be further," said Tara.

"I told you," said Yachi. "We have to go around the backside to sneak through a window. Follow me."

The further they went, the less Tara worried that she was in a trap. Cusco wasn't the scary place that Hualpa, Umita, and the others made her believe it was. It was beautiful and peaceful. The towering walls of Cusco were draped in moonlight and varied in color. Some were plain stone, others gold, some blood-colored, and others glimmering like the moon. The monumental buildings gave her inspiration and belief in herself. The tranquility of the city absorbed her anxiety.

Tara, mesmerized by the city, bumped into Yachi.

"There," said Yachi, pointing up at a window with a small rope tied to it. "Hualpa is in that room. We have to climb the rope to get to him." The rope was coarse and the color of dry wood.

"Wait, no. I can't climb that high, I might fall. How do I know that Amaru Tupa Inka isn't up there waiting to push me down?" said Tara.

"Says the woman who survived two fires?" Yachi hesitated and looked side to side, "I'm doing this as a favor to you, stop making me feel you don't want to go."

"No, I'm going. But you're going behind me, so if I get pushed off at the top by Amaru Tupa Inka, you'll fall with me," said Tara.

"I don't think he'd care," said Yachi. Her voice was more monotone than usual.

They both removed their sandals and grabbed the rope. Tara jumped and grabbed onto the rope and pushed herself up with her feet. Half way up, her hands became sweaty and she slipped down a little ways and stepped on Yachi's face.

Yachi hit her foot.

When Tara reached the top, she stalled before entering through the window, She looked around; she was twice as high as the surrounding buildings, but the tower itself blocked the view of the Acllahuasi. If the view was unobscured, she supposed she would see Viracocha and his friends waiting for her. She looked behind at the silhouette of Sacsayhuaman. She nodded in amazement that such a building existed. It was so big.

"Are you ever going to go in?" said Yachi.

Tara moaned and rolled into the small window and into a small dark room. She scanned the dark room. It was warm and humid, like Milagro. It had a thatched roof and stank of rot, and thousands of bugs moved within it the leaves. Alpaca and wool rugs covered the moist brick floor. Hualpa laid upon a stack of the blankets in a cockeyed position. His arms hung limp off of the rug and laid on the brick floor.

"HUALPA!" Yelled Tara. She ran to him and hugged him. She kissed his cheek. He opened his eyes and gazed at the wall behind Tara.

"Hualpa, can you see me?"

He didn't move or speak.

"Hualpa, look at me, it's Tara. Remember me? Tara from Milagro? You conquered my—I mean, you led me here to Cusco safely. You are supposed to marry me. Look at me. My scars are gone, well almost. Hualpa!"

She grabbed him by the shoulders and shook him.

"Yachi, what happened to him!"

Yachi who stood near the window looked back and forth, "I don't know."

"Don't lie to me." said Tara. She held Hualpa's head slightly off the floor and stroked his long oily hair.

He closed his eyes again.

"Um, well, I was told that he was leading warriors into Chachapoyas and he became very sleepy and then one day when they woke him up he was like this. I guess." She paused and went to the opposite corner and mixed some liquids together. "Amaru Tupa Inka told me that several Hampi Kamayoc visit him daily to administer herbs and perform healing rituals. That's why he is here in Cusco. Here, you can feed him this boiled maize flour. It's one of the few things he will eat," said Yachi.

She gave Tara a pottered bowl.

"The Hampi Kamayoc, the best healers in Cusco, are working on him in a place like this?" Said Tara. She yanked the bowl from Yachi and with her other hand scooped some up with her fingers and put it to Hualpa's mouth. He didn't move.

"You have to put it inside his lips. Make sure you pull your fingers out quickly or else he'll bite them," said Yachi in a voice that one uses to bore the listener.

Tara obeyed. She fed Hualpa the contents of the bowl. Meanwhile Hualpa did nothing more than stare into the distance.

"I need to come here each night," said Tara. Her jaw shook while she tried her best to remain strong.

Tara thought she saw Yachi smile when she said that.

"I don't think that's possible, in fact, we have to go. People are going to wake up soon," said Yachi.

She went to Tara and pulled her up.

"Wait, let me straighten him up. Apparently, the Hampi Kamayoc that visit him daily, are incapable of doing so."

She repositioned him so that he laid comfortable. She placed several blankets beneath him to soften the stone floor and one over him. She kissed his cold forehead and left with Yachi.

"Hualpa will recognize me tomorrow. I know he will," she told Yachi as she passed her to go to the window.

Yachi whispered, "Doubtful," from behind her.

Tara poked her head out and experienced vertigo. She gasped. Her breath froze in the frigid air.

"Hurry up," said Yachi.

Tara gripped the rope with her gloved hand: The rope was crunchy with speckles of ice frozen to it.

Yachi and Tara visited Hualpa almost every night until Tara lost count of the number of times they went. The few nights that they didn't go, she visited Viracocha and told him stories of Hualpa. She spoke so much of him she forgave and forgot the evil parts of him.

One night Hualpa was in particularly poor condition. He laid in his own bowels and reached for non-existent items in the air.

"Oh Hualpa, oh Hualpa," said Tara. She grabbed his hands. "There isn't anything there." She turned to Yachi. "What good are the Hampi Kamayoc? I've never seen them, nor is there any sign that they were here," said Tara.

Yachi tumbled into the room through the window. She stood back up and fixed her tunic, "They come."

She stood and watched Tara run back and forth to gather water and towels to clean Hualpa.

"Speaking of what good the Hampi Kamayoc are, you're not going to like what I'm going to tell you," said Yachi. "So next time will be the last time that I'll be able to bring you to Hualpa," said Yachi.

Tara placed the covers over Hualpa, kissed his forehead and looked up at Yachi.

"If you can't bring me, I will find my own way to him. I'm apparently the only one caring for him, and he can't be without me for anymore than a single night."

Yachi glanced back and forth, "Well, the Hampi Kamayoc want to care for him better so they are going to move him to a huaca outside of Cusco to, um, a place of a natural fountain. It has healing powers." Yachi scratched her head and then continued, "You can visit him there."

Tara crawled to Yachi and kneeled at her feet, "Oh Yachi, do everything you can so he isn't moved. Please, don't allow it!"

"If you try to visit him without me, Amaru Tupa Inka will find out and have him moved immediately and you won't ever be able to visit him again. The next time that I bring you here will be the last time if you won't leave Cusco," said Yachi. She spoke calmly and stood erect. She showed no remorse in telling Tara the devastating news.

"I CAN'T LEAVE CUSCO! Last time I tried to leave, Inti almost killed me. I'm no use to Hualpa if I'm injured and confined to the healing chambers. Please, Yachi, do everything you can. He has to stay here!"

"Ugh, don't ask me things I can't do. We have to go."

Tara ran back to Hualpa, "If you can hear me I'm going to bring you something next time I come. I promise you I will return. I made a small bag with the image of the speckled bear upon it. Remember the speckled bear? It's because of it that we met."

Chapter Twenty-Eight

Share the Burden

Tara and Yachi returned to the Acllahuasi. Yachi assisted Tara in getting to the top of the wall to sneak back in. She proceeded to check if Viracocha was waiting for her.

"You're here so late!" said Viracocha when she came into view.

"You're here so late." said Tara.

"I watched you leave and waited for you to come back. Most nights you don't come here anymore and I see you sneak off almost every night. It's for that Waranga Hualpa that you tell us about, isn't it?"

Tara scratched the ice off of her nose. "It's just you tonight?"

"Yes, the others left long ago."

Tara didn't reply immediately.

Viracocha didn't wear his medallion, and Tara had difficulty seeing where on the roof he was.

"You shouldn't leave the Acllahuasi, especially at night when Inti isn't in the sky to protect you."

"Can I share a burden with you?" She said.

"Haven't you been already?" said Viracocha. He spoke in a particularly raspy voice. Tara attributed it to the cold weather.

"But I need the help of your friends, too. Only those that can be trusted, and I don't know which to trust."

"All of my friends that come can be trusted," said Viracocha.

"No, they can't. I made them promise not to spread the word about our nightly gatherings, but every time there are more boys. This isn't just a meeting, this is important and no one can know what I want to ask," said Tara.

"None of them did say anything," said Viracocha. He sounded insulted. "Each *man* that comes to hear your stories was invited by me. All of my friends promised, yes, but you never had me promise. I'm the one that invited each one of them based on the fact that I can trust them."

Tara paused and thought through their previous conversation.

She laughed. "You sit there and listen to my stories and I've told you everything about me, yet I know nothing about you. Who are you that have so many trusted friends? I don't have any."

"You finally ask, after all this time. Well, I'm a man that suffers from insomnia. I am also the son of the Apu of Cusco."

Tara laughed.

"I've been talking to one of the most powerful men in Cusco this entire time?"

"Who did you think I was?" Said Viracocha.

"A gift from Mamaquilla; a man that was kind enough to provide me company."

"Mamaquilla and not Inti?" said Viracocha.

"Whichever god, it doesn't matter to me," said Tara.

"I can be a gift from either," said Viracocha.

"Promise me that if I tell you anything, if I tell you secrets, promise me you will only tell those that you trust the most."

"In Cusco, we don't promise. Each thing we say is the truth, so there is no need to promise. If you're going to ask me to help you leave, we can't help you. Inti will kill us instantly if we help an aclla escape. We shall be marked forever worse than traitors."

"And what if I wasn't an aclla, would you help me?" Tara spoke quietly.

"Well, I figure I would, but if you weren't an aclla, we wouldn't be in this situation."

Tara squinted at him

She bit her lip and tapped her fingers on the roof.

"Wait for me," she said.

"Where are you going?" Said Viracocha.

"If I ask you this thing, I am putting everything in your hands. I will no longer hide behind darkness."

She left the roof and went back into the Acllahuasi. She grabbed the first torch she found and returned to the roof.

Viracocha was still there, but he ran across the roof to a place that concealed him from the light, so Tara didn't see him well.

"I don't need to see you," said Tara. "But look at me. I'm not an aclla. I'm not Inkan. I'm not who you think I am. I am from Cañari, I was brought here by Sapa Inka Tupac Yupanqui's command to become an aclla, but I haven't done the ritual yet. I am not bound here by Inti or by the rules that real Inkas and acllas abide by. Will you help me?"

"Tara, you are from Cañari?" He paused. "You ask for my help after you lied to me this whole time. Why would I help you?"

"Please, remember everything I've told you. Those stories you loved so much. They were about me. Please remember that before judging me."

"I won't help you, Tara. How do you expect to tell the stories of your people and correct history if you can't be honest with those closest to you? You claim a desire to spread the truth about your people? You can't even be honest with me. What's the difference between Amaru Tupa Inka lying about the history of your people and you lying about who you are?"

"I won't lie about who I am anymore," said Tara. "I really need you Viracocha. I won't be able to see Hualpa anymore without you."

"You already lied. Good night, Tara."

Chapter Twenty-Nine

Tara's Pacha

Tara held a wooden beam upon her shoulder. It seemed she had held the position the entire day, but the sun hadn't moved since she last looked. Her thoughts wandered to Hualpa.

"Tara! Lift it a little higher!" Yelled the woman holding the other end of the beam. Tara was assisting in the assemblage of the tower that Mama Ocllo was to sit upon to observe Quicuchica.

"How much longer?" Said Tara.

"Just lift it higher!"

Tara did so.

The acllas, mamacunas, and servants ran about the lower courtyard of the Acllahuasi preparing it for the thousands of women expected to arrive after the moon came up. The women moved urns of chicha around the courtyards, others stacked wood to burn, some prepared statues, and acllas rehearsed their dances.

Thousands of vibrant flowers carpeted the stone ground throughout the Acllahuasi, which released an aroma. It created a sense of peace when it wasn't overwhelmed by the smell of the roasting maize and meat.

Torches were lit and the sun was less than a palm-width above the horizon when Tara and the acllas finished the platform. Women trickled into the courtyard to greet the prompt moon.

Tara returned to her workshop to fetch the tunic of the speckled bear that she wanted to bring to Hualpa. She emptied a sack that contained scores of textiles onto the ground, but the tunic was nowhere to be found.

"Are you looking for this, my dear?" said Umita. Tara didn't notice her step into her little workshop.

Tara threw the empty sac over the pile of textiles to hide them from Umita and sat on top of the stack. She looked at Umita, who stood in the doorway with the tunic of the speckled bear in one hand and her cane in her other.

"How did you know I was looking for that?" Tara lunged forward and grabbed it, but Umita didn't let go. Tara was surprised at her strong grip.

"Calm down, dear Tara." She poked her with the cane.

Umita glanced across the room and fixated her eyes on the stack of textiles. "Why are you in such a rush?"

"I want to leave here, I want to leave right now," said Tara. She pushed the pile of tapestries to Umita, "Here, if you like them so much, you can keep them all but this one I need." She pointed to the one in Umita's hand.

"If you want to leave Tara, then go. I will tell the guards to let you out. Walk through the festival and if you please, tell all of them what you are doing because none of them can or will stop you."

Tara's shoulders fell and she took a deep breath of relief.

Umita continued, "You see, dear woman, all you must do is tell the guards the consequences of leaving the Acllahuasi." She set her cane against the wall and put her arm on Tara's shoulder. "I hope you don't go because I want you to show the other women your art. I want you to speak about it and answer the women's questions about what these wonderful images depict."

Tara froze.

"Yes, yes, tell the stories behind the images you weaved," said Umita.

"They are all pictures of Cañari. To speak about them would be to let me speak the truth Cañari. That's not allowed," said Tara. She spoke louder than she expected to. She shivered due to her excitement and nervousness.

"You see though, word comes from Sapa Inka Tupac Yupanqui that he and Colla have given birth to a child. The Achicoc, you would call him a prophet, and huacas have declared that this child is to be the future Sapa Inka. It is desired that the boy has clothes depicting images of his homeland, Cañari. The boy's clothes much be weaved by an aclla of the Acllahuasi in Cusco. Who better than you? And should you make the boy's clothes with these unknown images, there will be questions about what they mean, so teach us!"

Tara stared at Umita as if she were lost in the wilderness.

"Can I share my stories another time?" said Tara. She thought of Hualpa alone in the Sondorhuaci tower, waiting for her.

"The time for you to speak about Cañari has arrived and you shun it?" said Umita. She stepped backward and looked at Tara with a cocked head. "No Tara, you cannot do it another time. Only tonight."

Tara bit her lips, but then smiled and hugged Umita so hard that Umita squealed.

"I will go to Quicuchica," said Tara. "I will tell them all about Milagro and Cañari." She let go of Umita.

"I know you will, I know you will" said Umita. She put her hand on Tara's shoulder.

Umita placed the tapestry of the speckled bears upon the pile of Tara's other works.

Tara left it there and went to the festival.

Chapter Thirty

Quicuchica

The drums pulsated the stone walls of the Acllahuasi, Tara trembled at the sound, the beat was similar to those that were played when the Inkas invaded Milagro. She paused and took a big step toward the drums.

"I will still be there for you tonight, Hualpa, after they are all too drunk to realize my absence."

Quicuchica attracted more people than Tara expected; there were more women and girls crowded into the Acllahuasi than she thought could fit inside of Cusco. She pushed them aside as she made her way through the corridor to the lower courtyard.

At the entrance of the lower courtyard, there were litters with the mummified wives of the previous Inkas. They were carried upon the shoulders of several women dressed in matching checkered clothes as vivid as a frigid night sky and reflective snow. Their tunics and skirts were inlaid with feathers along the edges, resembling a mountainside covered in thousands of blooming flowers. Tara recognized the tunics as those made by Tata and Ñuestra.

Alongside of the litters, which were made of silver and wood, stood a female, adorned in silver and the color of fresh snow. There was a line of women waiting to speak with the lady that stood beside the mummy.

"Hello Tara," said Yachi from behind her. "I've been looking for you. I figured you'd come sooner or later."

Tara jumped.

"Where are you off to?" said Yachi.

"Oh, um, just looking at what this festival is all about. It's the first Quicuchica I've been to. The last one I was recovering from the fire."

"I remember," said Yachi. "Are you waiting in line?"

"No?" Said Tara. She noticed the line Yachi referred to. It consisted of tens of women. "What is this line for, anyway?"

Yachi pointed at the start of the line. There was a woman standing beside the mummy of the wife of a deceased Sapa Inka. "They are waiting to speak to to that beautiful lady. She speaks for the mummy. The women in line want advice, or to ask for a favor."

"Inkas are so weird."

Yachi stepped in front of Tara to force her gaze, "You don't belong here at Quicuchica. Come, you want to visit Hualpa one last time, don't you? That's where you belong, by his side."

"Yes, I have to see him." Tara didn't move.

"Then let's go!" Yachi grabbed Tara's arm and tugged. "With these women here, it'll be the perfect distraction for you to get out."

"I don't need a distraction anymore, I have permission to leave. I can walk out the front gate should I want to."

"Excellent, then let's go!" Yachi tugged on Tara's arm again.

"I can't, not yet." She took her arm back. "Later though, Mamacuna Umita wants me to—" Tara paused and figured it was better not to tell Yachi what Umita told her.

"—wants you to?"

"Wants me to be here for the opening ceremony. She said it's important."

"Tonight isn't only about seeing Hualpa, though, come with me. Come on! There's someone you should see."

As they spoke, they made their way to the middle of the courtyard, past the platform that Tara help erect earlier that day. Upon it sat Mama Ocllo, the Lady of Cusco.

Yachi's animation and her rapid speech surprised Tara.

"We snuck him into Cusco with the crowd. He's just outside the Acllahuasi. You can come right back, but you must see him. To have him in Cusco is very dangerous for him." She grabbed Tara's hand from within her cloak and pulled her. "We'll come right back."

"Who is it?" asked Tara. She pulled her hand back from Yachi.

"Someone you love and never thought you would see again."

Tara bit her lip and looked into the distance. "He's just outside the Acllahuasi? Like really close?"

"Just outside and down one of the quiet alleys where he is hiding. You said yourself that you can leave, so leave and come right back. It won't take longer than just a moment and this visitor will make you happier than you've been the entire time here," said Yachi.

Tara smiled, "Fine, but I have to come right back and will you still take me to see Hualpa after the opening ceremony?"

"Yes, yes, of course I will. But we can't be seen leaving the Acllahuasi together, so meet me outside. I'll exit via my secret path," said Yachi. "Go as if you were going to the Sondorhuaci Tower. I'll meet you out there."

Tara made her way to the exit and recognized the guard that stopped her before. Tara took a deep breath and marched toward the exit. She mixed with the crowd and didn't stop until she was outside in the crowded street.

She continued past Huacaypata and onto the narrow streets. The crowds thinned as she got closer to the corner.

"Tara, over here!" said Yachi. Her disguise was of the mourning clothes of a widow whose husband died within the past moon.

Yachi slipped into a narrow and vacant alley.

Tara ran to her.

"I'm starting to worry," said Tara.

Yachi shrugged. "Follow me. He's close by."

She grabbed Tara's hand and led her down a monotonous brick walled alley. Tara ran her finger along it as they walked.

"Don't," said Yachi. "That's Cusicancha, the place where Sapa Inka Tupac Yupanqui was born. It's a very sacred huaca."

They went a short way further.

Yachi stopped and turned to her.

"Don't mind me, I have to call the signal," said Yachi.

"What?"

"It's a good night," Yachi called again down the alley.

"What?" said Tara. She took a couple steps backward.

There was a small doorway in the stone about halfway down the narrow corridor. From it, two hooded men emerged. One had a large composure and the other was slender in comparison.

"Don't worry," said Yachi. She led Tara toward them. "Promise me you won't run."

Tara didn't respond. She clenched her fists and calculated how far the exit of the alley was behind her.

The larger man stepped forward and removed his hood. The darkness hid his face.

"Is that her?" said a vaguely familiar voice. Tara raced through her memory to place it, but it had been so long since she heard a male's voice besides Viracocha's. She shrugged it off.

"Of course it's her. I told you it would be" Said the other man who's voice Tara matched, it was Amaru Tupa Inka.

Tara ran to the exit of the alley, but Yachi moved quicker and grabbed her cloak.

"Don't worry, Tara, you're safe. Look who the other man is."

"LET GO OF ME!" She yelled in a wretched voice she didn't recognize to be her own.

She pushed Yachi.

"LET GO!"

"LOOK WHO THE OTHER MAN IS!" said Yachi. Her jaw was clenched.

Tara pushed Yachi to the ground and jammed her knee into her abdomen. Yachi let go.

Tara jumped up to run.

Yachi grabbed Tara's foot.

"What are you waiting for, Amaru?" Yelled Yachi.

"Speak up!" said Amaru Tupa Inka to the other man. "Tell her who you are."

"Tara? Is that you, sister? It's me, Achache."

Tara froze. Her leg stopped mid-air above Yachi's face.

"NO! No! It can't be. That's impossible!"

She placed her foot on the ground and turned to the men. The other man removed his hood and held a torch close to his face. It was her brother, Achache. He ran toward her.

I'm safe.

Her head felt light. She tried to smile but lost strength and she collapsed.

Achache caught her.

Chapter Thirty-One

The Catch

A chache looked like a grown man, a skinny replica of their father. Tears rolled down her cheeks and ike a jolt of lightening, she lunged onto him.

Behind them, and as if a world apart, Amaru Tupa Inka blabbered something about how sorry he was, and how he mistreated Tara. She didn't listen, nor did she believe that her brother stood before her.

"Tell her, Achache," said Amaru Tupa Inka. He spoke in his smooth, wispy voice.

Achache ignored him, then he whispered to Tara, "On the way back to Milagro we have a special privilege to teach the Cañari stories and legends to the settlements we pass."

Tara released Achache from her grasp.

"All of them?"

"That's right, Tara," said Amaru Tupa Inka. He stepped closer to them. "I am a man of Inti and cannot bear the thought of the evil I did to you, and so I wish to gain your forgiveness by allowing you to share them. Now, let's get you back to Milagro. We can set everything right again."

Tara didn't want to hear his late apologies. He knew nothing of her sacrifices.

"Oh, Achache! I didn't think you survived that damned day when I was taken. Oh, my brother! My brother!" sobbed Tara on his shoulder. She bastioned his cheek with kisses.

Achache kissed the top of her head and gently pushed her away. He looked straight into her eyes, "Tara, there will be time to hug and tell each other all about each other's lives but only after we leave Cusco. We have to leave right now. We have to get as far from Cusco as possible before they realize you are gone."

"Yachi will be your guide out of the Cusco valley," said Amaru Tupa Inka. He pointed at Yachi, who stood nearly out of hearing range at the end of the corridor.

"I'll get you out of Cusco safely," said Yachi.

Tara shuttered and hugged Achache to keep herself from running.

"Tara, look at me," said Amaru Tupa Inka.

She refused.

"Look at me, Tara!"

She didn't move.

He grunted.

"Look, Tara, it's only a matter of time before the Inkan soldiers look for you. They will search inside and outside of Cusco. They will canvas the Qhapaq Ñan and question anyone who saw you. Chances are that you won't be able to make it back to Milagro. You need each moment of a head start."

"That's wrong, Mamacuna Umita told me that I was free to leave and that I wouldn't be pursued."

"Who said that?" said Amaru Tupa Inka. Then he laughed, "Mamacuna Umita?" He looked toward Yachi and squinted his eyes. "Oh yes, she's the one that tried to burn your huasi when you were supposed to escape? You trust her?" He laughed again. "It's not her you should fear, it's the Inkan soldiers. They are ordered to chase you down and kill you if you leave the Acllahuasi. They have spies everywhere. Mamacuna Umita lied to you. Again."

"I can't trust anything you say," said Tara.

"He's right," said Yachi. She stood beside Achache now. "She is the one that lit the fire. Now, follow me."

Tara looked back and forth from Achache to Yachi. All of this was so sudden.

"We must go," said Achache. He stroked her hair.

"Oh Achache, your voice is so deep now and you can say 's' now. Do you remember that lisp you used to have? Do it for me one time so I know it is really you."

Achache laughed. "Tara! Time isp running out. I' wath a miracle I mathe i in hewe. Pleath thop thelaying an' leth uth go."

"Yachi," said Tara. "You say I can't trust anyone, but can anyone trust me?"

"Um. No, not really. You're not one of us."

"Then I must keep my word to Hualpa and bring him the tunic I told him I would bring. I must go to the Acllahuasi to get it and then to the Sondorhuaci Tower and deliver it to him and say goodbye."

"Tara, you can't because—" started Yachi.

Tara saw a flash of fire behind Amaru Tupa Inka's eyes, the same she saw before he tried to kill her. It disappeared as quickly as it rose.

"—No, you are not going back to the Acllahuasi," said Amaru Tupa Inka. "We are going now. Imagine what would happen to you. Imagine what would happen to your brother if his presence was discovered, his fate might be worse than that which befell Waranga Hualpa in Chachapoyas. You would be responsible for his torture and death. Not even I could stop that."

"Wait, THAT Hualpa?" Said Achache. "That's the guy you want to go see? The same guy that invaded Milagro and nearly killed us. You're risking all of our lives for that man?" He was on the verge of yelling. "No, you will not go to him!" Achache grabbed her arm.

"I am going to marry—I was going to marry him until you showed up and he got sick," said Tara. She avoided Achache's heated gaze. "It's more than that. Achache, understand, and don't be mad at me. Please! I'm going back. If Pachayachachic desires us to live through the night than it will happen whether or not I go back."

Achache sighed through his teeth, "Tara, I can't be mad right now. You sacrificed yourself so that I could live. But you're risking everything for what? It's not worth it."

"It's not worth it, Tara," echoed Amaru Tupa Inka.

"My word to Hualpa is worth it. My honor to Umita is worth it. The reputation of the Cañari people is worth it," said Tara.

"NO! Everything is set that we must go now! There is no time! My distraction will only work for a little while longer!" said Amaru Tupa Inka.

"Are you going to burn me alive again?" Asked Tara.

She sprinted off to the Acllahausi. Amaru Tupa Inka and Yachi gave chase but were too slow.

Chapter Thirty-Two

Mama Ocllo

Tara blended with the other ladies when she entered the Acllahuasi through the large trapezoidal doorway and into the first courtyard where the main event was being held.

Tara went between the different groups of women to the far wall and followed it to the corridor entrance. One of the few songs Tara learned while at the Acllahuasi overtook the crowd, she hummed a version of it to herself as she tried to remain inconspicuous.

She found the tunic of the speckled bear folded upon her work bench and next to it was the tapestry that Umita gave her of Machu Picchu. She reverently picked them up, slipped them beneath her cloak and left for the last time. On the way out of her huasi, she noticed that the sack of her tapestries was gone. She swept the room but didn't find it. She shrugged, it didn't matter where the tapestries were; she was planning on leaving them.

She made her way back to Quicuchica and avoided everyone's gaze. The large mass of women formed into several groups, each huddled around one of the mummies that were now spread across the courtyard. Each group dressed the same way and busied with their own kind of celebrations. She remembered that the kin of each mummy, and those that adhered to that community's customs, formed tight groups called Panacas.

"They are so weird," she said to herself.

She didn't have to look over to know that she was passing the group that followed the teachings of the ruler, Cinchi Roca Inka. Each of the women wore small decorative drums that hung from their wrists, and they carried a fresh bouquet that perfumed the air. These two hundred or so women were famous for their bouquets, and their elegant demeanor matched the flowers. She peaked over, they were so beautiful.

Her quick glance was met by that of a woman trying to get her baby to latch to her breast to feed. She stood on the outside of the group.

Tara resisted the urge to run.

"You're the girl from the savage lands of Cañari," said the woman.

"There's nothing savage about the people of Cañari," said Tara. She replied without contemplating the consequences.

The woman held her baby's head up with one arm while she tapped the shoulder of the woman next to her.

"Where is the tapestry I gave you, I'm certain this is the girl that made it," said the woman.

"I've never made any tapestry, I don't know what you're talking about," said Tara.

The woman laughed. Her laugh seemed patronizing to Tara.

"Your face is evenly split between day and night," said the feeding woman while she waited for her friend. "Everyone here knows about the outsider girl with the face of Yanantin."

Tara touched her face. "That's why, huh? Well, I have other places to be. Goodbye."

"Wait!" said the woman. "Here's the parchment, okay."

Tara ignored her and started toward the exit. After a few steps, she froze. She saw that her tapestries were being passed around by everyone.

The woman ran after her while holding her baby close. The baby came off the nipple and cried. "You made this, right?" She pushed a tapestry into Tara's hand and almost dropped the crying baby.

It was an image Tara made of a monkey in a tree, eating a fruit. Meanwhile, a snake in the branch above it was readying to attack. A jaguar eyed them as it climbed the tree toward them.

Tara forgot she created the near comical image. She chuckled. "You should see my better ones."

"Tell me if I understand the image, okay? It's a representation of the three worlds, the lower world, this world and the higher one each balances each other with the reciprocal, okay? Okay, and each feeds and serves one or the other. Am I right?"

"Yes, that is what it means," said Tara. "Now, I really must leave."

The woman grabbed her shoulder.

"Okay, so you aren't from a savage land then, because if we believe the same thing you are just like us, Tara from Cañari." She ceased speaking for a moment but didn't let go of Tara's shoulder.

"We were calling you to tell us about these images but you weren't here, why don't you do so now? Tell all the women what you just told me, okay? No one knows these things and we're all wondering what these tapestries mean."

Tara twiddled her fingers. She remembered what Umita told her: she could present the truth about Cañari tonight or never.

Isn't this why I came to Cusco? Achache can wait.

Tara went to the platform. The ladder was blocked by guards. They dressed in moon colored llama furs. A third guard, one that Tara recognized, parted the two.

"We thought you left," she said. She pulled out a small mantle that Tara created one sleepless night. "I'm glad you didn't. I always thought that Milagro was like Lima, a desert, and then I saw this tapestry, it's of Cañari, isn't it?"

"Yes, that is what Cañari looks like."

"What a beautiful place," said the guard. She stepped out from below the ladder, "Mama Ocllo is expecting you upon the platform."

The crowd hushed as Tara ascended the ladder to the top of the wooden platform.

The view from the top reminded Tara of watching the celebration in Cañari when Amaru Tupa Inka threw her into the fire. The scent of burning human flesh and hair entered her nose. She shook her head. She heard the sounds of the beating drums, the drums made of her friend's skin. She saw a woman dressed in white and thought it was Amaru Tupa Inka, dressed in his pompous cape made of snow feathers. She caught herself at the edge of the platform. Umita was at the bottom, her forward leaning gait seemed all the more evident being surrounded with vibrant young women. She gave her an encouraging smile. Umita transformed into Sycri.

"Tara!" She said to herself. "That is Umita, not Sycri! I am not in Cañari, I am in Cusco! I am in the Acllahuasi! I am safe!"

She took a small step away from the side. She shivered.

"I am Tara, and Tara is in Cusco. These are women below me, they are my friends and they want to learn. They aren't soldiers here to kill me. They are friends. I am—"

"—Tara Inka of Yanantin, are you okay?" Said Mama Ocllo. Her voice was smooth and high pitched.

Umita poured some chicha on the ground and closed her eyes in prayer.

"I am Tara, I am in Cusco. These are friends. I am safe—"

"Tara," said Mama Ocllo, a little louder. "Are you going to speak?"

Tara glanced up and acknowledged Mama Ocllo. She stepped into the center of the platform.

She locked eyes with Mama Ocllo. "I am Tara. I am in Cusco and I am among friends."

"Yes," said Mama Ocllo. "Are you going to tell us anything else?"

"She closed her eyes, turned to the crowed and opened them with a long exhale. She stared at the crowed with the deathly stare of a jaguar on its pray.

"The images weaved onto the tapestries that you have seen are of a place called Milagro and the surrounding area of Cañari—" she yelled.

Each word she said was echoed by special women posted throughout the crowd.

"—It is the place where I was born and where I resided until I surrendered myself to Sapa Inka Tupac Yupanqui."

She spoke of the history of the Cañaris, from their beginning with the union of a condor and of uncivilized men to the end, "But since the men learned of the ways of the higher world which the condor taught them, they became civilized and wise."

She told them about the rare items found in Cañari that were prized in Cusco. She told them about the conquest of Cañari by Sapa Inka Tupac Yupanqui. She finished and descended the ladder when one of the ladies yelled, "What are the flowers that are in most of your images? Are they special flowers in Cañari?"

Tara ceased her descent, and while clinging to the ladder with one hand she said, "The Cañari's use them to create medicines and to flavor foods. With them, we can remove parasites and clean our body. And the other one," Tara paused. Silence sat upon the crowd. "I don't know what it is. I think it guides me."

"You mean Cañari's bath and are clean?" yelled a woman.

"Yes. Yes we, I mean, they are."

At the bottom of the ladder, she embraced several women and visited each group. Several women crowded around her, each with a tapestry in hand. She glanced at the exit of the Acllahuasi. "Achache, I'm coming as fast as I can"

She felt the tapestry for Hualpa tucked against her chest. "Oh, Hualpa. I'm coming for you too."

"I'm so proud of you," said Umita from behind her. "We all know more about Cañari. It seems like a magical place like Cusco used to be."

"Thank you," said Tara. She hesitated, "It might sound crazy, but was it you that started the fire in my huasi that night I was going to leave?"

Umita snapped upright, "Me? You think I started that fire? Aren't I the one that healed you from the scars from it?" Umita placed her hand on Tara's shoulder, "Tara, it does not matter who started it like it doesn't matter who planted that floating flower on your ear in Cañari. Or, who buried that Mullu shell, or who prompted those two speckled bears to play that day when you met Waranga Hualpa. Who does not matter, it if you realize it's the gods."

"Of course. It was the gods," said Tara.

"Exactly. And it was they that healed your burns. Do you know that your burns were beyond healing and people burned half as much as you were, don't survive?"

The crowd ceased to exist in Tara's mind, "How did you heal me then? And how do you know everything? It's like the magic that used to exist in Cusco still does, but only with you."

Umita smiled. "It's the gods, Tara, not I. Magic doesn't happen to anyone, but a few people are led along a path by the gods, a path of hardships that prepares them to do something that they need done. They lead these few people along this path of lessons until there is a choice. One choice is to return to what we, as humans, always desire: a simple life. Most people take it. The other is a choice that requires all the lessons and hardships that the gods gave along the path. Using what we learn, we can accomplish what the gods need and we are those that will find that magic happens around us. Not because of us."

She stood alone. She was in on the mountain in Cañari again, staring at the floating flower in the rain. She gazed at the horizon, at the smoke ascending from the camps of the invading Inkan soldiers.

"—Tara," Umita interrupted her thoughts, "If you are to return to Milagro with Achache, your time is running short. You must go soon."

"This is our goodbye, Tara." She kissed both sides of Tara's face and then the midline. She disappeared into the crowd.

Tara ignored the line of women waiting to speak with her and ran to the exit.

Tata ran alongside Tara.

"TARA! You were amazing there." She said. "Cañari seems amazing. You seem amazing."

"You're a spy for Amaru Tupa Inka," said Tara.

The guard at the exit signaled for them to stop running.

She complied.

"I'm sorry I treated you so badly," said Tata. "I didn't think you were going to make it here, you are an—you were an outsider. But look at you now! You're still here and even sharing a platform with Mama Ocllo. Please, share some chicha with me."

"I forgive you. But look, you won. I'm leaving."

"Don't leave. They are going to kill you."

Tara slipped through the exit. The guard stepped in front of Tata to prevent her from following. She didn't try to.

Chapter Thirty-Three

Bloody Pulp

"I was worried you weren't going to return!" said Achache. He stood up.

Tara looked for Yachi but didn't see her. She was gone.

Amaru Tupa Inka pushed past Achache, who fell back to the ground. He grabbed Tara by the neck seam of her gown and pulled her close, "You dared speak of the history of Milagro to those women without permission! That's right, I heard you all the way out here."

The veins in his face and neck pulsated.

Tara pushed him off and ran to Achache. She helped him up and hugged him.

"I got the tunic and look, I got the one of Machu Picchu, Look! Look how beautiful this place is."

The torch light beaming from the nearby Acllahuasi reflected off of the stone walls and gave a depth to the image of Machu Picchu that wasn't seen in the daylight. The roaring rivers were darker against the more dramatic cliffs and the stone citadel emerged from the lush vegetation. It made a visible impression of Achache.

"That can't exist. There is nowhere that magnificent," he said.

"It does, I'm telling you, Mamacuna Umita lived there. I make tapestries like this too and people love them. You should have seen—"

"—Tara, we go this instant. No more talking," said Amaru Tupa Inka. He held a club.

Tara's eyes got big when she saw the club, then she bowed her head.

"I'm sorry, but I'm not leaving. I understand you came all this way, and it hurts me to think I can't go with you, but I remembered why I came here." She raised her head and glanced at Achache. "Pachayachachic, Mamaquilla, and Inti need me here. The women in the Acllahuasi need me here. Cañari needs me here. I must stay here, even if it leads to death, but after tonight I think I'm safe.""TARA GET DOWN!" Yelled Achache. He jumped onto her and pulled her down.

Amaru Tupa Inka's club swooped though the air where her head had just been, "If you won't die outside of Cusco, you will die here and so what if I be damned," he yelled.

He raised the club over his head. She rolled out of the way, but it struck her hand and crushed it.

She yelled.

Achache wrapped the Machu Picchu tapestry around his neck and strangled him.

Amaru Tupa Inka seemed not to care that Achache was on his back strangling him. He kicked Tara in the belly and knocked the wind out of her. She curled into a ball and heaved to try to breathe again. He stomped on her neck.

Achache yelled as he pulled with all of his strength. Amaru Tupa Inka fell on his back to crush Achache. Achache didn't let go.

"Run, Tara!" Yelled Achache. He held Amaru Tupa Inka down.

She stared blankly at her crushed hand.

She looked at Achache but didn't seem to hear him. She glanced at Amaru Tupa Inka. His face looked as though it was about to burst. He struggled to loosen the gag.

Her gaze returned to her crushed hand.

Amaru Tupa Inka stood and slammed Achache into a corner of a nearby brick. Achache let go and stumbled to keep his balance. Amaru Tupa Inka grabbed the back of Achache's head and slammed his face into a stone wall.

Achache fell to the ground and didn't move.

Amaru Tupa Inka caught his breath and went back to where small Tara was still lying.

She wanted to stand, but her body didn't respond.

Amaru Tupa Inka grabbed the back of her torn cloak. She tried to kick him, but he resisted. He picked her up and dropped her on the ground. He stepped on her throat. It popped and cracked and sent shooting pains throughout her body.

"On second thought, I really shouldn't kill you," said Amaru Tupa Inka. He let her go and went to pick up his club, which he left near Achache's limp body.

Tara coughed uncontrollably.

He returned with the club and jumped on Tara's uninjured arm and put his full weight on it.

"I really shouldn't kill you, but—"

He slammed the club into her uninjured hand and crushed it. She tried to push him off with her other hand, but it was too badly injured and gave up. The pain echoed through her body. Each heart beat more painful than the last.

"—if I—"

He slammed the club into her hand again. It made a sound like when Achache dropped a large stone on top of an unsuspecting coy, thus crushing it. She laid limp, spread out on the stone ground.

"—can't kill you—"

The club slammed again on to her hand. This strike was his club hitting the stone road instead of flesh. Tara realized her hand was gone.

"—then I will be sure—"

He pounced onto her other arm and slammed the club into that hand.

"—you'll never weave—"

Another strike. There was a blood mist in the air.

"—ever again."

He got on his knees next to her and whispered into her face.

"I'll let the gods kill you or save you depending on what they want. You have no voice, you have no hands, you're as good as dead to me and anyone else," he said.

Achache rolled over and tried to crawl. He collapsed and laid a mere arm's length from Tara. She now laid in a pool of her own blood. His extended arm reached the stream of blood that flowed into the middle of the street.

Amaru Tupa Inka threw him over his shoulder. "Your brother is now my captive. If you ever give people suspicion that it was I that did this to you, I will kill him. Do you understand?" Yelled Amaru Tupa Inka.

Tara didn't comprehend what the Amaru Tupa Inka said.

He got close to her, "If you tell what I did, your brother dies. Do you understand?"

Tara moaned, "uhh."

"I'll take that as a yes."

Music from the festival in the Acllahuasi echoed off of the looming spinning walls. A strange sense of peace overcame her.

So this is the music that will play when I die. It could be worse.

She closed her eyes.

"Tara," Whispered a low voice. "You can't die. You still have to tell me stories."

She didn't move.

Small footsteps ran away from her. They infuriated her. They disturbed the perfect music that absorbed her.

Several hands grabbed her and lifted her onto a cold board. She heard the voice of a condor explain to an unknown person that he had followed a trail of while flowers to find her.

Chapter Thirty-Four

How Death Happens

Tara woke screaming. She sat on a dank straw mat on the floor. She screamed, but no sound came out. She paused and looked around the dark room; she wasn't in the Acllahausi anymore: The stones were smaller than those in the Acllahuasi and they were colored with gold and blood. The bed she slept on was covered with itchy llama wool instead of smooth vicuna wool.

Voices of men and women from outside flowed into the room, accompanied by a small beam of light where the wooden door and stone doorway met. The voices were mumbled and she only made out her name, which was uttered continually and each time in a negative tone. She recognized the language they spoke to be that which only the Sapa Inka's family were allowed to speak.

A hand touched her shoulder. She jumped and threw the hand off of her.

"Are you going to stay awake this time?" said the hissy voice she recognized to be Viracocha's.

Tara tried to answer, but her voice sounded like a wind blowing through a deep canyon.

She gasped and covered her mouth with her nobs. Everything came back to her and the little she saw in the darkness spun in circles. She felt herself slip back into a doze, but she resisted and yelled again. Only air emerged.

Viracocha lit a candle and held a wooden cup to Tara's lips. She sipped it. It was hot coca tea. The consistency was slightly thicker than water, and it felt like what a dry rock feels when it's overtaken by a flood after a long drought.

She put the cup on the ground beside her and gazed at Viracocha. It was the first time he showed himself to her.

He wore a cumpi tunic and cloak that draped over his short bony body with un-humanly wide shoulders. His head was far too small for his body. In middle of his face was a substantial nose the color of urine. His skin was worn and scaly and had a hue of a sunset. His earlobes had plugs in them the size of a babe's arm and his black oiled hair was braided and mixed with the thick dark hair that protruded from below his cloak from his chest. A small patch of hair in the middle of his head was the color of snow. It too was braided, but was much shorter than the rest. He wore a square breastplate made out of feathers with a golden idol of Inti in the middle of it.

"I'm Viracocha," he said. "You finally see me."

"I'm Tara of Milagro."

Viracocha smiled, his teeth showed, and they protruded from his mouth in a point.

He kissed her on the cheek and then ran out and hissed, "She's awake!"

The door opened and the incoming light blinded her. When her eyes adjusted, she was surrounded by several men and women she didn't know, none of whom were Viracocha.

From the appearance of those around her radiated of nobility. They wore llautus with deep colored feathers and had large gauges in their ear. Their robes looked similar to the ones that Umita weaved. Tara later learned that these were curacas, apus, and Nina Kamayacs, the most powerful people in Tahuantinsuyu.

Without introducing himself, the man that Tara assumed was the leader among them asked what had happened to her. She tried to respond, but no sound came out. He turned away from her. The men and women resumed their conversation, this time in Quechua, and Tara understood.

"She's useless here. She can't sew, she can't be married off, she can't even do basic servant skills," said a man dressed as a Nina Kamayac.

"No, let her be married off to a man without legs. She has no hands, he has no legs. It will be a perfect match," said another man, but this one was dressed as an accountant.

"You're both wrong, she's part god, let her be offered as an ice sacrifice. She has the legs, she can walk up the mountains to the glaciers. That's all that's needed," said a different Nina Kamayac.

"No, she can't do that. The god's won't accept her. Didn't you notice that she's missing her HANDS?" Said the original Nina Kamayac. He threw his hands up when he yelled the final word.

Amaru Tupa Inka came into the room and stood near the back.

Tara clenched every muscle in her body. She kept one eye on him while she looked around for items that could be used as a weapon.

He jutted his chin toward the door. There, two guards lifted Hualpa off of a litter and supported him as he walked into the room, one guard under both of Hualpa's arms.

The guards put him down on the ground with his back supported against the cold stone wall.

Hualpa gave a faint smile to Tara.

Tara forgot about her situation, just for that instant a euphoric feeling overtook her. He was okay! He was awake. Her suffering was worth it to see him up.

Amaru Tupa Inka gave him a bloody tunic to hold and then smirked at Tara. Tara, perplexed why he smirked, looked at the tunic. It was the tunic that Achache wore the last time she saw him.

Tara stood up and tried to yell, "Where is Achache?" But only a wince of her voice came through, and with her accent no one could understand her. She got light headed and fell over. One of the nearby men caught her.

"ACHACHE" She yelled again once she regained her strength.

The men stood around her and looked at each other, confused. "You want coca tea?" One of them asked.

"MY BROTHER ACHACHE!"

Everyone glanced at each other looking for answers, everyone except Amaru Tupa Inka.

Tara broke down and cried. She didn't know what else to do. She tried to demonstrate for them to get a needle, thread, and parchment for her to sew pictures of Achache. Then she remembered she didn't have hands. And even if she did, how could she ever draw Achache? She was useless. No hands, no voice.

Useless.

Viracocha returned to the crowded room led by the Lady of Cusco, Mama Ocllo. She walked alongside a decorated man with plaited hair and the largest earplugs that Tara had ever seen besides those worn by the Sapa Inka. It was the Apu of Cusco.

Viracocha went to Tara and stood on the mat she used as her bed.

He was even uglier in the light. His legs were substantially shorter than his arms, his body much too large for his arms, and his eyes were much too small. She pulled herself away from him.

"Can you guys back up and give her some space? Imagine how hard this is for her," said Viracocha.

No one moved.

Viracocha ignored them and stroked the dark side of Tara's face, "What do these people want with you?" asked Viracocha in raspy voice.

A man with a llautu the color of fresh blood with feathers the color of the noonday sky and an enormous nose laughed, "She's trying to tell us stuff, but she hasn't a voice. It's almost as funny as you trying to direct us, little man," he said. He rubbed the patch of snowy hair on Viracocha's head with his large palm.

"Be mindful of what you say to my son," said the Apu of Cusco. "This 'Little Man,' has more favor with Inti than you do."

The crowd backed up.

Viracocha knelt beside Tara. "What is it you wanted to tell them? I always understand you."

Tara gave a sideways glance at Amaru Tupa Inka and at Achache's bloody tunic in Hualpa's hands.

Viracocha leaned forward, "Talk to me, Tara. Please."

"Before the little savage girl speaks, I need to say something," said Amaru Tupa Inka. He looked directly at Tara, "Waranga Hualpa Inka here has told me some disturbing things that happened while he was sick. We all know that many girls want to be with this hero of Tahuantinsuyu, and many go to great lengths to do so. He is handsome, and fierce it's easier for him to vanquish an army by himself than for the army to scratch him. He emerged from his sickness demonstrating that not even death could take him. He was brought to the Sondorhuaci tower to recover from a sickness, which he only received from Inti to keep him humble. The first thing that he told me when he regained speech was that certain girls snuck out of the Acllahuasi and into the Coricancha to see him. For a woman that was sworn to the Acllahuasi to leave without extenuating circumstances is a crime punishable by execution. To enter the Sondorhuaci tower without first performing the fasts and rituals has a penalty of a tortured death. Since Tara is before us now, perhaps she can tell us who it was that snuck out of the Acllahuasi. If not, I think Hualpa would like to tell this audience exactly who it was."

Amaru Tupa Inka avoided looking at Tara.

"Nice speech, Amaru Tupa Inka," said the same man who insulted Viracocha. "But if you didn't notice, the girl can't speak. Should he husk her like maize to see if she'll reveal the perpetrator like that?"

Tara tried to speak again, "I want to say something to them."

Several men and women in the group threw up their hands.

"What do you want to tell them?" Asked Viracocha to Tara.

"You can understand me?" Asked Tara.

"I can," said Viracocha.

Tara smiled.

"If you can understand me, tell these people what I say."

"I don't know who you all are, but I am Tara, the daughter of Raura and Guaman, they are what you call curacas of an allyu called Milagro in Cañari—" she paused to let Viracocha repeat to them what she said.

Viracocha stood as tall as he could, which was a head shorter than the shortest person in the room. He repeated her words verbatim.

"How do you understand her?" Asked one of the men.

"How do you not understand her?" Asked Viracocha. "She speaks as clearly as I do."

The man crossed his arms and cocked his head at the Apu of Cusco.

"My son always understands," said the Apu of Cusco. His voice was deep, like the voice of the stones that constructed Cusco.

"On second thought," said Amaru Tupa Inka, He shuffled back and forth. "Maybe we shouldn't let her speak. She is not right in the mind. The loss of her hands has made her crazy. This little girl might try to lie to you about her home, which can I remind you is not in Cusco, it's in the savage lands of Cañari. I've been there and it is a terrible place. A horrible place. Anything she says is a lie and will spread the filth here. The walls of Cusco shouldn't have to hear such things."

"Is that a bloody tunic that Waranga Hualpa has?" Said the Apu of Cusco.

"Oh, it just needs washed," said Amaru Tupa Inka.

"Whose blood?" Asked the Apu of Cusco. He put his arms on his side.

As they spoke, Viracocha went to Hualpa and said something to him. Hualpa returned the bloody tunic to Amaru Tupa Inka and leaned upon Viracocha's wide shoulders. With Viracocha supporting him, he went to Tara, who stood upon her straw mat.

Tara watched Hualpa as he stumbled toward her. For the first time, he appeared human. He was flesh, just like her.

Viracocha set him down gently beside Tara on her bed. She sat next to him.

Hualpa leaned into Tara and remained with his mouth close enough to her ear that she heard his faint breathing.

"Tara, now is the time to make everyone fall in love with Cañari," said Hualpa.

Tara felt goosebumps on her skin when she heard him speak. She looked at him with her tear laden eyes.

He continued, "Make them fall in love with Cañari by telling the stories that you told me when I was sick. Now is the time for the truth. Now is the time that truth means life. Life for you. Life for your brother. If you fail in this moment, you will be killed and there will be nothing standing in the way of the total dehumanization and ultimate death of Milagro and Cañari."

Tara peered at Hualpa. The way he looked at her, the way he spoke to her. A fire was lit inside of her belly and the world became brighter. The birds that would sing with her in Cañari sang so loud that everyone looked around. No one but Tara understood them, they were saying "Speak and tell them."

Hualpa nodded at Viracocha and he helped him back to Amaru Tupa Inka's side.

Hualpa said something to Amaru Tupa Inka, who patted him on the back in an approving manner. Hualpa lowered his head.

Tara realized that Hualpa was supposed to threaten her, not encourage her.

Tara whispered to Viracocha, "First tell Amaru Tupa Inka that he can kill me, he can kill Achache, he can kill my entire village. I will sacrifice all of that, so the truth of my people lives. And so my story begins—"

She wheezed the story of her people, beginning with their forefathers, the female condor that snuck into the cave of men while they were out hunting. She cooked for them and departed before they returned. One day they returned early to see who was cooking for them. Their decedents became the first Cañaris.

She told them of the deluge and how Sapa Inka Tupac Yupanqui invaded. She told him of the fight and why she offered herself as a hostage, even though she thought she would be raped and her children killed.

Many of the stories that Tara told she had already shared with Viracocha. His familiarity with them gave him the ability to recite them with more conviction and passion than Tara would have been able to, even if she was well.

"—It was all because a history, it must be remembered, or else it's the greatest insult to the dead. A person only dies after they are forgotten and a people are only vanished from time after their gods, legends, and stories cease being repeated." Finished Tara.

When she finished, there wasn't a sound in the room. She noticed Amaru Tupa Inka was gone.

Each man and woman looked at Tara as if she were a goddess. After a moment they retreated to the courtyard outside to "Discuss things."

Tara went back to sleep.

Chapter Thirty-Five

Amauta

Tara slept for many days and each time she woke Viracocha was there beside her. He brought her everything she needed, and she felt safe. She told him what happened to her and gave him permission to tell his father.

One morning, she woke from her dream to the Apu of Cusco sitting upon her mat bed.

He put his hand on her leg and spoke in his stone voice. "Good morning."

"Good morning," she replied. She shook from the surprise of hearing her voice. It had returned.

"Sapa Inka Tupac Yupanqui is two days away from Cusco. There shall be celebration and you will be honored for your bravery and obedience in Cusco."

"Me honored by the man I—?" She stopped before she said hate. "—the man that—" she paused again and kept herself from saying, "destroyed my life."

The Apu of Cusco slanted his head and looked at her.

"—the man that sent me here." She said.

"Yes, which wouldn't that make sense? He honored you by sending you here and so he wishes to honor you again."

Tara paused and looked around.

"And what of Achache and the Amaru Tupa Inka?" Asked Tara. Her voice flowed smoothly, like a small bird flying in an empty canyon.

"The Sapa Inka is Amaru Tupa Inka's brother, and it will require a punishment from him. He is hiding in the Coricancha and we cannot go and look for him without performing elaborate rituals. I'm sorry, Tara, and about Achache. No one has seen him except Viracocha the night that you were attacked. We will keep looking. We shall worry about that later, for now there are many preparations to make so that Cusco is ready for the Sapa Inka and his entourage of hundreds of litters and thousands of people."

"Why do you tell me this?"

"Because it's time for you to leave the healing chambers. You are better," said a stranger. He emerged from a dark corner with a jar in his hand.

"Who are you?" Said Tara.

She moved closer to the Apu of Cusco.

"Tisk, tisk," said the stranger. "I'm the Hampi Kamayoc, the healer, that saved your life. You can call me, Paqo. Drink this thick tea. It will restore some of your previous strength. Be aware, it doesn't taste good. Actually, you will probably want to spit it out because it tastes to bad but don't. Just swallow. The taste doesn't linger." Paqo attempted to life a heavy sack. "AND THIS!" He dropped the sack. "And this—" he repeated. He kicked the sack "—will be rubbed all over your body. It will make your arms and legs return with vigor. It will burn but," he paused and smiled, "for you and your experiences, it probably won't burn all that bad."

Tara glared at him for an instant and returned a large smile. A plump coy sprung up from beneath the wall and ran to the middle of the room. Paqo quickly jumped and tried to capture it with the jar containing the tea meant to heal Tara. The coy escaped its capture and the herbal sap spilled over the dirt floor.

Tara laughed. She tried to stand but was unable instead she waved Paqo to her.

Paqo complied.

She leaned forward and kiss his hands. "Thank you for keeping me alive."

"It was the gods, not I. We did a lot of work on your kawsay. I'll be back with more of the healing sap."

He disappeared back into the shadows and returned with another jar.

Tara drank it and as he said, the taste was putrid. She resisted spitting it out and swallowed. The taste didn't vanish as he said it would, but grew worse.

Paqo smiled and gave her a vessel of chicha.

She chugged it and it eliminated the taste.

"Now, rub this all over your body," said Paqo.

She did as he suggested.

She went to sleep and woke again later that day with some energy restored. She stood up and didn't feel like fainting. She took a step, her knee locked, but she didn't fall. She took another step and it felt natural.

"It worked!" said Paqo.

Tara jumped from the scare.

He was hiding in the dark corner. He emerged. "It doesn't usually work. I just like to see people's face when they drink it. Leave here and rest woman! Recovery will take a long time. The Apu of Cusco will be here shortly and tell you where your huasi will be. Go there and rest."

"I will wait for him outside. I must see the sun again."

"Oh yes, you must miss Inti."

"Thank you for keeping me alive! And restoring my strength."

Tara went outside. She closed her eyes and inhaled the sweet air of Cusco, but instead got a breath of dust. There were scores of people on the road, all seemed to be in a rush and many of them carried items.

The Apu of Cusco came up beside her. "Look at you!" He tried to raise his voice to sound friendly, but it was just as deep as always. "There are a lot of people, aren't there? They have come to prepare Cusco for Sapa Inka Tupac Yupanqui's arrival. His return will make

Quicuchica seem like a child's celebration. For his return, there will be no detail forgotten for his arrival. It is the first time he will be in Cusco in four years. It'll be the most elaborate festival you've ever seen." He leaned over and felt the brick ground. He stood up and yelled, "Get someone over here to fix the masonry. The road isn't smooth here."

Tara breathed quickly and bit her lip. The noises, people hollering, sacks of maize being dropped, urns being rolled, echoed in Tara's head. Everyone seemed to be looking at her.

"Do you know where I can find Viracocha?" said Tara in a rapid spill of words.

"I don't know. He disappears and reappears as he pleases," said the Apu of Cusco.

One of the urns that was being rolled down the road broke into several pieces and caused a woman carrying sacks of dried food to trip. She cried out in pain.

"Excuse me," said the Apu of Cusco as he ran to help.

Tara thanked him and went confidently in the direction of what she thought would lead her to the Acllahuasi. After she took a couple turns and meandered down several streets, she realized Cusco was much larger than she thought and that she was lost. She turned down an empty and narrow alley and sat on the cold stone road with her back to the wall. She attempted to place her head into her hands but only found her foul smelling stubs. She hid her arms in the folds of her skirt, leaned her head back onto the wall and closed her eyes and wondered where Viracocha would be.

She retraced her steps to the healing chambers and entered.

"Paqo, are you still here," she yelled.

"Hey stop delaying and help out," he yelled back.

"How do I go to the Acllahuasi from here?" she asked him.

"You have no need to go there with those hands, or lack of hands," said Paqo, you're done with that place."

The insult hurt Tara almost as deep as the losing her hands. "I'm not going to go in the Acllahuasi! It's just I'm looking for—Nevermind. How can I get to the Sondorhuaci tower?"

Paqo approached Tara. His countenance changed, his shoulders lowered, and he avoided eye contact with Tara.

She took a few steps backward.

"Come here," said Paqo. He led her down the street in the opposite direction. "You can see it from here."

"If you want to go to the Acllahuasi, I will give you the directions, but I suggest you run far away if you can."

"I've already run away from there," said Tara. She examined his burdened face. It looked familiar in the sunlight, awfully familiar, like she knew him in a former life.

"Have we met?" She said.

"Besides caring for you for the entire dry season, no." He said.

She jumped "You are Tata's father! I know your daughter! She is the most beautiful girl in the Acllahuasi."

He froze. His face less than a hand's width from Tara's. Tears welled in his eyes. He sniffled and then shivered. He regained control over his body and looked back and forth, ensuring that they were alone.

"She is still alive?" He whispered.

"Very much so and is living a happy and joyful life. She's an amazing dancer and her voice sounds like the wind when she sings."

The man smiled, "I'm sorry for insulting you, when I hear about the Acllahuasi or see anything associated with it, as you are, I become very angry and sad." He looked back and forth again, checking to see if they were still alone, "It's an honor to have one's daughter chosen to go to the Acllahuasi, but the pain of her leaving is great. She is being prepared to be a sacrifice because of her beauty. It is a difficult honor for me. I can save others, but I can't save the one person that meant the world to me."

"I think they may have other plans for her. I don't think she'll be sacrificed."

He grabbed her and held onto her for a moment.

He let her go and told her how to go to the Acllahuasi. She thanked him and kissed his forehead.

"Wait," yelled Paqo. "Wait, please. If you happen to go into the Acllahuasi, bring her something for me. Please."

The pang of the Tata's betrayal emerged as a flash of rage in Tara, but the eager hope of a destitute father quenched it. In that moment, she felt the repugnant and vile filth that vengeance was. In the instant that it takes for lightening to strike, the ugly creature of resentment and vengeance was rid from her soul.

He returned and smiled at Tara, realizing the transformation he inspired. "Forgiveness is a great feeling, isn't it?" He didn't wait for Tara to answer and gave her a small woven llama doll to Tara.

"It was her favorite toy before she was taken," he whispered to her.

Tara tucked it into her cloak and kissed him on the forehead again.

She ran to the Acllahuasi, pushing her way through hundreds of people. She found it and went to the building next to it, where Viracocha sat during their late-night conversations.

She stood at the base of the building that stood three times as tall as she. The wall of the building was smooth, but there were a few stones along it.

"Viracocha!" She yelled.

There was no answer.

"Are you up there, Viracocha?"

She placed her foot on one of the stones and pushed herself up. She reached to grip one of the stones above her head but hit it with her stub. The sharp rock struck a nerve and sent a tickling sensation to her back. She fell back to the ground and landed on her butt.

"What are you doing, young girl?" said a woman passing by with two children in her arms.

"Trying to get my fingers to work," she said. She showed the woman her stubs and the woman scurried away.

Tara continued to try to climb the wall. Each time she made it a bit higher, but finally she realized it was hopeless.

"Viracocha! If you're up there, help me!"

She tried again. She nearly got to the top when a hand gripped one of her stubs and pulled her up. Her feet scraped the edge of the building. Once upon the roof, she saw it was Viracocha. He gripped the reeds with one hand and pulled her with the other until she was at the top of the pitched roof.

"Get down there," said Viracocha. He pointed to a spot below them on the opposite side of the roof than the street crowded street.

Tara quickly glanced below her at the surroundings of the building and there were scores of people, several of whom were pointing at them.

She slid along the side of the roof to where Viracocha indicated.

The roof muted the sounds of the street and they sat in silence. She saw the place where she sat in the Acllahuasi those countless nights talking to to Viracocha and his friends.

Viracocha slid down the steep roof and stopped right beside her.

One of his braids looped through his ear gauge. Tara took it out for him and straightened his hair.

Chapter Thirty-Six

Llama Doll

"T hank you for your help," said Tara.

"I thought I heard someone call me but wasn't sure. I went to look several times but only saw you this time," he paused. "So now that you're healed and free of the Acllahuasi, what are you going to do?" He removed his cloak made of weaved feathers and beads and straightened up his checkered tunic.

Tara shrugged. "I was going to weave the clothes for the Sapa Inka's child, Hualpa, but now I can't weave." She raised her stubs. "And all of these people, I can't handle them, there's so many! I can't even find my way around Cusco. I'm completely useless."

Viracocha moved in close to Tara, "Those gowns they make you wear in the healing chambers are ugly and look and smell like dirt," he said. He placed his magnificent cloak over Tara. After having done that he said, "I don't think that you are useless and none of the other people who heard your stories think so either."

"So then, I can tell you guys' stories for the rest of my life. Will you provide me with a place to live and food? I see you're already providing me clothing." She tried to fake a laugh, but nothing came out. "Is there a huaca nearby that I can ask to give me knowledge of what I can do without hands?"

"There is, but before you go, I may have the answer for you."

Tara leaned her head to Viracocha, "You're a huaca now?"

He laughed, "I can be, if you need." He grew serious, "All those nights when you told me stories you changed my, and my friends' view of Cañari and of the world. You did that with your voice, not your hands. Your stories made our boring lives filled with rituals and tasks enjoyable. Do you remember that story you told me about that time you and your brother Achache were lost in the Yumba's territory and they captured you? You never told me the end of that story and how you guys escaped. I've thought about it almost every night, of such a place that I never knew existed.

Tara chuckled at the memory.

"How does it end?" He asked.

Tara told him the rest of the story.

She sat quietly for several moments after finishing it, having forgotten about her lost hands. She felt purpose burn within her.

"I can still teach the child of Sapa Inka Tupac Yupanqui! I must go talk to him now! Your father said he was two days from Cusco. Let's go!"

Viracocha puckered his lips and concealed his laugh. "You may want to tell stories, but maybe that's the wrong approach because you'll likely die. If Inti allows you to find him, you will be killed if you try to approach him. If you aren't killed trying to approach him, he won't speak to you."

"Viracocha, this is what I'm supposed to do. You're still the only one I dare trust and if I'm going to travel outside of Cusco."

She paused for an instant and continued in a higher pitched voice. "I need you. I don't know the roads, I need you so they will provide me food and lodging at the tampu, and so they will allow me to cross the bridges. They know who you are and will treat you well."

"You don't need to find him, just speak to his statue here in Cusco."

Tara thought of the line of people waiting to speak to the statue of Sapa Inka Tupac Yupanqui the night that Yachi led her to meet Achache.

"I will not speak to a rock. I want to speak to the actual Sapa Inka, the one that conquered my country, the one that ordered that I be taken from my home, that one. Not a rock shaped like him."

"It's the same. The rock shares his kawsay and speaks for him."

"Not in my world."

"Then use a chasqui. Send your message via a chasqui, they'll run it to his entourage—"

"—Fine, don't help me. I'll go find him myself." She looked up at the pitched roof and stood up. "Can you at least help me get off of the roof?"

"Tara," said Viracocha. "You're unable to get off of the roof alone. You have just emerged from an entire season of rest. Your strength isn't strong enough for a multi-day hunt to find the Sapa Inka in this vast land."

"There is a fountain in the courtyard of the Acllahuasi." Said Tara. She pointed toward it.

"Yes," he said.

"When I arrived, Umita told me that the waters used to heal injuries. She let me drink a little of the water and I felt energized after the long journey here. Help me get off of the roof, I will sneak into the Acllahausi and drink it. If it gives me the strength to carry on, I will know this is the right path for me and you will help me. If not, I will heed to the gods and surrender my idea."

"I've heard of that fountain. It doesn't have water anymore. It dried up long before anyone alive now was born. But, if that's your proposal, I will take it." he smiled and his pointed teeth poked through his lips.

"If my strength returns, you will help me find the Sapa Inka?" Said Tara.

"I will accompany you to the most sacred huaca, the Huaca of Inka Ayar Uchu. He will tell us if you are supposed to go. This is the huaca that I went to during my Huayacuacha and he gave me guidance. You should know though, this Inka Ayar Uchu—" he paused and smiled, "—is a rock."

"You Inkas think way too much of rocks. But fine, I'll talk to that rock if it means that you'll help me. Only that one!"

"You'll need an offering to give Inka Ayar Uchu if you want something from him."

"Right," said Tara. "an offering of Ayni for the rock."

Viracocha assisted Tara off of the roof and to the secret entrance of the Acllahuasi that she used to escape to see Hualpa. He gave her a small vessel of chicha from Machu Picchu to pour into the fountain as the offering.

Tara, unafraid of any consequences, went to the fountain. She gasped when she saw its flow was bountiful, just as it was depicted in the old artwork she came across throughout her time at the Acllahuasi.

She tried to place the llama doll for Tata next to the fountain gently, but it fell out of her two arm grasp. She clumsily poured the chicha into the fountain and then leaned over the edge and put the basin in the water to fill it. The water, as if it had hands gripped her invisible hands and pulled her head first into the fountain. The water was icy to the skin but warmed her inside. She sunk deeper and deeper into it. As she descended, the warmth within her grew. She grew weak and craved a breath of air, but the heat within her gave way to comfort and it erupted like a volcano. With the explosion of lava from within her, she felt herself explode into millions of pieces. She opened her eyes and found herself laying beside the fountain. She was dry and so was the ground upon which she laid. She felt whole again. She felt she had hands, but looked and she didn't. She felt that her face was beautiful again and peered into her reflection, but it was still scared.

It didn't matter anymore.

She bent over to pick up her clothes and noticed that the llama doll was gone, where it was stood the sac of the textiles she weaved. On the top was the scarf that Umita was weaving when Tara arrived at the Acllahuasi.

The courtyard was vacant.

"Thank you, Umita," she yelled. "Thank you, Tata. Your father loves you," she said in a softer voice.

She left.

Outside the Acllahuasi, Viracocha helped her select the textiles that meant the most to her to be offered: A llautu with the story of the creation of Cañari; a blanket for an infant that replicated the image of Machu Picchu that Umita gave her; a chuspa to carry coca leafs with the Mountainscape as seen from the Acllahuasi, and others that she felt a connection with.

Chapter Thirty-Seven

Mountain Streams

They departed Cusco and just as Tara hoped, the city guards didn't question their departure because she was with Viracocha. He led her along secret paths that ascended Huanacauri, the most sacred and highest mountain near Cusco.

The mountain smelled of sweet fresh air, the scent that is only created in a forest after a soft rain. It was a scent that Tara missed so much from Cañari. Hundreds of coy ran about and purred along the sides of the path as it meandered past high points with vistas of Cusco and along grass meadows that were colored every color that grass grows. Through these meadows, animals and birds abounded. They made as much noise as the people did in Cusco.

"I've never seen the animals so lively," said Viracocha.

Tara stayed silent and absorbed her first experience in the open since her arrival in Cusco.

The most magnificent mountain vistas had platforms constructed upon them. Viracocha explained that ceremonies were performed there to remember their past.

"What if the ceremonies are celebrating a history that is incorrect?" said Tara.

"It doesn't matter what we think, Tara, just what Inti wants. Here, we're almost at the Huaca of Inka Ayar Uchu. Ask him. He has access to Inti in Hanaq Pacha."

They followed the path to the backside of Huanacauri.

"That's it?" asked Tara.

She pointed at a small enclosure. It was hidden in a mountain cove. It was painted in such colors as a vibrant jungle bird.

"Yes, remove your sandals," said Viracocha. He sat upon a large log and removed his. Tara sat on the other side of the log and struggled to do the same.

"Here, I'll help you." He said after watching her.

After removing them, he pulled out the offerings.

"I think this one is good."

He gave her the blanket with the image of Machu Picchu that Umita gave her.

"You're not coming with? I don't know the proper way to ask Inka Ayar Uchu for guidance."

"You must go in alone. It's easy, don't worry. At the center of the enclosure is a boulder, it's the huaca, the reincarnations of Inka Ayar Uchu. Burn your offering there and ask him what you wish from him. Either you'll receive inspiration or you won't. It's that simple. When I asked him at Huayacuacha, I felt that I must help you. It was a mellow feeling, but recognizable. It's different for everyone though."

Tara looked back and forth and scanned the horizon. She hoped to see the entourage of Sapa Inka Tupac Yupanqui so she could skip this whole ordeal. Seeing nothing, she turned back to Viracocha.

"How can I burn it? There is no fire."

"There is a fire next to Inka Ayar Uchu."

Tara bit her lip and entered the small enclosure through the small trapezoidal doorway. Immediately, she was in a dark, empty, and narrow passageway which led to a small light at the end. The walls were heavy and colored as blood. It was silent besides the echo of her deep breaths.

She scratched her nose as the aroma of burnt llama meat and maize entered her nose. It grew more pungent as she drew nearer to the central chamber. There, she found a small room that only fit one person. In that room, and pressed against the walls and the roof of the building, was a large boulder-Inka Ayar Uchu. There was a small plain platform at the base of it. On one side of the platform was a pile of llama bones and a few kernels of maize that stood as high as her knees. On the other side of the platform was a wood burning fire.

She looked around but saw no one.

She lit the blanket on fire and placed it on the platform. The stench of burning hair made her dizzy and she covered her nose. With her other hand, she lifted her tunic to breathe through it.

"Dear Inka Ayar Uchu, hear my plea," she said. She spoke through her tunic. "I realize I must go ask Sapa Inka Tupac Yupanqui to allow me to teach stories to the future ruler of this land. I was going to make clothing for him and teach him that way, but I no longer have hands. My voice is all I have left. To ask the Sapa Inka such a privilege is likely to get me killed, if I can be killed. This blanket that I give to you is one of my most valuable possessions. Please give me guidance as to what to do in exchange."

She sat in silence and waited for inspiration. Nothing came. No thought or feeling. The smell was too much for her. She stood up and turned to leave. The passageway was gone.

She heard something move behind her. She pivoted to see what it was. Out of the corner of her eye, she saw the boulder had transformed itself into a young man. His face was smooth and innocent. His eyes red with hurt, but his thick lipped smile conveyed understanding and empathy. He wore a smooth cloak the color of the tender grass outside of the building, with lacings the color of the flame before him.

She quenched her impulse to run, there was no where to run. She resisted biting her lip and took a bold step around and locked eyes with him.

"Inka Ayar Uchu?"

"That's me, Amauta Tara Inka of Yanantin, Huaca of the Spring of the Floating Flowers. To answer your question, follow the signs that have led you to this point in your life and they will lead you to where you must go," said Inka Ayar Uchu.

He spoke in a high voice filled with an innocence that matched his face.

"What did you call me? Huaca of what?" Said Tara.

"I called you by your name, that is all. Now go!" He said.

"But will I be safe? Every time I try to do something, I am faced with an insurmountable challenge, attacked, or betrayed!"

"How do you think I ended up as a boulder during my youth? I was betrayed by my brothers after having discovered Cusco after a lifetime of searching. It was the betrayal of all betrayals. But look at me now, speaking to a beautiful woman and they are forever gone."

Tara put her hand forward to feel the man. As her hand touched him, he transformed back into the boulder.

"Wait, what will the signs be?"

There was no answer.

She lowered her hand and said, "Thank you."

The passage way reappeared and Tara departed the building.

Viracocha stood on a nearby platform that overlook the untamed jungle. He threw small rocks off of the ledge.

Tara ran to him and grabbed his arm, "Don't throw the stones. You never know who they are!"

"Huh?" He said. He lowered his arm and dropped the rock.

"Well, what happened in there?" said Viracocha.

She looked over the mirador. A cluster of condors flew in the distance.

"I don't remember those condors there before, I would have noticed them. Did you see them?"

"No, I didn't, but they were likely there and we missed them."

"You know," said Tara, "A condor is the mother of the Cañari people? It was a condor that started everything."

"To us Inkas, condors are the messengers from the Hanaq Pacha. It's how Inti and others that reside in Hanaq Pacha bring their favor upon us."

Tara bit her lip and then smiled.

"That's where I need to go, to the condors! That's where we will find Sapa Inka Tupac Yupanqui. It's what Ayar Uchu wants."

Tara looked at Viracocha to see if he showed willingness to lead her.

He examined the landscape, "It looks like they are flying over the small city of Cusibamba. I'm not sure if there is a path that goes there from here."

She bit her lips while looking at him.

Viracocha analyzed the landscape for a moment longer, "I think there's a way, but we'll have to run to get there by night.

"You'll lead me!" She said.

"That's what I agreed to, and I don't lie. Let's go."

He set off in a slow run. Tara followed behind him with a renowned sense of energy. She didn't know where it came from.They followed a series of small paths until one intersected with the Qhapaq Ñan at Cusibamba. The sun was a finger's width above the mountains, and the condors were still flying over the settlement.

Tara paced up the Qhapaq Ñan a little ways and looked around. She returned to Viracocha, who leaned up against a small wooden structure and searched for something in his small bag.

"This is where I passed by on my way to Cusco," said Tara. "It's the same road."

"It probably is." He put down his bag and pointed in the direction Tara returned from, "It's the Qhapaq Ñan and in that direction it goes straight to Cañari. It's the way that the Sapa Inka and his entourage are mostly likely to come from. It'll be best to wait here."

He put down his arm and moved in closer to Tara. He put his hand on hers. "If you want to go home, back to Cañari, this is your chance. I will make sure you get there safely and go with you as far as needed. You're no longer be a hostage. You can go."

Tara grabbed his hand, "Cusco is where I belong now and that's where I will teach young Huayna," said Tara. She expected the words to hurt, but instead they provided warmth.

She let go of his hand and stepped away from him. "Where is everyone? It was crowded and busy when I passed by here."

"Probably in Cusco for the festivities. While we wait for him, let's go to the tampu," He pointed to the side of the hill to a stone structure. "There will be people there and we can wait for his arrival and they should have food. I'm starving."

"We will only wait if there's a sign that we must," said Tara.

"Sapa Inka Tupac Yupanqui will be coming through here, it makes sense to wait," said Viracocha.

"Yes, it makes sense, but logic doesn't always follow what the gods do."

"So, do you see another sign?" Said Viracocha. He pointed to the setting sun. "It'll be dark within moments."

"Maybe there will be one tomorrow."

They went up the hill to the tampu.

"Wait out here," said Viracocha. "I'm going to go inside and get permission for us to stay. It's best that you don't speak, they will probably know your accent is not from here."

Viracocha went inside and Tara examined the unique tampu.

It was made of two long and skinny buildings. One consisted of the typical assortment of rooms of a tampu. The other was a giant kitchen consisting of fifteen large basins built over a corresponding number of fire holes. A small manmade creek ran in front of the length of both buildings and a pathway followed between the creek and buildings.

Viracocha snuck up from behind, his approach was muted by the sound of the flowing water. "That's where the women that accompany the armies prepare the meals," said Viracocha in an accentuated voice.

Tara jumped.

Viracocha laughed.

"We have permission to stay," he said once his laugh passed. "Come on, they'll even provide food for us."

They went inside the plain stone tampu. It was well lit, yet frigid. A woman led them to a room in the back. There was a large bowl of stew and roasted maize.

They ate and laid down.

Tara, unable to sleep, rose late in the night. She picked up the bag of offerings between her arms and made her way to the small creek in front of the tampu. She followed it until it joined with its source, a nearby mountain stream.

She pulled out one of her textiles, the llautu with the creation story weaved into it. She placed it in the water.

"Dear Pachamama, you have always guided me by the way of water. Accept this llautu as a thank you and grant me a sign of where to go next so that I may find the Sapa Inka. Have him accept me as a teacher for his child that has Cañari kawsay within him."

She removed her sandals, using one foot to pull off the other, and put her feet into the frigid water. Her worry of finding the Sapa Inka disseminated into the water and washed away. The sky lit up with lightening and the ground shook with earth-splitting thunder.

She spread her arms and embraced the rogue raindrops that escaped the oncoming storm. The wind carried the scent of Milagro. She smiled.

"Thank you," she said.

She put her sandals back on and went toward the tampu. The wall of rain close behind her. She jumped inside the tampu as the wall of rain caught her. She ran to the back room and slid onto the floor beside sleeping Viracocha. She laughed.

She laid awake the remainder of the night and listened to the deluge. It reminded her of the deluge that saved her from the fires in Cañari.

Chapter Thirty-Eight

Unexpected Find

Tara departed the tampu when the sun rose. Viracocha found her shortly thereafter, sitting on a rock overlooking Cusibamba.

"That rain came down really hard last night," said Tara.

"Rain?" said Viracocha. He looked at the clear sky. "I didn't hear anything."

"It was a huge storm and went on for at least half of the night. The thunder—"

"—Tara, the ground is dry. You were dreaming."

"No, I definitely wasn't dreaming."

An elderly man walked out of the tampu and Viracocha called to him, "Did you hear any rain last night?"

"There weren't no rain," said the man. He kicked the dirt. "The ground dryer than in Atacama. The crops gonna to die. Inti knows, we sure do need that rain. Sapa Inka Tupac Yupanqui coming all the way from yonder land where there's no shadow to beg to Inti to deliver the rain." He kicked the dirt again and went the opposite direction.

Viracocha scratched his head, "The land where there's no shadow?"

"I know it rained," said Tara. She stood up and left Viracocha, who stared at his long shadow cast by the morning sun.

"Land of no shadow?" Said Viracocha.

"It's the land near Cañari called Quito," called Tara. "At high sun, there are no shadows."

"No shadows like no rain, huh?" said Viracocha. He smiled.

"I'm going to show you, it rained."

She departed and looked around the vacated tampu to find a sign of rain, but found none. She went to the stream expecting to find a high water level, but it flowed at the same level as before.

"Okay then," she said to herself. "I guess it didn't rain."

She turned to return to the tampu. As she swept the landscape, she saw a tall tree, the tallest in Cusibamba. It was split in a way that only lightening does. It was smoking.

She went to it and found it surrounded by deep mud and puddles of water. Water from the storm. She stepped into it, the seductive mud engulfed her foot. She took three large steps until she was close enough to the tree to place her forearm on it. As she expected, it was cold and wet.

"It did rain!"

She admired the tree and saw that it stood at the trailhead of a path that followed the nearby mountain stream she prayed to the previous night. The path and stream wandered into the altiplano, toward a small mountain, and disappeared in the knolls.

She ran back to Viracocha and found him finishing his morning meal of boiled quinoa and squash.

She told him about the previous night and what she found.

Viracocha put his plate down, "You want to go down a small path that leads us into wild land, full of animals and snakes, and away from where the Sapa Inka will certainly pass by today or tomorrow? All of this based on a lightening strike from a storm that didn't happen last night. I don't think that is a good idea."

"It's exactly what we need to do," said Tara. "We have to go now!"

"I see." He stood up and glanced at his half finished bowl. "I'll follow you then." He picked up a small sack of supplies and followed her to the trail and into the altiplano.

The path followed the small stream across the grasslands to the mountain. By the time the sun rose to its zenith, they were on the far side of the mountain where the stream joined with a small river. The terrain broke into the mouth of a forested canyon and the path descended into it. A little way into the canyon, the river went over the edge of a large plateau.

Tara ran along the trail, down several switchbacks, to the bottom of the waterfall and jumped into the plunge pool.

When Viracocha caught up several moments later, Tara called to him.

"Isn't this great! And the water, oh my, it's so cold. Much colder than anything in Cañari."

"You should join me!"

Viracocha stayed a little distance back from the water and looked around. He pulled a branch out of his braids and threw it into the pool.

"Do you think you received the sign from the huaca to come this way to jump into the pool?"

Tara had difficulty hearing him over the sound of the waterfall and swam to the edge. "No, but that sun is so hot. I needed to cool off."

She got out and tried to put her clothes back on. She found it difficult to put her dry clothes over her wet body. Viracocha noticed her troubles and came and helped her.

As he tied the final knot to secure her tunic, he said in a whisper. "I don't think we're alone."

Tara focused the tree line where he was watching, "We're definitely not alone. Let's leave."

"Agreed."

"Not that way!" said Tara. "We're going to keep going down the path until we discover what the huaca wanted us to find."

She slipped her sandals back on.

"I think we found it," said Viracocha. He pointed at the waterfall.

Two speckled bears, one chasing the other, ran in front of them and jumped into the water.

Viracocha jumped between the bears and Tara.

"Where there are cubs, there's a mother." He said.

"Viracocha?" said Tara, "How often do you see two speckled bears playing like this right in front of humans?"

"I mean, there're tons of animals in these woods, it's to be expected."

"No, how many times have you actually seen two speckled bears playing like this so close to humans? And without a mother nearby."

She went past Viracocha and looked at the bears closely.

"Never, I guess," he said.

"That's what I thought." She returned her sharp gaze to the tree line.

"What?" said Viracocha.

"He can't be."

Viracocha stepped in front of her and glared at her, yearning for an explanation.

Tara pushed her way past Viracocha and approached the tree line.

Viracocha crept just behind her. "Can't be what?"

The bears continued to play in the water, oblivious to Tara and Viracocha.

Tara saw movement in the trees and heard voices. "Ha! I see you. Just come out," she yelled.

The bears looked up at her and ran off.

"Who's in there?" said Viracocha.

A spear flew by her head and landed in the water.

Viracocha pulled out his knife and lunged past Tara.

"I don't believe it!" said Hualpa.

He jumped out from behind a tree that was near Tara.

Viracocha ceased his attacked and stood stunned.

"It's not you, it can't be. Who are you really?" said Hualpa. He stood half naked and stared at Tara.

Tara lost her balance and fell backward onto her butt. "Aren't you sick, trying to recover in some healing chambers?" she said from the ground.

"Waranga Hualpa?" Said Viracocha. "All of Cusco is looking for you." He turned to Tara. "How did you know he was—"

"—I didn't." Said Tara.

Hualpa approached and leaned in close to Tara, who was still on the ground, and stared at her face.

"I guess it really is you, no one else has a face like that." He gave her a hand to help her up, but pulled it back when he saw she didn't have hands. "You're missing something?" He said.

She put her stubs forward and he grabbed her arm and pulled her up. He brushed the dirt off of her back side. "Being so beautiful as you are, why did you leave Cusco with that guy? He's the ugliest!" He pointed at Viracocha. "You chose him, over me? You chose him? I'm so much better."

Hualpa spent a longer than necessary time hitting the dirt off of her bottom. "And you let him help you get dressed and not me? Although I prefer the undressing."

He kicked a rock toward Viracocha, who kicked it back.

"HUALPA!" Said Tara. She spun around and jumped onto him and hugged him. "I thought I'd never see you again!"

"And that's your excuse for pairing up with Viracocha?" said Hualpa.

She let go of Hualpa. "I'm not playing your games right now."

"Very well, don't play my games. You can leave. My troops and I are quite occupied at the moment and can't be distracted by you." He turned toward the tree line. "Oh, and I most certainly don't have time to show you *what* I have for you," he said as he walked off.

"HUALPA!" said Tara. "I'm not playing your games."

"I know. You just said that," said Hualpa. He yelled at the tree line, "Let's move out boys and don't let Tara see anything she hasn't already."

"There is nobody with you," said Viracocha. "You're out here alone."

"You suck! What are you hiding?" said Tara.

"I'm hiding my two hundred men first of all," he said. He gave Viracocha a dirty look. "And among them, there is something *she* may want."

"You only command one hundred and ninety-nine," said Tara. She shrugged and raised her stubs, "You have my hands?"

"Oh Inti!" said Hualpa. "No, I don't have those but I have something better."

He turned toward the woods, "Men come on out and bring ACHACHE! Come on out!"

The still woods became alive and the men emerged from the trees. They split into two columns and Achache walked down the middle to Tara and smiled at her.

"I command two hundred today, Tara," said Hualpa.

Tara fell to her knees and then onto her face, crying.

Achache ran to her and picked her up.

She examined the fresh scars on his head and he lifted her arms and kissed her stubs.

"We are going after Amaru Tupa Inka and we will kill him!" said Achache. "He is going to die."

"That's right!" said Hualpa. He jumped over to Achache's side.

Achache continued, "Hualpa and his men attacked him and his treacherous hordes yesterday when I was with them. They rescued me." He reached up and grabbed Hualpa's hand, "Once he learned who I was, he directed his men to find and rescue me instead of pursuing Amaru Tupa Inka."

"Do you want to join us?" Asked Hualpa to Tara.

Tara, still crying, spoke in a broken voice, "I would love to come with you but I have my own journey. Viracocha and I are looking for the Sapa Inka."

"What do you mean, looking for the Sapa Inka?" Said Hualpa.

"I am looking for his entourage and once I find him I'm going to propose that I become the teacher for his son of Cañari descent, Huayna."

"Are you trying to get yourself killed? No one 'finds' the Sapa Inka, he finds you and you NEVER ask anything of him," said Hualpa.

"That's what I said," shouted Viracocha.

Hualpa ignored him.

"And you came down here looking for him?" said Hualpa. You thought the ruler of the world, the Son of the Sun, would hide down here in this filthy forest?" He put his face in his hands and shook his head "Viracocha, what is wrong with you for guiding her this way?"

"Wait, no, it was her idea!" Said Viracocha.

Hualpa ignored him.

"I'm going to find him," said Tara.

"I have no doubt that you will find him. Go back to Cusco and wait for him there, Tara. No one approaches the Sapa Inka's entourage. No one. NO ONE. You won't even get close. He is accompanied by thousands of highly trained soldiers that will kill you upon sight. They don't care who you are and if they don't kill you, the sickness that travels with them will kill you."

"What sickness?" Said Viracocha. He spoke loudly, not wanting to be ignored again.

Hualpa released a long sigh, "The sickness, Viracocha, the sickness. Haven't you heard? The sickness that has killed nearly half of the people that travel with the Sapa Inka."

"No, I haven't heard. How would Intl allow such a thing?" Said Viracocha.

Hualpa ignored him.

"Inti might allow his followers to get sick," said Tara, "but Mamaquilla and Pachayachachic won't allow it to happen to me. I will survive the guards and I won't get sick." She stomped.

Hualpa acted scared for a fleeting instant in response to her exclamation and then resumed his cautionary tone of voice. He put one step forward to Tara and put his palms toward her.

"We're not talking Amaru Tupa Inka's level of incompetence here, he can't even kill me after poisoning me. He can't kill you, but the Sapa Inka's men can and will."

"Goodbye, Hualpa," said Tara. She cried again but her voice remained strong.

"Let's go Viracocha, unless you think I'm incapable like Hualpa thinks."

Viracocha followed her.

Achache ran after them. "Wait!"

Tara stopped. She didn't turn to face him. She held back tears that if she let flow would rival that of the deluge of the previous night.

Achache came to a stop in front of her, "Mother wanted me to give this to you." He gave her a small llama leather bag. Tara reached inside and pulled out two locks of hair.

"One is from mother," said Achache, "The other is from father. That way they will always be with you." He tied them to her stubs.

Tara pressed them to her nose.

"Mother wants me to tell you that you are more of a Cañari woman than she ever was. She's so proud of you and every day, she tries to be as brave as you."

Tara squeezed her eyes shut.

Achache hugged her and held her tight for several moments.

Tara cried and a puddle accumulated at their feet.

"Tara," said Viracocha. He touched her shoulder, "We must go now if we are to make it back to Cusibamba before dark."

"Go back to Cañari, sister, go back. This is your chance. Everyone misses you and you'll return as the leader."

Tara stumbled between words to allow for her sobs. "Just as you have your calling to go get Amaru Tupa Inka," she sobbed and wiped her face. "I have my calling." She lost control of her voice.

"It's okay," said Achache. He held her closer.

She regained control of her voice, "I see now that Cañari isn't where I am supposed to be. There is something much more important here in Cusco. When you kill Amaru Tupa Inka, go to Cusco! I'll be—" Her voice cracked again and she buried her head his Achache's shoulder.

"I will," said Achache. He let go of her and took a few steps backward. He raised his hand to Tara, then turned and ran back to the Hualpa, whose back was facing them.

Tara remained quiet for the return journey to Cusibamba.

The sun slipped behind the mountains as they entered Cusibamba and the temperature dropped just as quickly as the sun and thousands of birds sang from the altiplano where they hid in the grass.

"I'll go to the tampu and see if the Sapa Inka passed by today," said Viracocha.

I'll meet you at the Qhapaq Ñan," said Tara.

A man, dressed in plain garb, laid beside the Qhapaq Ñan at the entrance of the city. He wasn't there that morning when they left.

He moaned.

Tara went to him.

"Are you okay? Did you see Sapa Inka Tupac Yupanqui's train pass by?" said Tara.

The man rolled over. "Who asks?"

"My name is Tara and I seek to join up with the train," she said.

The man opened his eyes, "Tara Inka of Yanantin? The Sapa Inka and Colla speak so highly of you." The man lifted his hand and stroked her face, "They passed by. I was in the entourage." He pushed himself into a sitting position and coughed. "I am one of the litter-bearers of the Apu of Antisuyu who travels with the Sapa Inka. Half of the men and woman as left Cañari will make it to Cusco alive tomorrow." He cleared his throat, turned his head and spit a blood stained gob of mucus, "Don't seek them, run away from that train. It is cursed."

Viracocha ran to Tara, "The Sapa Inka and his train already passed and will reach Cusco tomorrow!"

"I know Viracocha."

She continued to look at the man.

"You're going to chase them, aren't you," said the dying man, "Tara Inka of Yanantin?"

Tara withdrew from her bag a llautu with the different faces of Mamaquilla on it. She put it on the Apu of Antisuyu's head."

"Travel well to the Hanaq Pacha and guard me because I am going to chase him and will need all the protection I can get," she said.

She left her sack with the remaining offerings on the ground. She ran with Viracocha toward Cusco in the dark and moonless night.

Chapter Thirty-Nine

Cusco

Mist descended upon them in the already dark night. Despite the low visibility, they maintained their hurried walk along the Qhapaq Ñan, which was covered with trampled flowers, pedals, and vibrant colored bird feathers.

Sick, dying, and dead men and women lined the road. Those that could speak warned Tara and Viracocha to stay away from the train, that there was nothing there but sickness and death. They said that those who remained only did so because they were forced to. Viracocha implored Tara to listen to them, but she remained unwavered. They pressed onward into the depths of a ravine.

The first light of the day made out a silhouette of the lip of the ravine in front of them that formed the boundary of the Cusco Valley. Beams of light projected through the mist and hurt Tara's eyes. A measure of song traveled the narrow ravine and interrupted the wakening birds.

"I think that's them," said Tara. She pushed Viracocha along. "We caught up to them. Come on!"

They increased their pace to a slow run. The dying men and women cried from their death beds alongside the road. "Run the other way! You must run the other direction."

The train became visible through the fog as it ascended the wall of the ravine: masses marched in front of and behind the leading litter, which glimmered like a bright star. The other litters, none of which shined as bright as the first.

As they drew closer and the mist lifted, Tara saw more of the train. The columns that led the train were beautiful girls and women. These girls threw reeds and flowers in front of the throng of litters while singing praises. Their virgin voices cut through the mist like lighting through rain.

"What are they singing?" Asked Tara. "I don't understand the language that they sing in."

"They sing of Sapa Inka Tupac Yupanqui's glory and accomplishments in the royal language," said Viracocha.

Other women played the straight pipes and blew through sea shells. The sounds echoed through the ravine and filled the vast hollow.

Soldiers with spears over their shoulders and a bag of stones by their sides marched behind each litter of which Tara counted fifty occupied and many more empty. Each of the litters was accompanied with its own entourage and columns of women, men, soldiers, and children. Each group of people dressed differently, and the accompanying soldiers carried weapons native to their land.

Viracocha grabbed Tara's tunic, "We shouldn't get any closer. If you have any chance of getting to the Sapa Inka, we have to leave the Qhapaq Ñan and use the landscape as cover."

They left the Qhapaq Ñan and used a small game trail to ascend the cliff side. The fog dissipated at the top of the cliff. They ran across the open altiplano until they were a little way ahead of the train. They hid on a mound near the Qhapaq Ñan, behind a small outcrop of stone, and waited.

The train crested the cliff side and sprawled across the altiplano.

"It's still grander than anything I imagined, even with half of the people dead. How is it so big?" Said Tara.

"Because he's part God," said Viracocha.

The litter that followed the Sapa Inka's was a litter made of silver and resembled the moon. It was accompanied by all women, including female soldiers. They beat drums colored as dark trees in a dense forest. The beat set the pace of the train. Behind them was a crowd whistling a 'whoosh' sound.

In the litter sat a woman adorned in silver and glacial clothes.

"No!" Said Tara.

"What do you see?" Said Viracocha, he tried to match Tara's point of focus.

"That woman behind the Sapa Inka is Colla, the ruler of Cañari."

Tara jumped to her feet and was no longer hidden from view of the train.

"Get down!" Viracocha grabbed her cloak.

"It's time she learns what happened to me and what is going to happen because of her treason."

She let her cloak slide off and wore only her checkered tunic, freeing her of Viracocha's grasp.

Tara took a few steps down the small hill they were upon and turned around.

"Weren't you going to go to the Sapa Inka and tell him that you want to teach Huayna?"

Tara took a few more steps toward the train.

"Tara, they will kill you!"

"Once you've lost everything, death doesn't matter."

"Don't tell me I didn't warn you," said Viracocha.

Her cautious steps turned into a run.

The female guards that accompanied Colla saw Tara's approach and created a human wall between her and Colla. Scores of male soldiers from the Sapa Inka's group joined their female counterparts.

The hundreds of guards that blocked Tara's way placed stones into their slings and released them at the speed of flying stars. They shot past Tara. One clipped her hair and sheared it. Another went through her loose fitting tunic, and another nicked her stub.

The projectiles, so close to hitting her at the beginning, increasingly missed their mark. The train ceased its progress. Several of the litters were dropped by the litter-bearers. The guards fell to the ground and screamed and cried to their God, the rising sun.

The earth, all around Tara, shook.

The earthquake didn't hinder Tara. She ran past the fallen and crying guards to the litter of Colla, the only other object that wasn't affected by the quake.

Colla looked down on Tara from her litter and Tara glared at her with pressed lips heaving through her runny nose.

Colla said in her deep, smooth voice. "Tara of Milagro, to see you again is a delight. I wish your—"

"—Why did you do it?" Tara interrupted Colla.

The earthquake ceased and the guards surrounded Tara, their spears and knives pointed at her. Colla raised her hands to stop them.

"Why did you give our land, our people, our heroes to the Inkas? You caused us so much pain! And look what you have done to me!" She raised her stumps. "You could have stopped it before anything happened! You should have stopped it! You selfish, horrible person that only cares for herself! You just wanted to marry the Sapa Inka to make yourself the most powerful woman in the world. Ruling Cañari wasn't enough for your greedy desires. You never cared for any of us! You're a horrible person! Me, little Tara from Milagro, have done more than you!"

Colla stood upon her litter. Her smile turned to a scowl. "Take this ungrateful bitch away. Her punishment will make a good public display of how not to address me when we reach Cusco."

She spoke firmly and remained standing.

Two female guards grabbed Tara's shoulders.

"I'll go when I am done talking!" She spoke while attempting to shake free of the guards' grasp.

"I'm going to save the Cañari people, something that you failed to do even with a Mamaquilla, and soldiers willing to die for you."

Tara turned to one guard, "GET OFF OF ME!" She jabbed her stubs into the guard's eyes.

Tara turned back to Colla. "You're a terrible leader and even a worse person!"

The guard that Tara assaulted, picked her up and threw her to the ground. Three more guards jumped on top of her.

One of their chest plates hit Tara in the abdomen and she hurled.

"Cease!" Yelled a male voice. "Don't hurt her! The Son of the Sun, the Protector of the Poor, and the ruler of this land, Sapa Inka Tupac Yupanqui, commands so. He desires to speak with her."

The guards got off of Tara and backed away from her with their heads lowered.

Tara stood up. She tried to stand straight up but leaned forward because of the pain in her belly.

The man that spoke was a soldier, the tallest man Tara had ever seen. He dressed similarly as Hualpa dressed, but this man had larger bores in his ears, shorter hair, and a larger llautu.

He went up to Tara and without consulting her, examined her face and brushed some dirt off of it.

"Good, no injuries." He said.

He turned to the guards, their heads were still lowered and their silver adornments less radiant than moments before, "You should be ashamed of yourselves."

He kicked the ground and several small stones from beneath the rose pedals flew up and hit the guards' bare shins.

"Come with me, Tara Inka of Yanantin. The Sapa Inka wishes to speak with you."

The thousands of people and the 50 litters, not having resumed their progress since the earthquake, departed the Qhapaq Ñan and curled around to see the spectacle. They looked upon in silence, only broken by the sounds of coughing and the distant shouts from Cusco.

She humbly trailed the looming soldier without muttering a word or resisting. They passed the columns of soldiers that stood ready between the litters of Colla and the glamorous litter of Sapa Inka Tupac Yupanqui.

Tara looked back at the outcropping that Viracocha hid behind. She didn't see him.

They arrived at the front of the Sapa Inka's golden litter, which was carried on the shoulders of 48 men.

Sapa Inka Tupac Yupanqui looked visibly older than when she last saw him. His eyebrows covered his drooping, dry eyes and his cheeks sagged below the jawbone. His robes sat upon him as those that sit upon a skeleton after having been unburied.

"Don't look at the Son of the Sun, the Protector of the Poor, and the ruler of this land, Sapa Inka Tupac Yupanqui." shouted the tall soldier. "Bow!"

Tara complied, and lowered her face until it was on the flower covered, and sweet smelling, pavement.

"You're going to kill me, aren't you?"

There was a long pause.

"From what I hear, you cannot be killed," said the Sapa Inka. Her chest vibrated at the sound of his bass voice.

You want to know why I'm not in the Acllahuasi, as you commanded, don't you?" Said Tara.

"No," said the Sapa Inka.

"You want to know why I tried to approach you, despite not being allowed to?" Said Tara.

"No."

Tara looked up at him, but the soldier pushed her head back down. Another silence ensued.

"I want to know why you aren't in the litter as I commanded."

She raised herself to her knees and without looking at the Sapa Inka, raised her handless arms.

"They were compliments of your brother, the one you commanded to put me into the litter so no, he didn't give me a litter as you commanded him to do."

"STOP!" said the Sapa Inka.

Tara looked behind her. A soldier held his spear directly above her. She didn't flinch.

The guard dropped his spear beside Tara and fell to the ground. He bowed. "You allow a commoner to speak to you like that?"

"A commoner she is not," said the tall soldier. "Get a litter for Tara Inka of Yanantin."

The guard raised himself and without turning his back to the Sapa Inka, left to fulfill the command.

"I don't want a litter," said Tara. "I don't want your blessing. I want nothing from you because you took everything I love and now each thing you give me ends up hurting me."

"Bring the child Huayna to me," said the Sapa Inka.

The tall soldier lowered his head and left to fulfill the command.

"Tara, everything only ends up hurting you because you are not yet the person that Inti needs you to be."

"Is that what you told all of the people who died following you in your entourage?"

"No one has died," said the Sapa Inka.

"I speak of the hundreds of dead men and women that I passed while pursuing you," said Tara.

"No one has died," said the Sapa Inka.

The faces of the litter-bearers went pale. The soldiers that gathered around the spectacle gripped their weapons and leaned forward, all waiting for the order to kill Tara. The Sapa Inka put his head into his hands for a moment.

"You want me to forget everything, and believe the lies you and your people profess," said Tara. "The more you forget and deny the truth, the more it finds power in a force you cannot control until a pachacuti happens and you too will be forgotten."

"Maybe you're right, Tara Inka of Yanantin, maybe so. I shall consult the other huacas."

"Maybe I'm right, what does that mean? What part am I right about?"

Huayna arrived upon his own litter made of gold and silver with bright wood. It was carried by 48 men.

"He's the first child of Colla and I," said the Sapa Inka. He smiled as if the previous conversation never happened.

The toddler was small and enveloped in so many robes that at first, Tara didn't see his large dark head. His head was covered with braided black hair that poked up out of his urine colored llautu inlaid with two feathers the color of an alpine lake. His eyes were as dark as his hair.

Behind him, an empty wooden litter arrived for Tara. It looked much nicer than the previous one she had and was carried by 12 men.

"Get into it," said the Sapa Inka.

Tara approached the litter and realized it was the litter of an Apu. The image of the dying man she met in Cusibamba flashed in her mind. She sat in the wooden litter, it was lifted. The train resumed its progress to Cusco.

"I have heard that you want to teach him?" Said the Sapa Inka. "But if I were to bless you with such a privilege of teaching Huayna, won't it hurt you according to your logic?" He raised the infant to her. "Take him."

Tara stared at the child and at her stubs. She bit her lips and put her arms forward, worried she might drop the future Sapa Inka. The toddler cuddled to Tara's chest and laid upon her breasts.

She put a hand on his head and all anger left her.

"Does this mean I can teach him the history of Cañari?" She said, hardly audible.

The Sapa Inka moved his gaze from Tara to the sun.

"Waranga Hualpa is pursuing Amaru Tupa Inka and will bring me his heart and head. You will receive his hands."

Tara closed her eyes, "You give the child to me but you won't tell me if I can teach him."

"After Waranga Hualpa brings you Amaru Tupa Inka's hands, what will you do with them?"

"Can I reattach his hands to my arms?" said Tara.

"Do you want us to?" said the Sapa Inka.

"What I want is to teach Huayna the history of his mother's people, of Cañari. The true history that will make him proud of his heritage."

"You, little Tara from Cañari, want to teach the future ruler of the world? You shall corrupt him, you will teach him to rebel and to love Cañari more than Cusco. You dare ask me such?"

"Yes!"

He looked back at Tara.

"What do you want more, to teach him or for me to restore your hands?"

Tara paused a moment.

"I see, so you don't know. Then I don't know either. I think we are done."

Tara saw that she was about to be dismissed.

"Why me?" She blurted out. "Why was it I that you chose out of the thousands of women in Cañari and the millions in Tahuantinsuyu? Why was it I that you chose to bring to Cusco?"

"Because the magic that used to adorn us is still present in you," Said the Sapa Inka. He sounded surprised, as if he expected Tara to know.

She stood up on the litter and almost lost her balance and sat back down. She looked at the Sapa Inka. "Having me teach Huayna is what's meant to be, it's why Mamaquilla and Inti have placed me here. This is the path."

Tara waited for him to respond, but he didn't indicate doing so but stared at her, waiting for her to say more.

"Mama!" said Huayna.

"Take the boy to his mother," said the Sapa Inka.

The litter-bearers turned toward Colla's litter.

"No! Not to her!" Said Tara. "I command you, do not take me to her."

"We must obey Sapa Inka Tupac Yupanqui," said the chief litter bearer.

Tara set Huayna on the litter beside her and jumped from it. The tall soldier picked her up with one arm and put her back in. "Bring the child to his mother. It's not a request."

Tara and Huayna were carried to Colla. When the litters were brought close enough, Huayna jumped out of Tara's arms to Colla's.

Tara turned her head away from Colla and looked in the direction from where she hoped Viracocha was still hiding.

"You did as you were commanded," said Tara to her litter-bearers. "Now, take me back to the Sapa Inka."

"I never spoke to you in Guapondelig before you were taken," said Colla. She spoke in her normal airy voice as she put Huanya to her breast to feed. "I will tell you what I wanted to say then."

"I don't want to hear it," said Tara. "I lived without knowing it and I will continue to do so. You did as the Sapa Inka commanded, litter-bearers, take me away."

The litter-bearers obeyed Tara and led her away, but Colla followed her.

"Do you think I wanted to be Colla, the ruler of Cañari?" said Colla, just loud enough for Tara to hear but soft enough so the words landed upon her ear like a dream.

"Faster men, take me away from this evil woman!"

"No!" yelled Colla. Tara jumped. Her voice was louder than Tara thought humanly possible.

Colla returned to her soft voice, "I didn't want to be Colla, anymore than you wanted to be Tara Inka of Yanantin, but in order for Cañari to survive we must become and do things we don't want to. DON'T YOU UNDERSTAND THAT!"

Tara tried to cover her ears, but her stubs provided no relief. She raised her handless arms and turned to Colla, "Oh, is that what you call this? 'Something I didn't want to become?' Don't worry, Colla, I've come to terms with my life. It is a miserable one and it shall be miserable forever."

Colla switched from speaking Quechua to the native language of Cañari, a language that none of their litter-bearers spoke or understood.

"This child that feeds on my breast, the one that you want to teach. This child that Tupac Yupanqui thinks I love so much, was a product of him raping me whilst his guards held their weapons at the ready should I resist him. This was the night before you arrived."

"Stop," said Tara in Cañari to her litter-bearers. They continued. "STOP" She said again, but this time in Quechua.

They stopped.

Tara slowly turned to face Colla. "I'm sorry, I didn't know that." Tara stared at Huayna sucking at his ravaged mother's breast.

Colla continued in Cañari, "The Sapa Inka came to me to make a proposal, which after his guards killed mine, he told me his proposal. He told me the exact number of men and women in our defenses, where they were, and how many of his men he had hidden in the forest outside each post. His guards described to me in perfect detail what would befall each soldier, depending which gender and age they were, should I not submit. I hesitated, and the Sapa Inka told me that he'd demonstrate to me what would befall the women. He killed my husband in front of me and then turned to me. I don't think I need to finish the story."

Tara hung her head and bit her lip. The pain of holding such anger and wishing so much evil upon Colla, hurt like she was the one that betrayed Cañari. She cried.

"Now, can we return to the train?" Said Colla.

Without answering, Colla directed her litter-bearers to bring her back and Tara's followed.

Colla continued her story, "They outnumbered us fifty to one. After I was free of the Sapa Inka, I begged the huacas to use their power to release the fury of Mamaquilla upon them, instead they told me we must submit or we would all be killed. They described the exact thing that that Sapa Inka Tupac Yupanqui's guard told me, word for word." She looked down at Huayna and spit on him. "I tell the tyrant that I love our child, and that I love him. I tell him that all is well because that's what survival is. What I really love is the idea of this sickness that ravages our train. Take him, slowly and painfully. But then I remember that I gave myself so that you, your family, your friends and everyone else could survive. And so that no other woman would have to endure what I did, so that our hero's would be remembered, so that your brothers and your father would be remembered. I did this so everyone can love in peace.

Colla closed her eyes and took several deep breaths. "The love that I can never feel again." She opened them and looked at Tara's stubs and made a clicking sound with her mouth. "You and I have to live for something larger than ourselves. If we fail, then Cañari will be lost forever, the people will be massacred, and we will only be remembered by the stones that are left behind. Those lifeless stones. We will be like those whom we must call the Chachapoyas People: after the tyrant was finished with me, he went to our neighbors. Their leaders refused to submit. Now, anyone who utters their true name, speaks their language, mentions their gods, or remembers their heroes is thrown from the heights of Kuelap after being burned alive—"

A roar erupted from hundreds of onlookers as the train passed the final chasquihuasi before entering Cusco.

Colla smiled and waved at them for a brief moment and then turned back to Tara, who hadn't removed her eyes from Colla."

"—Don't you understand, Tara? It's not about living, it's not about honor, it's not about your hands. We suffer to save the others, that is what leaders do, what women do. And, as Cañari's, we fight when it's time to fight and we submit when it's time to submit. That is how we have survived longer than any other civilization in this land, and that's how we will outlive the Inkas. To be selected by the gods is to be chosen for a horrible life. We will have to use memories of happier times to fuel our life now."

The screaming crowds around them grew as they approached Cusco. The noise was such that it drowned out Colla."

"Forgive me," cried Tara. "Please, forgive me! Forgive me, forgive me, forgive me, forgive me. All the bad things I've ever thought about you, forgive me! No wonder I've been harmed like this, it's because

I was so angry and held on to such resentment toward you. I didn't know. Oh, please forgive me!"

"I already have," said Colla. "Now, we must please the crowds and make everyone believe that there is no discord and that no bad thing has happened to us."

"I won't be able to look at the horrible tyrant that did this to you ever again," Tara said in their secret language.

"No, Tara. Act normal! And if you find it in your heart, forgive him too. Being vengeful and angry at someone does nothing but harm yourself. Don't give him that satisfaction. Such feelings will lead to a pachacuti."

Her litter fell behind Colla's as the train preceded in a single file line. Tara imitated the motions of Colla in front of her, waving and smiling to the crowd. She did so as her tears created a stream of water behind her litter.

The procession took an indirect path to Cusco. It passed by many huacas where the Sapa Inka paid offerings. Following his example, each person that was carried upon a litter behind him paid an offering, mimicking his.

A mullu shell was given to Tara to offer at her turn. It was expected that she'd ask the huacas that the Sapa Inka's wishes would be met. Instead, she prayed in Cañari that in exchange for the offering, she would never feel anger or resentment again and be able to forgive. At the final huaca, she asked that she might be able to become as great a woman as Colla and forgive the Sapa Inka.

It was nearly the end of the day before the train made its way into Cusco and to Huacaypata.

Five men stood upon a platform in front of the Coricancha. They dressed immaculately, the principal one Tara knew to be Villac Umu. He was the man in charge of the Coricancha, the most holy man in Tahuantinsuyu. He wore gold robes and a condor skull was sewn into his llautu.

Sapa Inka Tupac Yupanqui was lowered from his litter and all went quiet. He ascended the stairs to the top of the platform where he joined the five men.

The crowd, numbering in the tens of thousands, roared for what seemed to be the better part of the remaining daylight. After they quieted, the train disbanded and several of the men upon litters were lowered and disappeared into the crowd.

Tara and Colla remained on their litters, which were still held upon the shoulders of the bearers and positioned near the entrance of the Acllahuasi.

Villac Umu stepped forward and gave a vessel filled with chicha to the Sapa Inka. The vessel was shaped and painted as an anaconda. The Sapa Inka poured a little upon the ground and then drank a little. He returned the vessel to Villac Umu, who poured a little upon the ground and drank a little.

The crowd yelled and cheered, including Colla. Tara watched her and forced herself to do so. Scores of women brought the attendees vessels of chicha.

During this time, the five men sacrificed hundreds of llamas and collected the blood in large urns.

Once everyone in Huacaypata had chicha, they poured a little upon the ground. They then drank but didn't stop drinking and wouldn't for days, as was the custom.

"We're going to the top of the platform to join Sapa Inka Tupac Yupanqui," said Colla. "Will you carry Huayna? He's not used to the mountains yet and he may not make it up the stairs."

"I'm in charge of Huayna?"

Colla smirked at Tara.

Colla put the boy down and he walked beside Tara until they reached the stairs. Tara picked him up and he sat upon her hip. She felt no disdain toward the boy, despite learning of his conception.

"Since I have been away," addressed the Sapa Inka to the crowd, "we have brought Inti and civilization to a faraway land named Cañari. There, I married the ruler of the land named Colla who joins me now and with her is our son Huayna who Inti has revealed to me a great destiny."

Colla and Tara reached the top of the platform and Colla stood behind the Sapa Inka. Tara, carrying Huayna, stood behind her.

Tara's clothes had changed from when she was on the ground. Her plain garb was now a brilliant tunic that shone like Mamaquilla and matched the outline of what Colla and Huayna wore.

The Sapa Inka turned and kissed Colla on the lips. She smiled and kissed him on the lips.

Tara shuttered. She remembered Colla's words and remained strong.

He then kissed Huayna upon the forehead and Colla followed suit.

Tara looked away when Colla kissed Huayna; the crowd yelled and drank in celebration.

"And this woman," said Sapa Inka, pointing at Tara. "Amauta Tara Inka of Yanantin Huaca of the Spring of the Floating Flowers, shall instruct all who seek permission for passage to Collasuyu in the hills above Cusco at the—"

"—What?" said Tara louder than she thought.

The Sapa Inka ignored her intrusion. "—There, the stones that absorbed the blood of her hands have been moved and produced a wondrous field of flowers. All who wish to know the stories of Cañari shall go there and pay her an offering. Only after doing that shall you receive my permission to travel to the fruitful lands of Cañari. She shall also be responsible for the upbringing of my son Huayna, so he knows the stories, heroes, and gods of his mother."

Tara didn't move. She could not look away from the Sapa Inka, despite every intention of doing so.

The Sapa Inka turned to Tara, "Go to your new home and rest. Villac Umu will guide you."

She raised a finger to point at Huayna.

"He shall join you at a later time."

Villac Umu placed his hand on her back and led her off of the platform back to the litter.

Chapter Forty

The Huaca

The litter-bearers met Tara and Villac Umu at the bottom of the platform with their litters, a wooden one for Tara and a golden one for Villac Umu. Tara sat upon the cushioned seat of the wooden litter. The 8 women bearers lifted her, and twenty-four men lifted the Villac Umu's golden litter.

The crowd split. She saw the grand entrance to the Acllahuasi across Huacaypata. Villac Umu's litter led the way going toward it. She bit her lip as they drew nearer. She tasted blood. But they continued past the entrance of the Acllahuasi to a narrow path that led out of the plaza and into the small streets of Cusco. She released her lip. There was a chunk of skin in her mouth.

"Where are we going?" She asked Villac Umu.

"For tonight, a tampu. It is getting late. Tomorrow, we go to a hill near Matagua, the place where the ancestral Inkas, those that were magic, rested on their way to Cusco." He spoke in a hushed voice. "A settlement has been built for you."

"I'm going to live on Matagua?" Said Tara.

"You're not going to Matagua but a hill *near* it. No one lives upon Matagua, it is too sacred even for many Inkas to go there. No more questions until we arrive."

"I'm going to be in charge of a settlement?" She said to herself. Goose bumps covered her body. She leaned back in her seat, it seemingly being made of a cloud. She laughed. The relief was such that she felt like she was a bird that escaped her cage and flew past her captors, who threatened to remove its wings.

As they traversed the crowds in Cusco, they entered a large cloud of dust that emerged from a number of moving people. Her laugh turned into a harsh cough which only passed after they left Cusco and settled into the tampu for the night.

The next morning, and outside of dust ridden city, the sun seemed brighter and hurt her eyes. The sweet aromas of chicha, roasting maize, and llama, and flowers were blocked by congestion.

Her litter followed Villac Umu's as it traversed the same hill that she traveled with Viracocha days before when they went to the Huaca of Inka Ayar Uchu.

"Oh, Viracocha!" Tara moaned. "Where are you?"

"What?" Said Villac Umu.

"Nevermind, I didn't mean to say anything," said Tara.

She looked around in the hills in hopes to see him and she was troubled when she didn't see him. She looked back at Cusco and thought of returning to find him to say thank you. She opened her mouth to call to Villac Umu, but she realized in that moment such a request wouldn't be wise. She'd see him another time.

They turned off the main path onto a small trail before they reached Huanacauri. They went up a small canyon of lush grass.

"That's your settlement," said Villac Umu. He pointed at a hillside covered in terraces, "And that," he said pointing in the distance, "is Matagua, and that," he said pointing in another direction, "is Huanacauri. You are in the midst of the most magical places in Cusco." He stared at Tara for a moment. "It should fit for you, Amauta Tara Inka of Yanantin Huaca of the Spring of the Floating Flowers." He pointed to a nearby spring and the creek that flowed from it. "That spring continually provides water to a pond just beyond our view. You shall be like this spring: continually feed the pond. You are the spring, the water is wisdom and stories of the birth place of the future Sapa Inka."

"And where will I live while I perform this undertaking of being Spring Huaca of Amauta Tara Inka Floating Flowers?" Said Tara in a sarcastic voice.

"Amauta Tara Inka of Yanantin Huaca of the Spring of the Floating Flowers!"

"Yes, that's what I meant," said Tara. She held back a laugh and thought of what Hualpa would think of her new title.

"You will live in the dwelling on the other side of these terraces. Follow me."

The litters departed to the terraced hill side. The terraces were laden with thousands of potatoes, squash, and maize plants. On the far side of the hill, halfway up, was a small dwelling.

"Servants will be provided to you to tend the terraces, so you don't have to work," said Villac Umu.

"The terraces are mine too?" Said Tara.

"Yes, so that you, those that live here, and your visitors will have food. There will be others arriving in the coming days to build more shelters for the workers. A chasqui will be here at all times to provide you with a communication link to Cusco for any needs."

She closed her eyes. The cool, moist air encapsulated her and she took a deep breath. The coolness caused another coughing fit. After it passed, she said, "Thank you, I will take anyone you deem appropriate, but I wish to tend to the plants myself."

"Never," said Villac Umu. "That is man's work."

Tara didn't argue because she would do as she pleased after he left.

She got out of her litter and ascended the steep stairs to her small house.

The joy she felt amplified.

From her small hovel, she saw the pond that the spring fed. It was surrounded by a field of flowers. "Oh my," she said. The flowers pulled her toward them like she was stuck in a river's current. She forgot about everything and everybody and ran down the cliff side to the field of flowers. The flowers floated above the dirt and matched her face, half the color of snow and the other half the color of the night.

Villac Umu's litter came up beside Tara. It created an imposing presence. Villac Umu spoke from atop.

"This is your home now Tara, you shall never leave here unless summoned. Communicate by the chasqui that shall be here in the coming days. Everything will be provided to you and of which, one third shall go to me at Coricancha, another third shall go to the Sapa Inka and the rest shall be your own to do with whatever you desire. A husband shall be provided to you too. He is coming from—"

She gave little heed to Villac Umu and focused on the flowers. She wished to smell them, but her nose was clogged and now it was running. Still, she felt peace and contentment as she listened to the flowers instead of to Villac Umu. There was a tickle in her throat and she coughed.

Villac Umu finished. "We are going to leave now," he said.

"Where did all of this come from? When? Why was it prepared for me?"

"During your time in the Acllahuasi, it was built for you. This was your calling long before you arrived."

"Why wasn't I brought here earlier, or told about it?" said Tara.

"Because it wasn't ready for you, or perhaps because you weren't ready for it. It doesn't matter. Inti wants you here now," said Villac Umu.

He got back on his litter.

"Goodbye Amauta Tara Inka of Yanantin, Huaca of the Spring of Floating Flowers," he said.

He ordered his litter-bearers to return to Cusco, and they left.

Tara sat down on the ground in the field of flowers and watched him depart. She didn't want to leave the flowers. Not ever. She wanted to be a part of them.

She coughed and a condor shrieked.

She looked toward the sound, but there was no condor there.

She waited for Huayna to come, but he never came. No one came besides the servants. Nothing happened. As she waited, her sickness grew worse and soon affected her energy. By the turning of the moon, she felt worse than she imagined Umita felt in her old age.

She hid her illness from the servants and when her energy allowed it, worked upon the terraces alongside them. Her handless arms prevented her from doing anything that she wanted to do, but she found menial tasks such as moving stones, compacting soil, managing the water through the aqueducts, and harvesting large vegetables. The servants commanded her to cease, but only did so when her fatigue forced her to.

Days later, while she was kicking stones across a terrace, she collapsed.

"Amauta Tara, are you okay!" Asked one of her servants. He ran to her.

"Yes, I'm fine. I tripped is all." She mumbled her words. She stood up, her head spun, and she fainted again.

The servant by her side yelled at the other, "Tell the chasqui to run to Cusco and get the Hampi Kamayoc. She is not well."

The servants carried Tara back to her small stone house.

The Hampi Kamayoc arrived shortly after the sun went down. There was no moon and it was a dark night. He went into her small chambers alone.

"Did you get that little doll to Tata?" he said immediately upon entering.

Tara smiled, "I think I did."

"You think?"

She explained what happened.

"Yes, she has it," he said. He hugged her. "She was always sneaky like that when she was in trouble."

Tara didn't have the strength to hug him back.

"Why are you so weak?" He said. "Why! Your energy must be off balance. What have you been doing? Here, here, I'm going to do a ritual that will balance you." He went to the exit to retrieve the material from his litter.

"I am more balanced than I have ever been since leaving Cañari," she said. "I just need you to give me that ointment you gave me last time. I just need a little energy and I will be fine."

She coughed.

"You mean that terrible tasting stuff?" He said.

"Yes."

He paused for a minute and then jumped, "than that's what I shall give you! Good for you, I brought just enough."

He gave it to her and performed a few short rituals.

"Oh, you'll be fine! You'll be fine!" He said afterward. "The gods love you!" He jumped and went to the door. "I must leave now, but I will see you again. Anything, ANYTHING you need, I will be forever your servant." He kissed both of her stubs and then her forehead and left.

Tara felt different once he left. Everything she saw and experienced was like a passing sensation, even the visit from Hampi Kamayoc. The field of flowers called to her. She went to it like a mother opening her arms to a lost child. It was the only thing that seemed real to her.

She collapsed in the field and laid there absorbed by the flowers. She heard a condor shriek. She knew there was no condor present, they didn't fly at night. Still, they shrieked. She gazed at the sky until morning came. Far above her, there were circling condors.

They shrieked.

She realized she was going to die. This time it was going to happen. She thought back to the old man she encountered at Cusibamba that was certain that he was going to die. The closed door of death she saw in her previous sicknesses stood open now.

The condors circled closer to her.

"How can I be dying?"

She cried.

There was so much for her to do, so much. Huayna was coming, Achache was coming to live with her. And Mother! Just to be with her one more time. Where was Viracocha!

She grew more tired. She tried to stand again but didn't have the strength to move an arm. The fatigue ate her from within. She focused her eyes on a nearby flower.

"This was the plan all along, wasn't it? You wanted me to die."

Keeping her eyes open became the most difficult thing she'd ever done.

"Tara!" She whispered to herself, "You can't die. You must save Cañari! You must teach Huayna. You can't—"

One condor landed next to her. It transformed into Viracocha.

He kneeled next to Tara and held her head in his hands. "I shall be your voice. Close your eyes and travel to Hanaq Pacha. Inti waits for you."

She let out a sorrowful scream and closed her eyes.

Chapter Forty-One

The Field

All things that Tara felt and sensed disappeared. In their void was a new existence of song, peace, and motion. The field of flowers was lost to her, and it was replaced by euphoria that freedom after bondage yields. She found herself in an unknown place where time no longer mattered. It no longer existed. The momentous peace and love that composed the euphoric song dwarfed the pain and suffering she endured while alive; they were a pebble compared to a mountain. The happiest moments in her life were as scattered and insignificant as small leafs in a vast jungle, whereas she was the jungle now; an icicle on a glacier when her happiness was now the glacier. Such life or death, she didn't know which, bore no semblance to the other just as a tree branch and a bird share the same space but are inconceivable to the other.

How long she remained in this heightened stupor never occurred to her because time was gone. She was in forever, and forever was the same as an instant. No one was with her in this space except for fulfillment, contentment, and acceptance.

In her sojourn, two large ukukus came to her awarenesses. Where they came from or what they were doing, she didn't know, nor did they arrive at any given time. She enjoyed their presence and the joy they brought. Within an instant that lasted lifetimes, they approached Tara and sang a song to her.

She recognized the sound of being a familiar voice. Each word pierced the vast abyss of her non-existence like a glowing insect in a dark cavern. The words appeared from nowhere and then disappeared. The sound lingered, but there was no echo. As the ukukus approached, she recognized a familiar presence so strongly that she saw the field of flowers where she died but not with her eyes; the image was placed within her mind like a snow flake falls upon a child's hand from somewhere beyond.

She realized for the first time that even in death she had eyes. She opened them. She was the flowers, the field, the spring, the water-all the landscapes around the area where she died. Within the field, the field that was her, stood two handsome, fully grown men dressed in Inkan regalia. It was Achache and Hualpa.

"Tara, I know you're here even if your body isn't," said Achache.

He cried. His tears watered the flowers. It was Achache's tears that held the magic that brought Tara from the abyss to Kay Pacha.

"You gave your life for Cañari but have left me here alone."

Each tear that hit the ground impacted it like Amaru Tupa Inka's club hitting her hand, but instead of pain it was the love and loneliness that Achache felt. Tara imagined placing her hands on Achache's cheeks and kissing his forehead.

Achache grasped his cheeks and cried harder. He stood up and looked up at the sky, "I shall see that you are never forgotten. My children, and their children, will tell stories of your courage, selflessness, and fearlessness."

Hualpa stepped ahead of Achache. "We brought you a gift, Tara" said Hualpa.

"She's Tara to me, to you, she's Amauta Tara Inka of Yanantin Huaca of the Spring of Floating Flowers," said Achache. He clung to Hualpa and cried on his shoulder.

Hualpa put an arm around Achache and kissed his head. He turned to the flower and said, "Look, whatever you want to be called I'm not calling you that huge name though, we have brought you a gift."

He gently released himself from Achache and lowered to the floating flower. He removed two severed hands from a sac he carried with him. He dug a hole below the flower and covered them.

"They are Amaru Tupa Inka's hands. We wanted to give you his head, but Sapa Inka Tupac Yupanqui had other plans for that. It's food for one of his animals, I think."

The offering satisfied Tara, and she desired to give something in return.

Hualpa continued, "I have been given 500 men to take to Cañari to protect it from all threats and to build canals and roads. Achache has been given 200 men. He is now Waranga Achache."

Achache ceased crying and lowered himself to the ground before the flower. "We ask that you to be an intermediary to us and the gods in Hanaq Pacha so that we will have success in protecting Cañari both physically and its history and culture."

Coy ran out from their hiding places and climbed on Achache and Hualpa's legs.

Achache laughed, relieved. Hualpa kicked them away, not knowing what they meant.

Viracocha landed beside them and transformed from a condor to the young man.

Hualpa jumped and fell backward.

Achache didn't flinch.

"Pisca Panhaca Waranga Hualpa Inka, and Waranga Achache Milagro," said Viracocha, "I am the voice of Tara. She speaks through me. She says that your gifts are well appreciated. They add to her peace and happiness in Hanaq Pacha. It gives her strength to intercede on your behalf. By the use of Amaru Tupa Inka's hands, Cañari shall be protected from its enemies for now and forever so as long as the Cañari's put the effort in to preserve their history and stories. It will be through the women that these stories must be preserved or else they will be lost forever."

"Why must it be the women?" Said Hualpa. He regained his composure. "And, um, you're a condor. Maybe next just consider telling people that before you literally drop in on them."

"It must be the women because your real enemies forget the strength of women," said Viracocha.

"Real enemies? What?" Said Hualpa.

Viracocha roared. He transformed back into the condor and left.

Tara closed her eyes and saw the ukukus play. They added some entertainment and pleasure that was unique to them. They played for as long as forever, but also disappeared.

Another came to her attention.

"Tara, dear Tara," said the friendly voice of an old lady. Her voice sounded like the wind. She felt Umita. She was disguised and dressed as a commoner. She stood in front of the small spring on side of the hill that fed the field of flowers.

"You finally learned that life was too small for someone as grand as you. Oh my sweet child, I wish you safe travels in the Hanaq Pancha. Maybe there you'll be able to fulfill your tasks that were too impossible for you here. I brought you something." She lowered herself to the ground and sat upon a small rock next to the small creek. She placed her cane next to her and opened her bag.

"I'm giving you a new tapestry that I created of Machu Picchu. I hope you will take better care of this one." She placed the folded tapestry into the water and it floated to the small pond. "In exchange, Tara, please, oh please, end the Acllahuasi practice. It is wrong. Let us be free! But there is something even more important that I ask of you. My dear, my dear, I ask for your forgiveness. It was I that set the fire while you were sleeping in the Acllahuasi. I learned that you were to leave eventually and I was jealous. Why you, a foreign girl, would leave the dreadful place of the Acllahuasi and I must stay for my entire life. I loved living at Machu Picchu! I dream of it each night and wake in tears. That night that you were to leave with Yachi, I decided that if I couldn't leave, neither could you. I tried to kill you, but you survived and I saw the damage I did to you. Envy is a horrible thing, horrible! It's a lesson I have learned several times, perhaps this is the last time I needed to learn it. I decided that I would do as you did all those nights and leave. I did so and I am here now. This is the first time leaving since I was younger than you."

Umita picked her cane back up and leaned upon it to stand up. She glanced down the stream, "I don't see the parchment anymore so you must have it, dear Tara, please remember me."

She turned around to leave and Viracocha stood there in the form of the condor.

Umita smiled and cried.

"I am here to take you to the Hanaq Pacha," he said. "Fetch me the best llamas from the royal heard and bring them to me so I may eat and have the strength to carry you there."

Umita cried harder and wobbled away toward Cusco.

She never returned.

Tara floated away into the void of music and peace for another eternity, longer than she had ever been uninterrupted. She was filled with music from sacred flutes. She forgot all things and lolled in the stillness that gave her company as her father did when she was young.

A man's voice repeated itself several times. It was a serene voice, but was fringed with anger and confusion. It tore Tara from her celestial song and pulled her back to the field of the floating flowers.

"Tara Inka of Yanantin," she heard this unknown man say. "Amauta Tara Inka of Yanantin *Huaca* of the Spring of Floating Flowers, please give me guidance—" he repeated. "Answer me!"

Tara's senses slowly returned to the field. She fought to stay among the peaceful sleep where she felt the company of her father but could not.

"—I have brought you a gift," said the young man. "So that you will give me what I ask for. Teach me of my mother's home and my birthplace, Cañari. I brought you a blanket. Accept it as an offering."

He dropped a small blanket upon a rock and burned it.

Tara felt the warmth of a vicuña blanket cover her. It wasn't a reverent offering, but one of anger. She opened her eyes and saw a young man standing before her at the small pond. He had a light complexion and a small stature. His cloak draped over him and was the color of the sky. His tunic differed from any she saw before. The top half of it blended with the lush leafs of the plants behind him and was checkered with the color of the beak of a toucan. The bottom half of the tunic which went to his mid-thigh looked like a clear sky early in the morning, checkered with light clouds. The gauges in this ear lobes were as she remembered Sapa Inka Tupa Inka's.

"Here is some chicha from the estate of my grandfather, Pachacuti Inka Yupanqui." He poured the chicha into the water. Her tranquility was restored, and she felt as if she were bathed in a lake of pleasure and relaxation.

"—I demand that you teach me the stories of Cañari in exchange for these offerings."

"Huayna," she said, not sure if aloud or in her fleeting solace.

The full meaning of his request came upon her as a jocund flame. She cried as the agony of desire returned and burned her like the fire at the Acllahuasi. But the anger that the offerings were given to her made her not want to give anything to the boy.

A torrential downpour overtook the field. There was a rainbow in the distance.

Huayna put out his hand and felt the drops. "Wait, do you hear me? You must!" He jumped. "There wasn't a cloud in the sky when I arrived and now it's a warm and comforting rainstorm, of such I've never experienced. You answered me!"

He fell on his knees before the pond and smiled. "Teach me of Cañari. My father tells me that you are the one to teach it to me. You briefly knew me as a child, did you not? Teach me! Please. I'm so, so lost. I can't tell anybody but I hate Cusco."

He looked around in the rain and saw nothing new.

"I have another offering for you," said Huayna Inka. He spoke kindly now, his voice full of hope. "My father says that this belongs to you."

He reached inside of his tunic and withdrew a mullu shell. The shell looked familiar. It was the same shell she gave as an offering to Mamaquilla in Guapondelig so long ago.

Huayna Inka dug a hole to bury the shell. He was about to drop it in, but paused for a moment. He stood up and waded into the cold water of the pond until he was chest deep. He held his breath and submerged himself. He gently placed the shell on the bottom of the pond.

Tara experienced an overflow of energy. It filled her with sorrowful remembrance, the painful and burning ambition to see that Cañari would be given its former glory.

When Huayna Inka emerged from the pond, Tara stood before him, having emerged from one of the floating flowers. The petals created her face and hair, she was half the color of snow and half the color of night. The even split complexion went beyond her face and covered her naked body perfectly down the midline. The leafs of the stem transformed into arms that bore hands. She floated above the ground beside him.

Viracocha landed next to her and transformed from the condor to human form. He gazed sternly at Huayna Inka as a condor hones in on its food.

Huayna Inka fell backward into the pond. He mouthed several words, but nothing came out but mumbles and grunts. He pointed at Tara and at Viracocha.

"I, but, you, how?"

"Do not look at Tara Inka of Yanantin, Huaca of the Spring of Floating Flowers," said Viracocha.

Viracocha went into the pond and returned with the mullu shell. He gave it to Tara. She slowly and gently rose her hands, admired them, and opened them.

Viracocha placed the shell into her open hand.

She held it to her heart.

"Why are you so nervous," said Viracocha. "Didn't anyone teach you about the gods and huacas?"

"Yes, but no other huaca has spoken to me, I have made offerings at hundreds seeking guidance. I give them the best gifts and they remain silent. They refuse to answer and I will destroy them when I am the Sapa Inka," said Huayna Inka. He blurted the words out. "My mother died today. She said that her people, that my people, are threatened and will soon be cease to exist. She said that I will find happiness that I can't find here if I reside there. Teach me of this place?"

"In Cañari, if you save them and embrace your mother's people, you will find a peace that you will not find in Cusco. From Guapondelig, the place that you call Tumipampa, you shall rule, and from there you will find magic that you will not find in Cusco. There, only there, is the magic that will save your own people the Inkas from the next pachacuti. Protect that land, protect those people, and protect their stories."

Chapter Forty-Two

Epilouge

Sapa Inka Huayna Capac took Tara's advice and ruled from Tumipampa where the ruins of his estate are still present at the Pumaponga Archeology site in Cuenca, Ecuador. No one knows exactly why he ruled from Tumipampa instead of Cusco but the leading theories are that he didn't like the over-ritualized Cusco with all of their traditions, that all the choice land was taken by his forefathers, and the last theory is that he wished to be closer to the frontier where he led many wars to expand his empire. No matter the reason that he resided in Tumipampa instead of Cusco, the effect he had on Cañari is likely why their culture survived into modernity.

The Conquistadors, already having discovered the Americas when this story ends, were only decades away from entering the Inka Empire. There are theories that Huayna Capac met the first Conquistadors that landed and settled in what was then the Inka Empire. These Conquistadors were never seen again, but there was a note discovered saying "There is more gold than you can imagine."

Once Pizarro, the Conquistador, executed the heir of Huayna Capac named Atahualpa, they were anxious as to how they might control such a vast land and extinguish Inkan leadership. Pizarro found many civilizations under the Inkas dominion that were all too ready to ally with him to overthrow their Inkan overrulers. The Cañari people played a large role early in the invasion to secure Spanish victory over the Inkas. They received preferential treatment in return. As Spain's power increased, as well as that of the Vatican, attempts were made to eliminate the ancient cultures of the former Inka Empire. It was the women in the Cañari Empire, and to a lesser extend other Andean cultures, that safeguarded the traditions that survive to this day. The paternalistic view of the 16th century Europeans was that only men could preserve the culture, and so they ignored the musings and work of the women.

The Acllahuasi tradition was among the first traditions to fall after the fall of the Inkas, but the women that occupied the Acllahuasi had a terrible future waiting for them outside of the walls. The brutish Conquistadors forewent their professed values and many of these women were raped, traded, or forced to marry. The stories of what some of these women had to endure is tragic. As significant a part as the Acllahuasi practice was in Tahuantinsuyu, it wasn't a staple of Andean culture and thus it never re-emerged.

The Acllahuasi that Tara resided at now provides the structural backbone of a shopping plaza in modern Cusco. The patrons of these shops do not know that they are standing in a sacred place that only a select group of women could occupy for hundreds of years. The services they performed kept the empire alive in wealth and culture. In this shopping plaza, there isn't even a plague depicting the significance of the structure.

Glossary of Terms

Achicoc

Inkan Prophet.

Aclla

An Inkan chosen women to be used for production, a gift to nobles, or as a sacrifice to the gods. Acllas were sequestered in the Acllahuasi and allowed no visitors.

Acllahuasi

"Girl House," is where the Inkan chosen women resided. They created textiles, chicha, and other products that were used throughout Tahuantinsuyu. There was an Acllahuasi in nearly each Inkan settlement.

Agave

Agave, the Spanish name, for a common succulent. The plant has many medicinal and practical uses.

ají

Aji is a pepper common in the Andes mountains. It is very spicy and has a unique flavor. It was one of the most common seasonings that the Inkas used.

Allyu

An Inkan social group that typically encompassed a group of common heritage. The rules of the composition of an allyu differed upon region. In northern Peru and Ecuador, Llacta is the word used and has nearly the same meaning.

Altiplano

The high plateau in southern Peru and Bolivia. It is characterized by vast grasslands called puna.

Amauta

The Quechua word for teacher or professor. Commonly, it was a position held by a noble. This station was typically heritable and a lifelong appointment.

Amboto

A city a short distance from Quito in Ecuador. It predates the conquest and holds a rich history.

Ancalluasu

The ritualistic white dress and shoes given to women on the 4th day of Quicuchica

Antisuyu

One of the four quarters, or parts, of Tahuantinsuyu. Antisuyu consisting of the mountainous region of central and northern Bolivia and southern Peru.

Apu

One of the most prestigious positions in the social hierarchy of the Inkas. It is a common title of the western equivalent of generals, governors, and mountains.

Atacama

The driest desert in the world. It is located on the western side of the Andes in Chile.

Ayahuasca

A ritualistic and sacred tea that produces intense hallucinations and is known to transform and heal people.

Ayni

A principle of reciprocity where it is more of an obligation to reciprocate the gift or act of service than an act of kindness. If Ayni is neglected, the balance of existence is lost. Ayni extends between humans and all objects in existence.

Ayrihuay

The month that would correspond with April in the Roman Calendar. In this time, crops were harvested. There were many festivals.

Cañari

A large an ancient empire that resided in southern Ecuador. Their traditions have fared better than many other cultures since the Conquest.

Capac-Cocha

A festival in the month of Ayrihuay. It included the sacrifice of children, often times by having them walk up a mountain until they froze to death. Their remains are found perfectly intact in modern times.

Casamarca

Known now as Cajamarca. A semi-important city in Tahuantinsuyu in central Peru. It is where Atahualpa was captured by Pizarro and the first major Spanish offensive against the Inkas.

Chachapoyas

An advanced and large chieftain in north eastern Peru. Their prolonged resistance to the Inkan invasion earned them the ire of the Inkas who took extreme measures to dismantle their culture to the point of executing anyone who referred to their nation by the common name, a name which is lost to history.

Chasqui

An Inkan young man who was tasked to be a relay runner in a vast network of runners to convey voice messages and small items.

chasquihuasi

The small house in which chasquis waited for a message. They were placed every couple of kilometers along the Qhapaq Ñan and other roads.

Chicha

The alcoholic beverage of choice. It was made from fermented corn. Acllas were the main source of it. They would begin the fermentation process by chewing moist corn paste and spitting it into a basin to ferment.

Chimor

Or Chimú, was a large and advanced civilization that co-existed with the Inkas until the Inkas, under the direction of Inka Pachacuti, conquered them, doubling the size of Tahuantinsuyu. The Chimor culture had a distinctive art style.

Chimu

See Chimor.

Chinchas

The biggest foe and threat to the early Inka state, having at one point nearly occupied Cusco. A decisive Inkan victory pushed the Chichas from their ancestral land to a distant place where they continued to be an embarrassment to the Inkas. Inka Pachacuti reengaged them and destroyed them.

Chinchi Roca Inka

The second ruling Inka. He had a large and loyal following. He transformed his people into a warlike and conquest minded culture.

Chuspa

A small bag that hung from the elbow. It was a common piece of Inkan clothes. It was often used to carry coca leaves.

Coca leaves

Coca leaves played a large role in Andean life as a stimulant, an item of trade, and for rituals.

Coca tea

A common way to consume coca leaves was to make a tea out of them. The tea holds medicinal properties and assists with overcoming altitude sickness.

Collasuyu

A quarter, or one of the four parts, of Tahuantinsuyu. It encompassed the southern portion of the Empire, beginning at Cusco.

Condor

A condor was commonly viewed as a messenger between Kay Pacha and Hanaq Pacha. They play a major role in Inkan Mythology.

Coricancha

The most holy place and temple in Tahuantinsuyu. To gain entrance required months of rituals. It was located on the main plaza, Huacaypata in Cusco. From it emerged the 4 roads, and four parts Tahuantinsuyu.

Coy

Guinea pig. Commonly used for food.

Cumpi

The finest clothing only worn by the Sapa Inka and his close relatives.

Curaca

A title given to someone in a minor position of leadership.

Cusibamba

A small town near Cusco.

Cusicancha

The building that Sapa Inka Tupac Yupanqui and Inka Pachacuti were born in It was located next the Coricancha.

Earplugs

The earplugs, or gauges, that were in the earlobes, were a sign of nobility. They ranged from small to as large as making the lobes touch the shoulders.

Guapondelig

The capital city of the Cañari Empire. It was changed to Tumipampa by the Inkas, and Cuenca Ecuador by the Spanish. There are ruins that predate the Cañaris at the location as well.

Hampi Kamayoc

An Inkan healer.

Hanan-Cusco

Cusco, along with all things in existence in the Inkan realm and to a larger extend, Andean culture, was divided into higher and lower. Hanan referred to the lower portion.

Hanaq Pacha

The higher world. Kay pacha is this world, and Ukhu pacha. Neither one nor the other was considered bad but part of a larger cosmos and they balanced each other as is required by Yanantin.

Hatun Cañar

A settlement known by the name nowadays of Ingapirca. It was an implanted community of Inkan loyalists in Cañari territory to help promote allegiance.

Huaca

A holy or sacred object. It can be animate or inanimate, manmade or natural. An object can be designated as such for magnificent reasons or for simply being different.

Huacaypata

The main plaza in Cusco. It was surrounded by the Coricancha, Acllahuasi, Cusicancha and other significant and important buildings not mentioned in the book.

Huanacuari

A sacred hill next to Cusco that was the site of many rituals. It was believed that this was the mountain pass where Manco Capac and his brothers first saw what was to become Cusco.

Huarachicoy

The initiation festival for boys to turn into men.

Huaraz

A city in central Peru.

Huasi

The Quechua word for house.

Huata

The Quechua word for a year.

Huayacuacha

The initiation for boys to manhood. It included a multi-day journey to Huanacauri and Matagua, rituals and ceremonies.

Inti

The sun and the principle god of the Inkas and the husband of Mamaquilla. The Inkas are believed to be descendants of Inti. The solar calendar was used for festivals.

Jaguar

The jaguar played a major role in Andean lore. There aren't generalities drawn across the different myths as to the significance of the jaguar.

Kawsay

The living energy that each object, living or non-living, possesses. It is mailable energy by such principles of Ayni and Yanantin. It seemingly never disappears but can transfer between objects. It can be loosely translated as the soul.

Kay Pacha

Refers to this world and time. It contrasts from Ukhu Pacha, the lower world, and Hanaq Pacha, the higher world. There is a lack of reliable information concerning the Inkan cosmos.

Kuelap

A large inhabitable structure in the Chachapoyas region. It took hundreds of years to construct and housed thousands of rulers. It is commonly refered to as a fort but there is no reliable evidence that it was used as such.

Llajta

A large inhabitable structure in the Chachapoyas region. It took hundreds of years to construct and housed thousands of rulers. It is commonly referred to as a fort, but there is no reliable evidence that it was used as such.

Llapa

In northern Peru and Ecuador, llajta referred to a social grouping that consisted of those of close or familial ties. There are no fixed rules of what makes a llajta and caused much confusion to the Conquistadors. It correlates with allyu in Bolivia and southern Peru.

Llautu

A head dressing that signified rank and position. It was made of a long woven textile and was spun around the head. Inlaid ornaments or feathers signified different positions and powers.

Machu Picchu

The most famous ruin in Peru, Machu Picchu was built by Inka Pachacuti to be one of his private estates. Due to the lost history, it is impossible to say for certainty that it was an estate and alternative theories abound.

Maize bread

A common stable in the Inkan diet made out of ground corn, water, a little salt and some seasoning such as aji.

Mama Ocllo
Women by the name of Mama Ocllo play a large role in Inkan mythology. The name also refers to several women throughout Inkan history, and many wives of the Inkas bore the name.

Mamacuna
Mamacuna directly translates of several mothers. In this book, and in most chroniclers, Mamacuna refers to the older generation of women at the Acllahuasi that mentor the younger "Acllas" in the ways of the Acllahuasi.

Mamaquilla
The moon goddess and the wife of Inti. She was the goddess that embodied female energy. The fertility and farming calendar was based on her.

Mamaquilla-Huasi
Used in this book to refer to the temple devoted to Mamaquilla.

Manco Inka
The first ruling Inka and founder of the Inkas in Cusco. Circa 1200-1300 AD.

Manta
A small Pre-Colombia city in Ecuador that is situated along the coast.

Matagua
The ceremonial location near Huanacauri where the migrating Inkas rested before their final descent into what would be the Valley of Cusco. It appears to be the birthplace of many other rituals and ceremonies.

Milagro
The fictional location where Tara and her family reside. A modern-day Milagro exists in Ecuador and is the inspiration for the fictional city.

Morada
A non-fermented Chicha, essentially sweet corn juice.

Moras
A large assemblage of manmade salt ponds sourced from a saltwater spring in the Sacred Valley about 40kms from Cusco.

Mullu shell

What is now called a Spondylus shell, was a highly sought-after item in Andean cultures. It is commonly found buried with nobles and rulers. In some areas, it was loosely used as currency.

Mummy

Many Andean cultures, including the Cañari's, and Chachapoyas, would embalm their dead and wrap the corpse as mummies. Many highly preserved mummies have been unearthed, unleashing a flurry of controversy and further archeological discoveries. The Inkas would embalm many of their rulers and treat them as living. The Conquistadors destroyed all but Atahualpa's mummy, which is lost.

Nina Kamayaq

A generic Inkan prophet or wise man.

Pachacuti

Translated as an event that overturns time or the universe. It is believed that when Yanantin, or the balance of life, was disturbed, a great disruption would occur to restore balance. This event is referred to as a pachacuti. Pachacuti Inka Yupanqui, was the most ambitious ruler and formed the Inkan Empire from a successful chiefdom to a powerful empire.

Pachacuti Inka Yupanqui

The ninth ruling Inka, during his long rule, he transformed the Inkan Empire from a well-run chiefdom to the Empire that is known today. He is likely the founder of Machu Picchu. He ruled over a time of much death, famine, and war.

Pachayachachic

Also known as Pachamama, is the earth god. This god is worshipped throughout the Andes mountains and retains relevance to this day.

Panaca

A group of believers that adhere to the teachings of a common person, usually a diseased ruler. Each ruler maintained their own version of truth and history and once they died their followers preserved their beliefs, maintained their estates and mummy, and formed a social group called a Panaca.

People of the Forest of the Flatlands

A fictional group of people in the book that refers to the communities in the Amazon Rainforest that were significantly less developed than those in the mountains. Most references to them cite them as being hostile.

Pucamarca

A compound that consisted of two temples near Huacaypata. In these temples, rituals such as sacrifice (including of children) and rituals would be performed. In the other temple was an idol of Chucuylla, a name for Llapa.

Puna

A defining landscape in the Andes. It is vast grassland above the timberline. It is very cold and ranges from very dry to very moist. In places, such as on the Altiplano, is large enough to support cities.

Purun Rur'a!"

A sexual predator, "wild or savage man. The closet thing the Inkas had to the devil Quechua.

Quechua

One of the common languages of the Tahuantinsuyu, the other being Aymara.

Quicuchica

A festival for girls that had their first menstruation during the previous year and a celebration for their entrance to womanhood. Many girls were selected for the Acllahuasi at this time. This name is likely a Spanish derivative of the Quechua name, which is lost.

Quillojos Llajta

A fictional llajta that Raura's friend Tanto is from.

Quinoa

A staple grain of the Inkan and Andean diet as well as an important crop in their economy.

Quito

The modern capital of Ecuador; at the time of the conquest, Sapa Inka Atahualpa had designs to create it into another Cusco. Before the Inkas, it was the capital of the Quitus tribe, which was controlled by the Scyris dynasty.

Royal language

The royal language of the Inkas was an exclusive language and died with the Inkan nobility. The only proof of its existence are references to it made by the conquistadors.

Sacsayhuaman

One of the most visited ruins in Cusco, this fort is an archeological marvel that served for Inkan resistance many times during their early days. This fort played a major role in the struggle for control over Cusco from the Spanish.

Sapa Inka

A loose translation of "The Ruling Inka." Although all ruling Inkas didn't take this name, for simplicity's sake, it was used as a direct translation in the book.

Son of the Sun

A name given to the ruling Inka, as he was believed to be the direct descendant of the sun.

Sondorhuaci Tower

The tallest building in Cusco, between 10 and 20 meters. It was created of the finest material. Its significance is lost.

Suyu

Translated as "part." In reference to time, it meant a month. In reference to geography, it meant a province. The word TahuantinSUYU refers to the same word in terms of "four parts together," referring to provinces.

Tampu

A state owned and ran inn that provided lodging to armies and those on official business. They were placed every few kilometers along the Qhapaq Ñan.

The land where there's no shadow

Refers to Quito and the land along the equator where at noon, there is no shadow cast by objects.

The Qhapaq Ñan

A royal road that spanned the entire empire. It consisting of four main highways that connected in the Coricancha in Cusco and spanned in each direction. It was well maintained and one of the biggest archeological accomplishments in the world at that time.

Tunic

A common article of clothing in the Andes. It spanned from the shoulders to the mid-thigh.

Ukukus

A mythological creature that is half-man, half-bear. Such animisms refer to those that are connected to more than one pacha, or space-time continuum.

Vicuñas

Small camelids. They have the softest fur to be found in the Andes. They cannot be domesticated, making them all the more valued.

Viracocha

Most commonly referred to as the God that created the Universe. Once he created the Universe, he disappeared. He was believed to be white thus when the Spaniards arrived. Some believed them to be "Virachocas" because of their white skin.

Waranga

A title referring to a military commander.

Yanantin

The Andean philosophy referring to the balance of existence and kawsay. When the balance is lost, a pachacuti can occur to restore the balance. Yanantin is maintained by Ayni, the principle of reciprocity.

Yumbas

The dominant mountain civilization in modern-day Ecuador. They were generally seen as uncivilized, yet unconquerable. The author pictures them as the Germanic tribes during the Roman Empire.

Character Glossary

Achache

The younger and only surviving brother of Tara

Amaru Tupa Inka

The younger brother of Sapa Inka Tupac Yupanqui. He holds a high position in the state religion. He takes it upon himself to cleanse Cusco.

Apu Atoc

One of the most important generals, or Apu's in the Inkan Civil War.

Apu of Cusco

The ruler of Cusco. A close relative to Sapa Inka Tupac Yupanqui

Colla

The ruler of Cañari. She is forced to marry the Sapa Inka and is a mother to the future ruler, Huayna Capac.

Cora

A princess in Tahuantinsuyu, a daughter of Sapa Inka Tupac Yupanqui. She resides in Tumipampa.

Guaman

Tara's father. He suffers from PTSD

Hualpa

See Waranga Hualpa Inka of Hana Cusco

Huayna Capac

The son of Sapa Inka Tupac Yupanqui and Colla. He serves as the ruling Inka after his father's death. He rules from Tumipampa for unknown reasons. He is the last Inka to have his rule undisturbed by the Spanish. There are arguments that his given name was Titu Cusi Hualpa.

Inka Ayar Uchu

A brother of Manco Capac. Different legends have different causes of death, but in all legends he dies and turns into a stone. In this book, he is killed by his brothers for a made up conspiracy based on jealousy.

Latacina

A friend of Raura's

Mama Ocllo

The wife of the Apu of Cusco.

Ñuestra

A fellow Aclla at the Acllahuasi. She is beautiful and very gifted at what she does. She is friends with Tata.

Paqo

Tata's father, who works as Hampi Kamayoc. He heals Tara from many injuries.

Raura

The mother of Tata. She is the ruler of Milagro

Sapa Inka Tupac Yupanqui

Also known as The Sapa Inka in the book. The 10th ruler of Tahuantinsuyu and son of Pachacuti Inka Yupanqui.

Sycri

The daughter of a ruler from the Quitu's tribe. She leaves an impression on Tara.

Tanto

A friend of Raura's

Tata

A friend of Tara's at the Acllahuasi. She is the most beautiful girl there.

The Sapa Inka

See Sapa Inka Tupac Yupanqui

Umita

A Mamacuna that mentors Tara along her journey. She is from Machu Picchu and longs to return.

Villac Umu

The older brother of Amaru Tupa Inka and Sapa Inka Tupac Yupanqui. He is the head of the state religion.

Viracocha

The mysterious son of the Apu of Cusco. They maintain a forbidden relationship by meeting on the roofs of buildings on different sides of the wall of the Acllahuasi.

Waranga Hualpa Inka of Hanan Cusco

An Officer in the military. He commands 199 men. He played a minor role in the conquest of Cañari.

Yachi

A servant girl in the Acllahuasi. She is also Tara's only good friend. She is in an alliance with Amaru Tupa Inka.

Thank You

Thank You For Reading My Book!

I really appreciate all of your feedback, and I love hearing what you have to say.

I need your input to make the next version of this book and my future books even better.

Please leave me a helpful review on Amazon letting me know what you thought of the book.

Thank you so much!
J.D. Lanctôt

Made in the USA
Coppell, TX
27 August 2021

61254107R00194